D0869192

"Should we?" Hannah whispered.

"Should we what?"

"Make out."

Good thing he'd put down his beer. "That's a joke, right?"

She shrugged, her shoulders rubbing against his chest. "Just thought we should make it look good. I promise — no bloodsurfing."

His reaction had sounded far more harsh than he had intended. "The plan is to stay off camera, not attract their attention."

"If you insist." She tucked her chin onto his chest.

Never let it be said impulsiveness wasn't also a family trait.

"Hannah."

She tilted her head back just as Scott lowered his to place the most gentle kiss he could manage on her lips.

"Oh..." She didn't say anything further. Instead, she slipped her arm around his neck and pulled his head down toward hers. His plan to keep it slow and short flew across the Bay with the breeze. He slid his arm down from her shoulders to her waist.

"I think we should move," he said, when she pulled back to catch her breath.

"Good idea."

They stood up, pressed together since neither of them was willing to let go of the other. She giggled.

"Do you want me to pick you up again?" he asked.

"That would be romantic."

He curled his left arm around her legs. In the next instant, without warning, a familiar series of staccato pops erupted. One instinct overrode another. He shoved Hannah to the ground and covered her body with his.

"Ow, Scott, not so fast..."

"Gunfire. Stay down."

DEDICATION

For my mother, Bonny, my father, Michael, and brother, Eric. I love you all so much and I couldn't have written this book without you.

Enjoy!

Debra Jess

CHAPTER ONE

"Are you ready to die?" one of the Left Fists yelled over the *whoop-whoop* of the helicopter's blades.

Officer Scott Grey took aim as best he could and spat his broken tooth square into the gang member's face. Not a bad shot, considering he was on his knees with a chunk of his hair gripped in the meaty hand of the asshole standing over him. The overpowering stench of half-chewed food and liquor battled with the blood already pouring down Scott's throat to force his gag reflex.

"Just shove 'im out," the Fist's partner said. "No 'chute. Watch 'im go splat on a sidewalk."

Bastards, Scott thought. *I shouldn't complain. I've been living on borrowed time for the past decade anyway. If I'm going to die, I might as well go out in a blaze of glory. At least it's me and not a bunch of kids caught up in tonight's wilding.* Scott glanced at the third Fist, who ignored the threats in favor of examining Scott's Glock. *No help from the peanut gallery.* Number three appeared much older than the other two Fists with a vicious scar across his cheek. He didn't have a blitz-head's full-body twitch.

"Open it," number two yelled.

Small relief as the nearest Fist let go of Scott's hair and yanked open the helicopter's door.

Wind whipped through the cabin, pulling in funnels of black smoke from burning garbage. Even through his swollen eyes, Scott could see flames snaking their way from the mouth of the Fairfax River to the flooded streets surrounding the civic center. The copter followed Star Haven's cross-city expressway. Outbound traffic from the Swamp — the Southern Point district — was at a standstill, with desperate residents trying to outrun the fires and the Left Fists. Emergency vehicles raced in the opposite direction, lights flashing, back-up from the other districts called to assist the already overwhelmed police and fire departments.

Up ahead, aircraft warning lights on the hospital roof pulsed red. Just a few more seconds and maybe he'd have a chance. Scott scooted back onto his feet, his sore knees grateful for the shift in weight.

"And there ain't any goody two-shoe Alts left in this city to rescue you neither." Number two slammed Scott's face with his elbow, rocking Scott back. Scott rolled with the punch, but kept his balance. "So don't be expecting one of them costumed fucktards to swoop out the skies and catch you at the last second. Captain Spectacular ain't your bitch today."

Scott tried to laugh through his split lips, but choked again on his own blood. Figures, even at the end of his life he couldn't escape his past. "Would you believe I hate Alts even more than I hate you?"

The Fist staggered, either at the idea that Scott could hate alternative humans more than his self-appointed murderers, or from the blitz in his system. Whatever the reason, the Fist lost his footing. Scott took advantage of the distraction and launched from his squat to slam his head into the underside of the Fist's chin. With Fist number one howling curses, Scott swung at Fist number two with all his pent-up fury.

As badly as they had beaten him, Scott still had a fighting chance against three Norms, normal humans like himself, though the third Fist still sat there looking bored. The pilot, paying more attention to the fight than his flying, lost altitude and Scott's stomach plunged with the copter, but he didn't stop fighting.

"Shake him out! Shake him out!" one of the Fists — Scott had lost track of which was which — hollered. The pilot tilted the copter at a crazy angle, squishing Scott between the Fists and the closed side of the cabin.

"The other way!" More shouting from the Fists.

Scott shoved against the wall of muscle, ducked the next blow, and tried an uppercut in the cramped space. The copter tilted again and this time he fell toward the open door. In a desperate move, he grabbed for anything and caught the edge of a denim vest. The larger man stumbled into Scott as they fell out the door. At the last second, the other Fist grabbed his partner's legs to keep him inside while Scott dangled below the door with a death grip on the larger man's vest.

"Shoot him!" the vest's owner yelled as he pounded on Scott's arm, twisted his wrist, but Scott held on. The third gang member with Scott's gun still didn't join the fight. The helicopter spun three-sixty. Scott slammed back and forth between the door frame.

"Cut it! Cut the vest!" the Fist who held him shouted into the wind.

The vest ripped, lowered an inch. Scott could see the hospital's warning lights reflected in the knife's blade as it sliced through the denim. He made one last grab before the vest tore free.

3

***

Hannah Quinn scrambled away from her hidden rooftop shelter seconds before the falling body obliterated it. Just her luck, the Left Fists had decided to drop their latest kill right onto her hideout. Now she was going to have to run for it before the police showed up.

She managed three steps towards the stairs before she looked back, her heart in her throat. *Damn it. Damn it. Damn it.* There was no reason to assume the victim had survived the fall, but she couldn't leave without checking. She just couldn't. What kind of person abandoned a mortally wounded person to die alone?

Your mother would. You know she would. You should listen to your mother. Like you always do.

Hannah groaned at her own stupidity, but her desire to not emulate her mother turned her away from her escape route. She picked her way through the collapsed lean-to that she had constructed out of filched hospital sheets and plywood.

The man's body lay splayed in an unnatural angle. The sun hadn't quite set, so she could see the blood pooling around his head where his skull had cracked. The armor he wore looked like the kind police wore, dark blue with thick fabric, but the badge and nameplate had been sliced away. Had the equipment been enough to protect him? Maybe.

She examined the swollen, bloody face before she reached over to brush away black hair from his right temple. No ear lobe. It could only be Scott Grey. An Alt-killer. Hero to the Norms of Star Haven.

I might be an idiot, and if I heal Grey I'll be a traitor to the Alts, but I'm not a murderer. I can fix this. I know I can.

4

First things first. Search for a pulse. There. Faint, but it tapped against her fingers. Now for the hard part. Inside. *Yikes!* She'd entered through the carotid artery, which sent her surfing in the wrong direction, up instead of down. Her panic rose, but not enough to keep her from locating the jugular so she could surf down to the heart. *Damn, damn, damn.* The aorta had split and blood was spurting into Grey's chest cavity.

She sped faster around his heart, sealing the ragged edge of the hole until it stopped leaking. She waited three beats to make sure he wouldn't arrest in the middle of her operation. Three of his ribs had shattered and two had punctured his lungs. What a mess. She could make a circuit of the major arteries and veins without difficulty, but the millions of tiny capillaries seemed endless. She finished with his lungs and surfed down to the liver, fractured but still functional. Time distorted when she healed. A minute felt like an hour. An hour felt like a day. A day like a week.

Okay, liver fixed. Next she needed to look inside his head, so she hopped into the inferior vena cava and rode up to his heart before transferring back to the carotid artery. From there she jumped into the vertebral artery.

No good. His brain had swollen too fast, keeping her out of his skull. She shoved harder, but the swelling pushed her back. She'd never tried to travel outside the blood vessels before, but she didn't have a choice. If she ended the operation and let Grey die like he deserved, an autopsy would show his half-healed body. Whether she healed him or not, the police would know an Alt still roamed their city, but if they thought *she'd* killed him, they'd redouble their efforts to find her.

She could feel his heartbeat slow and his blood pressure increase despite her repairs. She'd never lost a patient yet and Grey was not going to be her first. She pushed out of the artery. With no blood to guide her, she free floated. *Where the hell am I?* She grabbed onto the nearest bone and looked around. *Everything looks different in 3D. I'll have to guess which way is up.*

Luck stayed with her and she squeezed inside Grey's skull. A few jokes about Grey's swelled head crossed her mind. Instead of laughing, she skimmed along the brain's surface, maximizing oxygen flow while reducing water intake until the swelling receded. His heart rate increased as she surfed, so she kept at it until his blood pressure returned to normal. She'd make one last dash through the brain to repair any internal damage. If only she could change his thought patterns so he wouldn't hate Alts like everyone else in Star Haven. Unfortunately, her power to heal couldn't fix a hateful personality.

She stopped when she spotted the black thread. The odd, atrophied-looking tangle protruded from the interthalamic adhesion. How strange. A quick search showed a corresponding strand across the midline. She brought the two ends together. The ends fused into one and a spark of energy kicked her backwards. Whatever the thread was, it worked again. She had no more time to waste. She surfed down to take care of his broken legs, followed by his arms, then his shoulders.

One last repair, though he didn't deserve it. She pushed herself back into the bloodstream and surfed up to Grey's right ear. She'd never done something like this before, not with such an old wound. Too much stimulation to the cells could result in too much skin. She wouldn't do Grey any favors if she gave him mismatched ears. That would only make him hate Alts more than he already did.

Done, and not a minute too soon. Her own body was failing fast. She floated over to Grey's neck and drifted back into herself.

Her stomach roiled and every muscle seized at the same time as the migraine hit. She flattened her palms against the craggy cement on either side of Grey's head. *RUN! RUN! RUN!* her mind screamed, but her body refused to obey.

Grey's smoky eyes opened wide.

"Hannah Quinn?"

She managed a soft sigh before her body gave out and she fainted on top of him.

CHAPTER TWO

Scott rolled out from under Hannah. He was alive, which meant someone had rescued him. He glanced around the roof, looking for Left Fists, but saw only torn sheets fluttering in the cool breeze, a first aid kit, and a garbage bag filled with dirty paper plates. So this was where Mayor Dane's daughter had hidden herself all these months. Smart thinking, to hide on the roof of a hospital. He ran his hands along the light blue scrubs she wore to check her for injuries. The ID hanging around her neck read "Karen Smith", but even with her red hair dyed mouse-brown he knew this was Hannah. Her face had stared at him from a dozen runaway posters distributed throughout Star Haven's police precincts.

Finding no broken bones or bleeding wounds, he scooped her limp body into his arms, stood up...and almost fell flat on his back. On top of the beating he'd taken, he hadn't eaten anything since before he reported for duty yesterday — no, the day before, judging by the sunrise. He'd figure out the details once he got Hannah to the emergency department.

As he raced across the helipad to the elevators, he considered the broader implication of his current situation. A mid-air rescue meant there was an illegal

Alt in the city. The Alt-ban should have forced every Star Haven Alt out of the city six months ago. If the Alt who caught him had knocked them both out, he or she had only made a bad situation worse — first by assaulting a police officer, then by assaulting Mayor Dane's daughter. Defying the Alt-ban would only have resulted in the Alt's transfer across Mystic Bay to Thunder City. Assaulting a police officer guaranteed jail-time, and hurting the mayor's daughter was like begging for the death sentence. He pulled Hannah closer to his chest.

The elevator descended too slowly but with his energy sapped he couldn't risk the stairs. He leaned against the back wall, thankful that Hannah remained unconscious. She'd lived alone on a rooftop for months. What had happened to her? Why had she chosen such a desperate, lonely existence?

When the elevator doors opened onto the emergency department, he stepped into a tsunami of humanity — doctors, nurses, and orderlies raced about, their arms filled with equipment, charts, or worse yet, small children. He stepped into the path of the nearest empty-handed nurse. "I found her knocked out on the hospital roof."

The nurse shook off her confusion at Scott's sudden appearance and laid her fingers on Hannah's neck. Pulse taken, she jerked her head toward the nearest empty gurney and Scott followed. He laid Hannah down and the nurse repeated his check for injuries while shouting orders for blood tests.

An orderly shoved past him with a needle already in hand.

"Get out of here," the nurse said to Scott, not taking her eyes off Hannah. "We'll handle this."

Scott backed up and let the pros do their job. Star Haven Memorial was no one's first choice for health care, but beggars couldn't be choosers. The hospital was already overfilled with wounded created by the Left Fists's shooting spree, so Scott backed away. He'd check on Hannah in a few minutes.

At least something useful had come out of this fiasco. Miranda Dane was desperate to get her daughter back. There'd been no ransom demand after she'd disappeared, so the police had no choice but to classify her as a runaway. The mayor had offered a reward to anyone who found her daughter. Scott had already earned the mayor's favor and he intended to keep it.

Behind him another set of doors led to a hallway for the first floor ward. Maybe he'd find another first aid kit somewhere to bandage his own bruises. Oddly, he didn't feel sore, but he was also bursting with adrenaline. He'd feel the beating tomorrow for sure.

Thanks to the Fists, he also had no phone, no radio, and no weapons. What he wouldn't give to at least have his phone back. He shoved his hands into his pockets, and his left hand curled around something solid and rectangular. Confused, he pulled out his phone. He was sure the Left Fists had snagged it when they disarmed him. Everything had happened so fast though, maybe they'd missed it?

He'd solve the mystery later, after he speed dialed his partner.

"Juan, it's Scott."

"Fucking hell, man. We've been looking for you all night. Are you okay?"

He heard the underlying question. *Are you still a hostage? Who's listening to this call?* "I'm fine. I escaped. I'm at Star Haven Memorial right now."

10

"Hang on one sec."

Scott wandered over to a vending machine while Juan shouted across the din of the precinct that Scott was alive. The return cheer made Scott smile.

"Hey, do you want me to come get you?" Juan asked.

He was tempted to say yes and ask his partner to bring him something to eat. The vending machine only offered two bags of chips and a packet of peanuts. Not that he had any money to pay for it. "No, not right now. You're needed there and I need to get patched up. Any leads on how the Left Fists managed to get their hands on a helicopter?"

Juan's sigh spoke of long hours and volumes of unanswered questions. "Nothing, but the detectives are working that angle. I'm just trying to find my partner while the higher ups keep the riot under control."

Scott couldn't have asked for a better friend. "Thanks, man. I'll catch you later."

"Sure thing," Juan said. "Watch yourself, though. Left Fist activity has calmed down, but there have been reports of Alts in the area."

Scott's stomach tightened around nothing. Of course he'd guessed right. "Which ones?"

"We don't have confirmation on anything, but a guy called nine-one-one claiming he saw Captain Spec fly over the marina. Another woman swears she saw Ghost walk right through her front door without opening it," Juan said.

Alts knew better than to operate this side of the Bay, especially those two. "I'll keep an eye out."

"I know you will. If anyone can bag themselves an Alt, it's you."

11

Scott winced. Not even a month out of the Police Academy, when he was only nineteen, he'd shot and killed an Alt, earning himself a reputation as an Alt-killer. In Star Haven, he'd received a commendation and the public's adulation. Mayor Dane had used him as a poster child, proof that her decision to lower the Police Academy's minimum age to eighteen had been the right call.

If he showed his face in Thunder City, he'd get a very different, far more ugly reception. It'd been four years since he'd crossed the Bay. He had no reason to go back now.

Instead of dwelling on what he couldn't change, he disconnected from Juan and started to punch in the Mayor's number. Then he stopped. He'd been unconscious all night. That would make today Wednesday. Hannah's eighteenth birthday had been Monday. He'd kept track of that sort of information in case...well, you never knew when it would come in handy. Legally, she was an adult now, not a runaway. If she didn't want to go home, if she didn't want her mother to find her, Hannah had the right to make that decision. Even Mayor Dane couldn't force her daughter to return, no matter how much Dane wanted the reunion.

Against his better judgment, he put the phone back into his pocket. Hannah wasn't going anywhere for a while, and even starved as he was, he first needed to satisfy a different urge. Waiting a few minutes wouldn't hurt anything.

Inside the nearest men's room, the fluorescent light flickered in an unsteady rhythm, but at least he was alone. Blood covered his uniform and face, which wasn't as swollen as he'd expected. He opened his mouth to check which tooth he'd lost, but all his teeth appeared to be intact. Maybe he'd only chipped one? A quick swirl of his tongue over his molars didn't reveal any rough spots. He'd call his dentist anyway.

Scott lathered up his hands to wash away as much of the blood as he could. He had to have been rescued by an Alt, but which one? It would be easier to get an arrest warrant if he could identify the Alt first. God help him if it was Captain Spec or Ghost. He didn't need those two complicating things.

Hannah might have seen a face or a uniform before the Alt knocked her out.

Scott grabbed a handful of paper towels to blot away the water. As he did, his fingers brushed past his right ear. *What the hell?* He dropped the wad of towels and yanked his hair back. He'd been so focused on the blood and his tooth, he never noticed his ear, now complete with a lobe. A hallucination, it had to be. He'd had no food, no water in over twenty-four hours. A solid dose of protein would force him to see sense again. He'd beg a couple of dollars off someone and grab the bag of peanuts from the vending machine.

Exasperated, he rubbed his eyes, but the sharp scratch of plastic jabbed at his left eyelid. He pulled his hand away and found a packet of peanuts clutched in his palm. It was the same brand he'd seen in the vending machine.

Cold horror replaced his exhaustion. What the hell had happened to him?

***

"Well?" Miranda Dane snapped into her cell phone, while simultaneously checking her location on its GPS. Traffic leaving the Southern Point district still clogged the cross-city expressway, but she was scheduled for a press conference in front of the burned out civic center. Her driver would have no difficulties getting her there early.

"We have a possible sighting of your daughter."

Six goddamned months and all Police Commissioner Becksom could offer her was a *possible* sighting. She should have fired him after the first three weeks of failure. He was lucky to still be alive after six months. "Where?"

"Star Haven Memorial."

"Which one of your men *thinks* he saw her?" She'd be sure to have the badge of the son-of-a-bitch who didn't have enough sense to get confirmation before making the call.

"One of my undercover detectives attached to the Left Fists," Becksom said. "He broke a leg during the operation last night. They were stabilizing him in the ER when he saw a patrol officer come in carrying a girl who could have been Hannah."

"Identify that officer. Have him cuff my daughter and lock her up somewhere. If she disappears again, it's your head on the chopping block." Miranda disconnected the call and pinged her driver. "Head for Star Haven Memorial. Jump the lights if necessary."

The driver signaled his understanding.

Miranda dropped the phone back into its dock, then pressed her forefinger on the biometric lock to the hidden safe. The door popped open and she pulled out a padded envelope. She slid a manicured fingernail along the edge and let the contents spill onto her lap, careful to protect her custom tweed suit: three pre-filled syringes and their corresponding needles. Two syringes went back into the envelope.

Her nursing days at Memorial were long behind her, but she still remembered how to administer injections, both to save her patients and to kill them as ordered. She couldn't kill Hannah, but the girl was becoming more of a problem than she'd anticipated. Without her stepfather to protect her, Hannah was alone. This time Miranda would employ stronger methods to see that the girl stayed where Miranda had put her.

The security video showed the cracked plaster of SHM as her driver slowed to swing the vehicle through the crowded parking lot, forcing other, smaller cars out of the way. With no place to park, her driver cut off an ambulance and maneuvered the limo into the last space in front of the emergency department's main entrance. A minute later, he opened the door and Miranda stepped out onto the pockmarked pavement amidst a cacophony of sirens and shouting, all of which she ignored.

"Wait here. This shouldn't take long."

He bowed, but didn't respond.

CHAPTER THREE

A siren blared as Hannah woke. Months of paranoia kept her eyes closed to the barest slit. Cool air scented with antiseptic could only mean she was inside the hospital. That buzzing noise...no, not the helicopter...voices. Loud...angry...desperate.... Oh, God, Grey? Was he in pain?

Her eyes snapped open as a gurney sped past her surrounded by colorful scrubs. She tried to sit up, but her pounding headache knocked her right back onto the flat pillow. *Wait, think*...Grey fell, she healed him and...crap, she must have fainted after. Maybe right on top of him, because the last thing she remembered was his eyes, wide and confused. He'd seen her, identified her. She couldn't stay here.

He must have checked her into the emergency department, which would explain the honking and shouting and the IV needle pinching her elbow. Someone had parked her gurney at the end of the corridor instead of inside an exam room. So far, so good, though — no guards stood nearby. The lanyard from her fake ID still scratched her neck. Why hadn't Grey alerted hospital security?

Don't jinx your luck. Be glad he dumped you without a second thought. You can get away.

16

Still, he had dumped her, just like so many others before him. It stung, even though it shouldn't have. He hated Alts, had even killed one. He'd kill her too if he knew the truth.

The pain behind her eyes spiked as she turned her head. Making a run for it was out of the question, but all she needed was a head start and enough time to put distance between herself and the hospital. She had to assume Grey, dutiful Alt-killing cop that he was, had called her mother as soon as he dropped her here.

Keeping her movements slow so as not to attract attention, she slid her free arm out from under the scratchy blanket. With a pinch and a squeeze, she pulled the IV needle out of her vein and pressed her thumb to her elbow to stanch the blood. She curled onto her side so she could see the rest of the hallway and breathed past the headache. No one paid any attention to Karen Smith, hospital volunteer.

The crisis outside built to a crescendo. Someone shouted, "Get the hell out of the way," someone else shouted back. Mayhem erupted. The crowd surged as a fight broke out.

Time to leave.

The second her bare toes touched the cold floor, her legs buckled. Arms flailing, she caught hold of a nearby water fountain, her fingers white as they slipped on the shiny surface. Bile burned her stomach, then her throat, while she retched. Her weak hands pushed the button to release lukewarm water into her mouth.

Relax, breathe deep, count to three, get control of yourself, your body. You're stronger than this.

Three breaths later, she lurched toward the double doors leading to the first ward outside the emergency room. The racket behind her increased. A fight at the entrance gained traction and the noise rolled closer as she threw herself against the latch bar. Her feet slid across the polished linoleum. *C'mon, this shouldn't be so hard.*

The door inched open. Behind her, a voice rose above all the others. "Mayor Dane, if you would please wait and let us find..."

Fear shoved her through the doors. *Please-don't-let-her-find-me, please-don't-let-her-find-me, please-don't-let-her-find-me.*

***

"You stay with the girl." Becksom's voice rattled Scott's already raw nerves. "Cuff her to the bed and don't let her out of your sight."

Scott tossed the last bite of his soggy sandwich into the trash, heading for the cafeteria's exit. "Isn't that a little extreme, sir? She's eighteen now. If she doesn't want to return home, we can't legally force her."

Becksom ignored his question. "The mayor is coming to pick her up. Whatever you do, don't interfere."

Don't interfere. Not since he left Thunder City had he ever considered disobeying an order. Obeying orders, trusting authority...he'd channeled all his anger into becoming a better man when he entered the Police Academy, a different person. It looked like he hadn't overcome his inner rebel after all. The only reason why he didn't tell Becksom to shove it was because he was still numb after discovering his ear had grown back.

At least he could think on a half-full stomach. He'd wanted to escape the hospital ever since he'd dropped the peanuts on the men's room floor. Thank God the cafeteria cashier took one look at his bloody uniform and waved him through the line as he stuttered some bullshit explanation as to why he had no money.

The cell phone he could explain. And the peanuts, if he could convince himself the Left Fists had slipped those into his pocket as well. The regrowth of his right earlobe defied explanation. No one in Star Haven knew more about Alts than he did, and he knew of no Alt who could regrow body parts. It was easier to pretend the regrown lobe didn't exist. To make matters worse, someone had recognized Hannah and called the police commissioner.

He picked up speed and prayed Hannah hadn't disappeared. If he was lucky, he would have a few minutes to talk to her before her mother showed up.

An ambulance siren welcomed him back to the emergency department. A knot of hospital security surrounded a group of irate civilians, all pushing and shoving against the guards and each other. He couldn't see from this angle who they were trying to attack. Any other circumstance and he would have lent a hand, but he couldn't afford to lose Hannah. Again, he stepped directly into the path of a nurse.

"I'm looking for a patient. Karen Smith, brown hair, unconscious, transferred from the helipad?"

The nurse pointed down the hallway. "Gurney at the end. We're waiting on her test results."

Scott quick-stepped around the nurse before she finished and headed down the hallway. The gurney he found was empty, the sheets bunched up with the IV tube tangled around its stand. *Becksom's gonna have me assigned to desk duty for the rest of my career if I don't find her.* There was a long line at the restroom door. Doubtful she'd gone in there. Above his head, the CCTV monitor recorded his actions.

He backtracked out of the department, but this time he headed for the staff elevators. The ancient box cut off the sounds of chaos as its doors creaked closed and rose oh-so-slowly to the third floor. He should have taken the stairs. Scott squeezed passed the doors before they opened all the way, and took a left toward the south wing. Another left brought him to the security suite. He knocked and hoped that his uniform would be enough to get him inside.

"I have a security situation." He pushed past the uniformed woman who answered. A bank of computer monitors lined the wall. Two other guards swung around from their stations, their hands on their weapons.

Scott stopped, hands raised slightly, and addressed the guard seated at the nearest terminal, an older black man with salt and pepper hair. "I need to see the ER corridor leading to the first floor ward from ten minutes ago. Can you show me the footage?"

The guard's eyes swept Scott's uniform from head to foot. "I can, Officer..."

"Grey. Scott Grey. Call Lieutenant Pearson, Havenside Precinct. He'll confirm my identity."

"I know Lieutenant Pearson," the guard said, his hands easing away from his weapon. "Trained him when he was a rookie. I also know he's looking for a rookie of his own, named Scott Grey. He asked me to call him if your carcass wound up in our morgue."

Scott noticed a print of his academy graduation picture, the most recent picture anyone would have of him, taped to the guard's display. "The reports of my death..."

"...are greatly exaggerated." The guard finished the quote. "Who are you looking for, Officer Grey?" He typed a command into his keyboard and one of the monitors flickered. Scott checked the time stamp. Ten minutes ago, main doors at the end of the hallway off the emergency department.

"Girl. Blue scrubs, long brown hair. She's a volunteer. Karen Smith."

"I know her." The guard typed another command and fast-forwarded at a speed they could both follow. "From Mainland High School, a couple of blocks down. Found her a couple of times in the boiler room. She was studying for exams — anatomy and physiology. Wanted to find someplace quiet while she was on break. What sort of trouble is she in?"

"I don't know yet," Scott said, appreciating that the guard sounded genuinely concerned, and that someone had been keeping an eye on her. A second later Hannah appeared on the screen. "There she is."

The guard stopped the tape. Hannah stood frozen against the doors. She looked over her shoulder at something. The grainy monitor image focused on Hannah's face. Fear. No, not fear. Terror. Someone in the ER had put that look on Hannah's face. Scott clamped his hands into fists, grinding his fingernails into the meat of his palms. He understood her fear, if not the cause. No one should ever have to experience that sort of terror.

"Can you track her?"

"Sure can." The guard set the video running, then clicked a few more keys. The camera recorded her turning right, then lost her. "Looks like she headed toward the cafeteria."

"I would have seen her." Which made no sense. "What else is between the ER and cafeteria? Any place with its own exit?"

The guard scratched his chin. "There's the old billing office. It didn't have a separate entrance until two weeks ago when a drunk and disorderly overshot the parking lot and slammed his SUV into the wall. Admin is still looking at the budget to see if they can repair the hole. In the meantime, it's only covered in plastic."

"We're supposed to have someone stationed there," the second guard said. He pulled a clipboard off the wall. "Jackson, in fact."

Scott didn't even have to ask. His guard pulled up that station on his monitor. No Jackson.

"Son-of-a-bitch, he knows he's not supposed to..."

"He probably got called to the entrance," Scott interrupted. "Some sort of ruckus broke out."

"Not your usual ruckus," the third guard said, rehooking her walkie-talkie to her belt. "Mayor Dane parked her limo in the emergency lane and her chauffeur refuses to move."

The look on Hannah's face. Was she scared of her mother? Why? What could Hannah have possibly done?

Guilt for the blame-the-victim assumption rode him hard. Maybe she hadn't done anything wrong. He wouldn't know unless he asked.

Scott clapped his hand on his guard's shoulder. "Thanks for the assist. I have what I need."

The guard nodded. "No problem, Grey. Tell Pearson when you see him, he owes me a drink."

"Will do," Scott said over his shoulder as he pushed open the door. He ran back to the elevators, but this time took the stairs back to the first floor.

Halfway between the emergency department and the cafeteria, he found the billing office. He tested the door and found it open. Plastic crackled and flexed over the gaping hole in the opposite wall, where sunlight sneaked past the loosened duct tape. The room was empty except for a few filing cabinets and a wooden desk. Scott checked under the desk to make sure Hannah hadn't decided to hide there, but no, she had to have gone outside.

Since he couldn't possibly cause more damage to the wall, he ripped away the plastic cover and squeezed through. Smoke from last night's fires still lingered despite the salty breeze from the Bay. At this angle he could also see the pile of cars and ambulances jam-packed into the parking lot. The Left Fists had succeeded in bringing more misery to a district already steeped in it. Mayor Dane's presence didn't help.

A flash of blue scrubs and long hair caught his attention. Hannah crouched behind an industrial-sized garbage bin. No one could see her from the lot and there was no security at this end of the hospital. He ducked down and scurried over to where she knelt.

"Hannah Quinn."

She spun, her back pressed against the bin. Her chalky white skin emphasized her green eyes, glassy and bright.

"Hannah," he repeated, his voice low as he moved half an inch closer. "I've been trying to find you."

She shook her head in slow motion. "You better leave before we get caught, Officer Grey."

She knew his name, who he was. He never talked to anyone about what he did three years ago, and the media mostly left him alone now, but some people never forgot. Others would never forgive, but they were Alts. He didn't give a damn if they forgave him or not. Hannah had joined her mother on the stage the day he'd received the commendation from the city. Of course she would remember him.

"Hey, you can call me Scott, okay? Just Scott. I can't leave you like this." He dropped one knee to the pavement, prepared to run if she did, though the feverish look on her face made her more likely to pass out again than run off. "You can trust me."

A smiled ghosted over her lips. "No, I can't. You want me to go home with my mother. I won't."

Tough nut to crack. Six months on the street would turn even the softest woman hard. For now, he'd stick to what they had in common. "Let's not talk about your mother. Let's talk about what happened on the roof."

Her face scrunched a bit as she thought over his words. "What do you want to know?"

"I need to know what you saw."

She shrugged. "What makes you think I saw anything?"

Classic evasion tactic. "I don't know if you saw anything. That's why I'm asking the question."

She glanced back at the parking lot. Her mother's limo was still parked in plain view, sunlight bright against the tinted windows. "If I answer your question, will you help me?"

"Help you with what?" Two could play at the evasion game.

She turned back to him and took a deep breath. "Help me leave Star Haven. Get me across Mystic Bay to Thunder City."

"Why would you want to go to Thunder City?" She was eighteen now. If she wanted to cross the Bay,

24

there was nothing to stop her unless she had no cash or credit cards. Contrary to what the guard thought, Hannah attended Milldale, one of the hoity-toity academies in the Northern Star district. The cost of a ferry ticket was little more than spare change to the kids at her school. Any one of her friends could have given her the money.

"My mother has the port authority on alert." Her voice rose, brittle as ice. "And security demands a biometric scan before anyone can get on or off a boat. I can't cross without her finding me."

The biometric scans had been put in place to keep Thunder City Alts from using the ferry to enter Star Haven. Scott could see Dane bending a few rules to find her daughter, but why was Hannah so scared? He had to figure there would be tension between the two after Roger Dane, her stepfather, had died, but this fear...it was too extreme.

Helping her would have career consequences. At twenty-two, he hadn't scored enough cred to blunt a backlash if Dane revoked the favors he'd gained when he shot the Alt. And yet, despite what the Commissioner had said, he couldn't legally force Hannah to return home if she didn't want to.

"I can't cross the Bay to Thunder City," he said. Nothing would make him go back. Not ever. "But I'll see what I can do to help. Tell me what happened on the roof last night."

She blinked, her eyelids thick and slow. "I didn't see much because my shelter was behind the vent. A couple of helicopters had already landed to deliver patients. No one ever looks beyond the actual landing pad. I only noticed your helicopter because it flew around like a pissed off hornet, circling, like it was looking for a target. I was afraid the crew would see me."

Scott couldn't help his grin. "Yeah, I kinda picked a fight up there. The pilot was trying to shake me out the door. It worked, because I remember falling. Did you see the Alt who caught me?"

She shook her head, but her eyes looked down and away.

"C'mon," he said, settling back further on his haunches. "We both know there is no way I could have survived that fall. Who did you see? If you don't know their name or their moniker, just give me a description."

She licked her lips but didn't answer.

Scott sighed. As much as he hated to talk about the shooting, he had to say something to gain Hannah's trust, to convince her he really was the good guy. "Hannah, contrary to what the rest of Star Haven might think, I'm not some trigger-happy Alt-killer. What happened three years ago is a lot more complicated than what you've heard on the news. I can't change the law or make an exception. If there's an Alt defying the ban, I'm obligated to arrest them. I won't hurt them, I promise."

The muscles around her mouth relaxed — not enough to give him a smile, but enough to ease the harsh lines of tension. "Me," she whispered.

"What about you?" A pinprick of fear poked him in the stomach.

"I'm the Alt, but I didn't catch you."

Fucking hell! Even though Alts didn't necessarily look any different from Norms, he should have figured her out before now.

"What's your power?" He placed both hands on opposite sides of her head, flat against the bin, caging her, but careful not to touch her. *An Alt. Hannah Quinn — Mayor Dane's daughter — is a damned Alt.*

This time her eyes locked with his as her breath quickened. He was so close to her, a free strand of her hair, plucked by the wind, caressed his face. He understood her fear, the cold paralysis of having run yourself ragged in a maze only to discover there's no way out. He'd been in that maze, his escape a miracle. Now he found himself trapped between his loyalty to the law and his growing sympathy for Hannah. He dared to feel sympathy for her, but he couldn't let it show.

"Will you take me to Thunder City like you promised?" she asked.

He would throttle her if she continued to evade his questions. "Don't play games. What is your power?"

"Will you...will you help me?" she stuttered, delivering a stalemate.

"Damn you. Alt powers are dangerous if you don't know how to control them. I won't help you until you tell me what you can do."

Wrong threat. He knew he'd screwed up as Hannah straightened her posture and raised her chin, her slow trust replaced by defiant steel. "I assure you, I know how to control my powers. I've had them under control since I was five. I don't need a lecture from some Norm."

Yeah. That's what he thought. She saw him as just some Norm. Not even his uniform, covered with his own blood, would change her view. Alts might pretend to be superheroes, but at the end of the day, they protected themselves and their own. To hell with everyone else. A harsh lesson, that he'd learned the hard way. "Fine. No lectures. You were on the roof last night and saw me get pushed out of the copter. I fell. How did you break my fall?"

She shrank back. "She killed my stepfather. Miranda murdered Roger Dane. She murdered all of her husbands. I have to get away from her."

To think that Dane had painted Hannah as a sweet, confused young woman without a manipulative bone in her body. Scott looked over at Dane's limo, still idling. Nothing in the news reports had indicated Roger Dane died of anything other than a heart attack. He'd been driving along Bay Avenue when his Cadillac careened off the road, crashed through the barrier, and ended up in the Bay. "Can you prove it?"

She shook her head and sagged against the bin, rubbing her eyes with the heel of her hand. "If you're not going to help me, you'd better leave. It always takes me a couple of days to recover."

"Recover from what?"

Again, she didn't respond.

"Hannah, I need to know." He slammed his fist into the bin, making her jump. "Recover from what?"

"Why should I trust you?" Hannah looked him in the eyes, no flinching, all challenge.

Screw her attitude. "Because I'm all you have. If what you say is true, and your mother did kill your stepfather, and you really are an Alt, then you'd better start trusting me, because in this city, not even the daughter of Mayor Dane is safe."

She knew he was right. Her emerald eyes splintered into facets with unshed tears. "I don't know what other people call it," she said, her voice low, hoarse. "I don't know if anyone else can do what I do. I call it

28

bloodsurfing because that's what it feels like. I'm a bloodsurfer."

"What does a bloodsurfer do?" His hands squeaked against metal as he slid them off the bin, giving her room, giving her a modicum of his trust. He knew of Alts who could fly, crush concrete bare handed, outrun a jet, turn invisible; who possessed empathy, telepathy, and telekinesis. He didn't know of any Alt power that involved blood, unless Hannah meant it metaphorically.

"It's how I healed you, after you fell out of the helicopter."

Blood roared in his ears as Hannah's voice faded into the background. He hadn't been rescued. He'd fallen out of the helicopter and died, or damn close to. "My body?" Did he really want to know the details? "The damage from hitting the roof..."

"Most of your bones had shattered. You had a tear in your aorta, your liver was fractured, and your brain had swollen almost beyond what your skull could contain," she answered, as if listing groceries. "Two of your ribs had punctured your lungs. There was so much damage...."

"Stop!" He hadn't meant to shout, and they both ducked further behind the bin, his body covering hers, blocking any chance she would be spotted. The move was pure instinct, because he was a cop trained to protect, not because he cared about her. He couldn't afford to care. He wouldn't allow himself to care. She was an Alt and he was a Norm...wasn't he?

Doubts about his past rose like demons. His parents, his upbringing. More recent events: the appearance of his phone, the package of peanuts. He knew what Alts could do.

"Everything. You healed everything?" This was insane. He was a Norm and proud of it. He'd left his home to prove he could be a hero, to show that you didn't need special abilities to save and to protect. He'd accomplished so much these past four years.

She nodded. "Once I start, it's hard to stop. If it looks wrong, I fix it."

"What else? What else did you fix?" Damn his crumbling pride. Was his life nothing but a lie built on an accident? A defect?

"What do you mean?" she asked, but he looked away, so he could focus. How could he explain to her the damage she'd caused, the life she'd destroyed with a mere wave of her hand — if she even needed to wave her hand.

His hate warred with his training, but he'd been trained to protect Norms, not Alts. Only a few hours ago, he'd traded his life to save those innocent kids from the Left Fists. Yet, Hannah looked at him just like those kids had — wide-eyed and helpless.

"What other powers do you have? What else can you do?" One final desperate plea, hoping he was wrong.

"None. I can heal people. Other people. I can't heal myself. That's all I do."

The bitterness of her laugh sounded familiar, too much like his own. *Stop it. Stop empathizing with her.* If Hannah healed his bones, his heart, his lungs, and his brain, she must have also healed something else. The Left Fists didn't miss his phone and they sure as hell didn't give him a bag of peanuts. Hannah fixed something and turned him into an Alt.

Fate had once again kicked his ass. Any hope he had of making his own choices, controlling his own life, and establishing his future on his own terms was shot to hell. All because Hannah Quinn had decided his life was worth saving.

If he accomplished nothing else, he had to get both of them out of Star Haven today. Star Haven was a city built on the hatred of Alts, where laws were passed specifically to keep Star Haven Alt-free. If he stayed here and accidentally exposed his power, he'd be targeted for arrest, and worse, by the same cops he called his friends.

Hannah sat there studying him, judging him. She'd saved his life even though she didn't have to. Like it or not, he owed her. He could save her, but could he save himself?

CHAPTER FOUR

Instinct forced Hannah to reach out to Scott as she watched the blood drain from his face. Had she missed a crucial repair?

"Don't touch me." He knocked her hand away. "Whatever happens, you keep your hands off me. Understand? No skin-to-skin contact."

With his finger pointed at her nose, how could she not understand? Why would she want to touch him anyway? He'd gotten the best she had to give, and for her efforts, he'd turn her in. She had risked everything for him and now she had to pay the price.

She leaned forward to stand up, but before she could make a run for it, muscular arms curled around her shoulders and legs as Scott swept her off the ground. The mid-morning sun forced her to close her eyes. She could still hear the sirens in the background. Her head pounded in rhythm with Scott's stride. The smell of blood mixed with sweat didn't help her nausea when Scott hitched her tighter in his grip, pulling her closer to his chest. Next to his heart, which beat clear and strong thanks to her. As the saying goes, no good deed goes unpunished.

The rhythm paused. Why had Scott stopped walking? To flag down her mother? Or maybe to get the attention of Victor, the nasty chauffeur who dogged her mother's every step? A shiver rippled up Hannah's spine. If her mother had given the order to have Roger killed, then Hannah would bet her dirty scrubs that the chauffeur was the one who had killed him.

More walking, but at no point did Scott bounce her in a way that made her think he would drop her. She wasn't a tiny girl, but she'd lost a lot of weight while on the run. It wasn't hard when your diet consisted of discarded vegetables and leftover doughnuts.

She cracked open one eye, but the sun's glare put her surroundings into shadow. She closed them again and focused on what she heard. The ambulance siren dimmed, almost as if Scott was walking away from the hospital's entrance.

A sharp whistle pierced the grind of traffic. "Yo, Grey. Y'need help, man?"

Scott stopped and a minute later he slid her into the welcome coolness of a car. Without the sun in her eyes, she could see the interior. A taxi. Scott must have known the driver because he called the man "Mac" and gave him an address as he slid into the back seat next to her.

If Scott hated Alts like the rest of the city, why had he carried her away from the hospital? Her mother no doubt had one of the hospital administrators in a headlock over her daughter's disappearance, so it wouldn't have been any hardship for Scott to drag her back inside and get her off his hands. He'd already won her mother's admiration by shooting an Alt. Why would he pass up the chance to impress the mayor again? Heck, her mother would probably give him another medal.

She never should have trusted him with her secret, never should have told him about her power. When she had first seen him, standing on the podium with her mother to receive the medal of commendation, he hadn't looked particularly happy. Maybe she had imagined it, but he hadn't appeared to view his lucky shot as a victory for Norms. Rather, he had seemed sad, as if he wished he could be anywhere else but standing in front of a cheering crowd.

No one else had noticed his distress. Maybe that's why she had trusted him. If he didn't relish shooting an Alt, then maybe he didn't hate Alts with the same fervor as everyone else. How wrong she'd been about him.

After what could have been a few minutes or a few hours — her head hurt too much to track time — the taxi swerved to a stop. Scott coaxed her out of the back seat, his attitude cool, detached.

Brick mid-rise buildings surrounded the entire city block. West Gate Apartments, the sign read. Scott had brought her to Havenside, the university district. She had lived around the corner in the West Gate Villas about five years ago with her mother's fourth husband, the biology professor. It wasn't quite as upper-class as the Northern Star district, where Roger had moved them, but it wasn't the heart of the Swamp either, where she'd been born.

"Can you make it up the steps or do you want me to carry you?" he asked.

Carry me where? Why? What's your game, Grey? "I can make it up the steps, thank you."

He nodded, waiting for her to make the first move. She took a couple of deep breaths. The stars in her eyes faded.

"Okay," she said. "I'm ready."

He led her into the building, its narrow lobby dark after the brightness outside. No one saw them as they made their way to the elevator.

"You live here?" she guessed.

He nodded as he pressed the call button. The doors opened and he stepped in first. She hesitated. If she timed it right, she could run just as the doors closed. "If she knows you've helped me," she said, "she'll come after you too. She has access to everything. She can track you down in minutes."

"I'm not taking you to my apartment." He raised an arm to stop the doors from closing. "I'm taking you to a different apartment, someplace safe. At least until I can figure out how to get you out of Star Haven."

What had changed? He hated Alts, that much was clear, so why help her instead of turning her in? He shoved the elevator doors open again. Hannah glanced back through the glass doors of the apartment building. Was it possible he believed her story?

She had nowhere to run and she was too sick to try, so she stepped into the elevator. Scott had gotten his chance to back out, but he chose this path.

***

Scott could see Hannah's indecision, right up until she entered the elevator. He let go of the doors and pressed the button for the fourth floor. What he'd told her wasn't quite true. He was taking her to his apartment, but not to his official address on the third floor.

If Hannah had the power to heal his body after he'd crashed onto concrete, then she had a unique ability among alternative humans. Could it apply to diseases as well? Regardless, she would cause chaos among the Norm population if her secret became known, and not just in Star Haven. Was this why Dane kept her daughter under wraps, or had she been more worried about keeping her job as mayor?

He had to get Hannah out of the city. Even her mother's political connections couldn't keep Hannah safe. Once he delivered Hannah to Thunder City, he would make her break whatever it was she had fixed inside him. Without Alt powers he could return to Star Haven and the life he'd so carefully built. She owed him that much.

The elevator dinged and he led Hannah onto the fourth floor. When they reached the nearest apartment, he punched in his code, then pressed his thumb to the lock. The door buzzed, clicked, and allowed him to enter. He took it slow. Hannah didn't even turn her head to look around, so he kicked the door closed behind him and regretted it when she flinched, pressing herself against him. The sudden contact sent a wave of protectiveness through him. This was why he had become a cop. He looked down at the top of Hannah's head. For a brief moment, he didn't care if she was an Alt. She needed him.

He turned Hannah to face him, his hands on her shoulders, careful to avoid her skin. "Tell me what you need."

She blinked, her lids heavy. "I don't need anything."

"You're in pain, Hannah. You can hardly walk on your own." She didn't respond. "Look, I already said I'm going to get you to Thunder City and I'm a man of my word. But you have to help me. You can start by not lying when I ask you a question."

Hannah bowed her head, her matted hair not quite hiding her look of resignation. "I had some painkillers. The powerful stuff I...acquired at the hospital. They're still on the roof, though."

"I have painkillers," Scott said. "What else?"

She still hesitated. His question had sounded more like a command, but damn it, his whole future was at stake. He swallowed and tried again. "Hannah, I can't help you if you don't talk to me. What else?"

"The painkillers make me queasy. If you have something for my stomach..."

"Not a problem. What else?"

A single tear slipped down her cheek. Scott's heart skipped a beat, but he shoved away the call to sympathy. Her helplessness didn't mean he had to feel sorry for her. She was still an Alt, and eventually she'd learn how to use her abilities against Norms. Alts always learned those tricks first.

"Someplace to sleep," she whispered. "Someplace dark. Light makes the headache worse."

He used the spare bedroom for storage, but the bed had clean sheets and there were blackout shades over the windows to keep out prying eyes. He led her there, booting an empty computer box out of the way so she wouldn't trip. She didn't notice and lay down on the bed without pulling back the blanket first.

In his own bedroom, Scott pulled out his first aid kit. He kept it stocked with the usual, plus a few extra things for someone with a stressful job. He dumped two pills into his hand, then mixed a bi-carb with a tall glass of water. At the last second he grabbed a pair of socks out of his dresser drawer.

Hannah had wilted, but she sat up long enough to swallow the pills and drain the glass.

"You should put these on your feet so you don't get cold." He placed the socks next to her on the bed.

"Thanks," she hiccupped.

He waited while she slipped the first sock over her foot. Before she could pull the second sock over her other foot her eyes closed. She was fast asleep before her head hit the pillow.

He shouldn't touch her. The first rule of dealing with untrained Alts was to never touch them bare handed. If they couldn't control their powers, the results could be deadly. *Oh, what the hell. She's already touched me and wrecked my life. How much worse can it get? I should be dead anyway. Besides, she can't do much while sleeping.* He slipped the second sock over her foot without causing fireworks. At least not externally. The protective feeling he'd ignored earlier flared again in his chest, stronger than before. He bit the inside of his cheek until the fire cooled to a low simmer.

Confident she'd stay put this time, he headed into the living room and sank onto the sofa, his phone already in his hand. He dialed a familiar number.

"Scott?" His father answered, hesitant. He would have been watching the news, and would know of Scott's hostage situation from last night.

"Yeah, it's me. I'm fine, but I need an emergency evac. For myself and one other."

His father paused, just like Juan.

"I'm fine," Scott repeated with emphasis. "No one else is around."

"The Captain can be there in…"

"No, you," Scott interrupted. "Call her back. She's been spotted and so has Ghost. You have to get them out of Star Haven before they make things worse. I want you to come pick us up. Just you. No one else, understand."

"Us?"

Now that he had Thomas on the phone, Scott wasn't sure what to share. He'd promised Hannah he'd get her out of Star Haven, but how much should he tell Thomas? Scott hadn't promised Hannah he wouldn't tell anyone else about her Alt ability, and his father deserved to know who it was he was transporting.

"I found an Alt," Scott said. "She didn't make it out of Star Haven before the ban. She needs transport to Thunder City."

"What's her ability?" Thomas asked. His unspoken question was, *how dangerous is she?*

"She has control." Scott waited to see if Thomas would press the issue. Telling Thomas about Hannah's power would lead to more questions. Questions he wasn't prepared to answer, but would if Thomas asked them.

"Okay. I can be at the marina by one o'clock."

Security at the marina wasn't quite as tight as at airport or the seaport, but it was still there. He needed to get Hannah onto Thomas's yacht before Mayor Dane realized Scott was the one who'd taken Hannah from the hospital. They needed a meeting place that no one would connect to him.

"No. I want you to meet me under the Fairfax Bridge. There's an open-air café with a dock. Be there tonight, after dark."

"Who's your guest?"

"Hannah Quinn."

"Miranda Dane's daughter is an Alt?"

He didn't blame Thomas for sounding skeptical. Miranda Dane — author of the Alt-ban, leader of the anti-Alt movement — was the mother of an Alt. It made no sense. "Yeah. Crazy as it sounds, it's true."

"What can she do?" In the background, Scott could hear the flutter of a keyboard — Thomas issuing orders to his crew while he talked to his son.

"She saved my life." Scott had never lied to Thomas, and shame washed over him at his non-specific answer.

A short silence followed by more keyboard taps. "Saved you how?"

"I'm not sure," Scott said. True enough. "She said she calls it bloodsurfing because that's what it feels like. Direct quote."

The sharp click of a laptop closing signaled Thomas was ready to move. "Have you witnessed her power in action? I'm sorry to press you, but I need to know what she's capable of before I'll allow her near my crew."

"Not exactly." Damn, Thomas had asked, so Scott had to answer. "Juan and I responded to a call for back-up in the Swamp. The Left Fists...there was havoc all over the place. It's like the Fists knew how much damage they could create with no Alts around to stop them. A couple of Fists took hostages, kids on a playground. There was no time...we were spread so thin...no one I could call...the Fists were hyped up on blitz. I didn't know what to do, so I offered myself in exchange. I don't even know how the Fists got their hands on a helicopter, but there it was."

Scott stopped talking. All the terror he'd buried over the past day-and-a-half came pouring forth. When had he lost his courage?

"Shhhhh, it's okay, Scott. Relax. You're safe now, yes? In your apartment?"

It wasn't really a question. Thomas could track his phone with the special software he'd had programmed and installed before Scott moved to Star Haven.

"Yes, I'm safe," Scott said, the terror back under control with just a few words from his father.

"So Hannah saved your life. I already like her." Thomas chuckled, clearly not understanding the depth of Hannah's power or how close Scott had come to dying. "Tell me how she saved you."

"The Fists forced me on board the helicopter. They disarmed me and beat me to a pulp." Scott could feel each punch all over again. "I tried to fight back, but I couldn't...there was nowhere to go...then they shoved me out of the helicopter and I fell."

Thomas's silence froze anything else Scott might have said. "You were pushed out of a helicopter and Hannah caught you? Mid-air? With telekinesis?"

The clipped anger hurt more than his beating.

"No, she didn't catch me. No one caught me. I landed flat on the roof of Star Haven Memorial. I would have died, except Hannah was hiding up there and she fixed everything. She can heal people. By touching them."

More silence stretched through the distant connection. Scott was afraid he'd lost Thomas.

"Why didn't you call me from the hospital? Were you planning to keep this from me? Do you know what your death would do to this family?"

Scott knew what his death would do to Thomas. He didn't know, much less care, about the rest. "I'm calling you now. The hospital was chaos. Anyway, I'm pretty sure Hannah has to touch a person for her power to work. She's asleep right now. Healing me...there was so much damage...she's exhausted."

Silence again. This time it stretched on so long that Scott checked to make sure he hadn't lost his father's signal.

"I'll meet the two of you under the bridge, one hour after sunset," Thomas said finally, his voice laced with unshed pain. "Don't be late."

Scott disconnected the line and pressed the phone to his lips.

***

Hannah stepped out of the shower and found an oversized t-shirt and a *Star Haven Sabers* baseball cap waiting for her. She had slept through the day, but woke to discover her headache had dulled to a mild roar. She didn't want to risk reigniting the pain, so she kept the room dark while she dried herself and slipped on the pants portion of the scrubs she'd been wearing.

The t-shirt appeared black or maybe dark blue. She paused with it halfway over her head and inhaled. Aftershave mixed with the raw scent of Scott Gray. For the first time in six months she felt clean and safe. If only she could wrap that feeling around herself and hold it close forever. Hold Scott close forever. It was a pleasant but pointless fantasy.

The light knock at the door forced her to pull the t-shirt down until it fell free to her upper thighs. "Come in."

Scott poked his head inside. If he thought she looked ridiculous in his shirt, he didn't say so. At least he didn't appear angry anymore, or at least not angrier.

"I have transport for us across the Bay, but we have to leave now."

Hannah threaded her damp hair through the back of the ball cap and pulled it low over her forehead. "Who's taking us?"

"My father."

Father. Her sense of safety faltered. Roger had had all the security in the world and it hadn't kept him safe from her mother. "Does he understand the risks? What he's getting himself into?"

Scott nodded. "He understands. Trust me. I'm going to get you across the Bay."

A firm declaration. No doubts, no ifs, no maybes. Scott would accomplish his mission, but she couldn't afford to drop her guard. No police training could have prepared Scott for her mother's wrath. And Scott was still an Alt-killer. Even if the news reports hadn't gotten the details right, he'd still killed someone just like her.

Hannah started to put Scott's socks back on, but decided against it. They were warm, but far too big.

Scott had also changed out of his ripped uniform into jeans, a similar t-shirt, and a light windbreaker. Without all the police armor, he managed to look more dangerous, not less. He held something out to her. The foil crinkled in his hand.

"It's not much. I figured you wouldn't want to eat anything too heavy," he said.

A protein bar. Her stomach rumbled. She snatched the package and tore open the wrapper. Before she could think too much about the consequences, she took a bite. Sweet cherry flavor burst over her tongue and her stomach didn't protest. A small victory.

"Perfect," she said around the crumbs. "Thank you."

He started to say something else, but an alarm honked, followed by a muted bang that reverberated through the floor, like a neighbor had slammed a door. Scott mashed a finger over her lips before she could scream.

"Someone's in my apartment downstairs."

She followed him out of the bedroom on wobbly legs, grateful he kept the lights low. In the far corner, behind the sofa and next to the television, was a computer with multiple screens. As he sat, his jacket flared open revealing holstered gun. She slid up behind him as he typed.

The screens flickered. Each one showed a different streaming video of three men wearing the Left Fist insignia. They were ransacking an apartment similar to this one.

"The apartment below us?" she asked. Scott had mentioned that he had two apartments, but she hadn't thought to question it until now. "Why do you have two apartments?"

He didn't answer and didn't take his eyes off the screens. Hannah watched the destruction as one of the men yanked out file drawers and flipped through the paperwork. Another typed at another computer terminal — smaller than this one, and with only one screen, which didn't seem to work. A third man poked around the edges of the apartment, looking behind pictures, checking the vents. Hannah noticed a distinctive scar cut across his cheekbone as he slid his fingers along the top of a window frame.

"I know him." She pointed to the right-side screen. "He works for my mother."

"Your mother hires Left Fists?"

Stupid! Her trust in Scott had made her too chatty. How could she explain to a cop the depth of her mother's corruption? How could she tell him and not implicate herself? She couldn't risk Scott backing out of his promise to take her to Thunder City.

"I don't know anything about them. I just did what my mother ordered and I've healed this guy more than once. The last time he didn't even wait for me to finish, which is why he has a scar."

He accepted her explanation without further comment and checked his watch. "We're out of time."

He stood, but Hannah dug in her heels.

"Shouldn't we wait until they leave?" she asked.

"They won't leave." He pulled her sleeve. "They'll keep the building under surveillance. My father can't wait forever."

In the hallway, she expected to take the elevator, but instead Scott led her in the opposite direction, toward the stairwell.

"How do you feel? Can you make it down to the garage?" he asked.

She knew what he was asking. Did she want him to carry her? A very romantic, tempting notion, but how could he carry her and protect her at the same time?

"No, I'm okay." She chomped on the power bar to prove her point.

By the time they reached the garage, though, her headache had pushed its way past the painkiller. Motor oil and exhaust heaved the power bar in her stomach, but through sheer force of will she pushed the nausea back down.

"We're almost there."

Did he really understand how awful she felt, or did he guess? For a guy who hated Alts, his close attention to how she was feeling unnerved her. Hannah followed him through the doors, but a split second later Scott grabbed her around the waist and pulled her behind a cement barrier.

"Wha...what's wrong?" Her heart pounded so loud she couldn't hear her own question.

Scott pressed her head down to keep her from looking over the barrier. "They slashed the tires on my bike."

She couldn't see anything and Scott didn't look like the bicycle type, so she assumed he meant a motorcycle. "Now what?"

"We find another way out." He pulled out his gun. "Stay here and don't move."

Hannah readjusted her baseball cap and tucked her bare feet under her, ready to run as Scott crawled away. Her heart ignored her command to slow down. More than anything she wanted to peek over the barrier to see where Scott had gone, but she didn't dare. She waited, as she had waited for the last six months, hiding like a rat in a sewer, always one step ahead of her mother. She was sick of it.

Scott would know how to handle this, though. Not to mention he had a gun. Deep grooves appeared on her palms where she dug in her fingernails. Scott needed more time, then he'd come back. He had to. She didn't know where else she could go if he didn't.

The barrier made for a poor pillow, but she leaned her head back anyway, her eyes wide open, ready for anything.

***

Scott slid along the barrier until it intersected with the first row of cars. What was left of his bike stood twenty feet away, in the pocket of the lot set aside for economy cars and motorcycles. Careful to keep behind the larger trucks, he made his way around the perimeter.

Upstairs, he'd also recognized the Fist with the scar across his cheek. It was the third Fist from the helicopter, the bored one who had ignored his beating. The other two were unknowns, but their methodical search strategy told him they were pros looking for information, not your typical Left Fist junkies looking for drugs. But why would Mayor Dane need professional thugs?

By the time he'd crawled to the opposite side of the garage, he could see his target. The guy sat in the driver's seat of a slick street racer with a custom blue on red paint job that stood out among the mundane sedans Scott's neighbors drove. No doubt the guy was armed. Scott crawled a few feet forward. Now he could see his target's face.

Payback would taste sweet, but he couldn't afford a firefight. Not if he was going to get Hannah across the Bay alive. Determination erased his doubts, eased his fear. The police academy had trained him well. He could do this if he kept his head together and wits in check. Hannah needed him to succeed — though why had he thought of Hannah first instead of his father, who also needed him to succeed? He didn't have time to analyze this. If he could just lure the Fist, or whoever he was, out of the car, Scott could get a jump on him.

The Left Fist pulled out a lighter and flicked it open to touch the flame to a cigarette. Anything could be used as a weapon if put in the right hands. The windows to the car were down. Maybe if he reached for the lighter...

He discarded that plan as reckless, but before he could think of a better one the Left Fist jumped out of the car. "The fuck...?"

The Fist didn't appear confused, just pissed. Regardless, he was distracted, giving Scott his chance. He slipped his Ruger back into its holster — just as he curled his left hand around a square object.

A lighter lay in his palm, gunmetal polish with the Left Fist symbol engraved on the side.

Fucking hell, he didn't need this right now. The Left Fist looked under the driver's side seat. Scott slipped the lighter into his back pocket, then made his way toward the Left Fist.

"Hey, asshole."

The Left Fist twisted around, still crouched. One, two, three swift punches to the jaw and the Fist went down in a heap, alive, but very bloody. Scott rolled the man's unconscious body out of his way. Once he settled himself in the driver's seat, he found the car keys still in the ignition. Scott started the engine and listened to it purr. Oh, yeah. He would have no trouble getting Hannah to the river in this baby.

He pulled out of the parking space and swung around so the passenger side faced the barrier. He hoped she hadn't run off. If she had decided to run, he'd chase her down — all the way to Hell if he had to.

"Hannah!"

Her head popped up from behind the barrier. He waved her over, his tension easing at the sight of her. She scooted around the barrier and ran to the car.

"Nice." She flopped into the seat. At that moment, the doors to the garage opened. Scar walked through.

Scott watched the thug scan the area, reaching under his shirt, probably for a gun.

"Hold tight," Scott yelled. Tires screeched as he raced down the center aisle. No time to let Hannah buckle her seat belt. No time to check for oncoming traffic. He slammed the car through the guard arm blocking the exit just as the car's rear window exploded.

CHAPTER FIVE

"How long do I have?" Miranda asked the shadow on the other side of the video screen.

"Three days," the electronically distorted voice replied. "Your job is to prepare Star Haven for our arrival."

Three days to prepare. Three days to find Hannah. Three days to get Subject B under control. Only two decades of concentrated self-discipline kept the sheer panic planted firmly in her belly. "I understand. What sort of transportation do you require?"

"We're making arrangements now. Have your people ready to meet us at all major transportation hubs at all times. We'll inform you when we have arrived."

The shadow never shifted, never gave her a clue as to who was addressing her or where the Court of Blood might be located. She suspected they changed their location often, but she had never dared try to trace a call.

The speaker leaned into the camera, though not far enough to break the shadow. "Remember your contract."

The line disconnected.

Miranda sagged into her oversized executive chair, her headache expanding. From the day the Court had

50

elevated her from simple assassin to section leader they had made their orders clear and tolerated no failures. Keeping Hannah under Miranda's influence had been their primary expectation, above all other projects.

The muted television on the far wall of her office streamed video of the damage in the Swamp her men had instigated last night. It had taken an early morning phone call to the Capitol to remind the Governor of how much he owed her and how much support he would lose if he tried to send in the state's military reserve. Without outside interference, she'd succeeded in turning Star Haven's focus away from the security surrounding the trucks transporting Subject B, but it might have cost her Hannah. If she didn't find the girl by day three, she might as well just put a bullet into her own head. It would be far less painful than what the Court of Blood would do to her.

Miranda picked up the phone and speed dialed a familiar number.

"Coreville."

"What did you find?" she asked.

"Almost had her, but the cop got the jump on us."

"*Almost* doesn't count."

Coreville grunted. "We tore apart his apartment, but didn't find anything. It's clean. Even his computer."

"No one's apartment is completely clean unless they know they're being watched." *So why would a patrol officer think he's being watched?*

Coreville had no response, but she didn't expect one. He didn't get paid to think. It was only sheer coincidence that the helicopter and pilot she gave him for last night's operation had flown over the hospital.

Miranda closed the signal. The news crawl across the bottom of the television screen confirmed that her daughter's rescuer had been taken hostage last night. It said nothing about his fall from the helicopter or his *miraculous* appearance this morning with her daughter in his arms. It didn't take a genius to find Hannah's fingerprints all over Scott Grey's resurrection. Even if Hannah had told him anything useful, he still wouldn't have had time to scrub his home or his computer before Miranda found him.

With a vicious swipe on a tablet, she pulled up Scott Grey's record. He'd been born and raised in Thunder City, but moved to Star Haven four years ago. She'd needed a police force strong enough to deal with any Alt-related issues, young people with a strong anti-Alt sentiment that could be nurtured through the Police Academy's classes. Grey had proved his loyalty when he killed an Alt who had proved troublesome to the city. So, why the hell would he protect an Alt now?

Miranda skimmed his record. Grades above average, working-class family, no run-ins with the Thunder City police. A perfectly average past for an overachieving cop? It read as if someone had scrubbed his record just like Grey had scrubbed his apartment.

Any connection to Thunder City could mean ties to the Thunder City Alts. If Grey had any Alt connections, no matter how innocent, it could mean his anti-Alt sentiments weren't as solid as they should have been for a Star Haven police officer. If he'd had any sympathy for Alts before he found Hannah, then maybe Hannah hadn't used her power to manipulate him. The girl had a talent for hormone replication and she could have easily nudged Grey's sympathy in her direction if he touched her, just as Miranda had trained her.

It still didn't explain why his apartment was devoid of any personal information. Scott Grey was hiding something, and it wasn't Hannah.

Miranda speed dialed Becksom. "I want a trace on Scott Grey's phone. His, and anyone else who he associates with — friends, family. I don't care if they're in Thunder City. Find a way to make it happen. Keep tabs on any other accounts he has: email, banking, social networks — everything. He's the key to finding my daughter. Track him and keep me informed, no matter what it takes. You have until dawn."

She hung up before Becksom could respond, and then dialed her chauffeur.

"Meet me out front. We have another problem."

***

Hannah placed both hands on the rear bumper to help Scott push what was left of the racer into the river.

"Don't. Relax. I've got this," he said, waving her back.

Just as well. She'd screamed when the bullet hit the car, reflexively ducking her head into her lap. *Stay down*, Scott had yelled. She did and white-knuckled the high speed dash to the bridge. They were lucky they hadn't been pulled over. By the time Scott skidded the racer to a halt under the bridge, she'd almost barfed.

Her shaky legs made it hard to scramble back up the embankment. Below, Scott stretched through the driver's side window to let loose the emergency brake. With the brakes off it didn't take much effort for him to shove the racer down the slope of dirt and near-dead grass. Within seconds the entire front end was under water. Overhead, traffic returning from last night's wilding roared over the Fairfax Bridge, which connected Southern Point with the rest of Star Haven. Air bubbles gurgled up to the surface from the car's interior and belched out the sour scent of refuse.

"How deep is the river? What if it doesn't sink all way?" she asked as Scott climbed his way back up to her.

"Doesn't matter." He tugged down his windbreaker, but not before she saw a second gun holstered at his hip. "They're not after the car, they're after us."

"After me," she reminded him. "She'll find me. You can still walk away."

He hid his anger, but she'd learned long ago to pay close attention to body language. His short, clipped sentences, his refusal to look at her when she talked, said more about his feelings than his rescue plan.

"If what you told me about your mother is true, she already knows I'm protecting you. Those men in my apartment — they weren't Left Fists. There's no way Dane would let a true Fist anywhere near you. They were looking for information, using the Fists as cover. Anything they could use to track me down. Names, addresses, pictures."

She paused. "But you don't keep that sort of information in the second apartment, do you?"

He walked along the road toward the *Bottom's Up Bar & Grill*. The flashy sign beckoned to them through the twilight with a cheeky girl flipping her fluorescent skirt. "No, I don't."

He still didn't give her an explanation — why no information or why he had a second apartment in the first place. Fine. If he wanted to be a sullen son-of-a-bitch, she wouldn't bug him.

She doubled her pace to keep up with his stride. "She'll never stop trying to find me. Even if I get to Thunder City, I won't be able to live in the open. I'll still have to hide."

"We'll work on getting you settled with a new identity."

What did he mean by *we*? Would he stay with her once they crossed the Bay? Did his father have connections who would hide her? Scott seemed so certain everything would be taken care of, but she couldn't take a chance. If she couldn't hide herself in Thunder City, she'd have to move on, one way or another.

Regardless, she'd figure out how to pay back Scott for everything he was about to lose: his job, his home, his friends. She owed him big time, even if he was an Alt-killer.

Even at this distance, the scent of deep fried fish wafted through the humidity. In the pit of her stomach, the last bits of the power bar churned, digesting in anticipation of more food. If she craved food, then her sickness from bloodsurfing was over. She hurried her pace again.

A few minutes later, they reached *Bottom's Up*. Scott sidestepped a couple staggering out of the exit and led her along a narrow porch, down to a small dock. Lanterns ringed the outdoor seats, and the water lapped quietly underneath. The combination of bright lights, sweet fish, and salt water triggered her memories of Roger and his sailboat. He used to love sailing with her along the Star Haven coast, enjoying a picnic on the deck while they sailed past other boaters. Sometimes they'd hail the other boats, other times they just watched the world pass by.

She didn't see the approaching runabout through her memories until a firm hand reached out to grab the sleeve of her t-shirt and pull her on board.

"I got 'cha," a new voice said.

From under the rim of Scott's baseball cap she looked up at another man. He was tall, but not quite as tall as Scott, with dark hair and the tanned skin of one accustomed to the outdoor life. Unlike Scott's smoky gray eyes, the boat pilot's eyes were movie-star blue. He gave her a quick up and down assessment. She did the same, taking in the deep red polo shirt and black jeans. No weapons for this guy, who she assumed was Scott's father, but he appeared relaxed as if he rescued Alts all the time. There was also something familiar about him, but she couldn't quite place his face.

"What's *she* doing here?"

Scott's harsh demand almost sent Hannah backstepping over the side of the boat, but Scott's father kept her upright. Scott stared past her at a woman in the front passenger seat. In the low light, Hannah hadn't seen her at first, but now she couldn't help but notice the pink-streaked blond hair and chartreuse nails, which clashed horribly with her life-jacket. Whoever she was, she took no notice of the new passengers.

"Her job," Scott's father said, as he released Hannah's sleeve and sat in the pilot's seat. "Now keep quiet and get yourselves secured."

Hannah chose the seat behind the pink woman. Scott handed her a life vest.

"You can adjust the straps," he said, demonstrating.

"I've done this before." She proved it in less than ten seconds. Was that a small smile on Scott's face? It disappeared by the time she pulled the life vest over her baseball cap and sat down.

Scott tugged on his own vest before sitting next to her. The boat pulled away from the dock and headed under the bridge. No one talked. After five minutes Hannah leaned toward Scott. "Is she an Alt?"

"Yes," he said, his anger clear. "A low-level telepath with a talent for looping memories. She's making sure no one sees the boat by looping the previous few minutes through the minds of anyone close to shore. It's distracting, but usually not dangerous."

The way Scott bit off *usually* made it sound like he had experience with this Alt. Yet, how would someone like Scott know a telepath? How would his father know how to hire an Alt, especially for a job like this? "What do you mean, not *usually* dangerous?"

"It would be unpleasant if she decided to loop my memory of Left Fists beating me up and shoving me out of the helicopter."

"Good point." Her worry ate any other questions she might have asked out loud. Could the telepath pick her brain and discover all her secrets? What would the telepath do if she discovered what Hannah had been using her powers for over the years? If she discovered the things Hannah's mother had made her do would the Alt refuse to take Hannah any further? Would she go to the Thunder City police? Hannah surreptitiously unhooked the belts to her life vest. If she had to, she could jump overboard and swim to shore. She'd evaded Miranda's men for six months, she could do the same with Scott.

When the runabout glided to a dock at the Star Haven marina, Scott's father leaned over and touched the Alt on the shoulder. She blinked as if waking from a dream.

Scott collected the life vests as they exited the boat. "This way." He pointed toward a yacht moored in a berth not far from the runabout. The three of them formed a protective triangle around Hannah as she made her way up the plank. She couldn't help but sneak a look at the Alt's face — she appeared to be sleepwalking, with her eyes half closed.

A minute later, they stood on the deck of the *Elusive Lady*. The name pinged a memory. Hannah took another look at Scott's father.

"You're Thomas Carraro," she said.

Carraro signaled the Alt to leave. The Alt turned, but not before tossing Scott a saucy wink over her shoulder.

Hannah's desire to talk to the Alt turned into an urge to punch her. Instead, she channeled her anger at Scott. "Why didn't you tell me your father was Hack-Man?"

"How do you know who he is?" Scott asked.

"We've met before," Carraro said before she could. "At Roger Dane's warehouse. Two years ago, as I recall. I wasn't sure you would remember."

How could she forget? It had been her sixteenth birthday and Roger had managed to secure some time away from Miranda. He'd promised Hannah a day on his sailboat, just the two of them, but first he had an appointment to keep. "Roger suspected someone had hacked his business computer. They changed the shipping schedule around. Messed up his import records. He asked you to track down who did it."

"Anyone could track the hacker." Another signal from Carraro. The yacht's crew worked around the guests to get the boat underway. Carraro's voice rose so he could be heard over the engine. "Your stepfather needed someone like myself to look at the system, study the damage. He thought I might know who the culprit was. I didn't, so I left. Did he ever discover the miscreant?"

"He never said anything to me afterwards." True enough, though she wouldn't be surprised if her mother had something to do with it.

"I remember you, though." Carraro caught a flyaway strand of dyed brown hair. He rubbed it between his fingers before setting it free in the wind. "You had your pretty red head buried in a book while you waited."

Well, crap, it didn't take much to drain her lingering outrage and get her to blush, just a near-stranger calling her *pretty*. At least she still had the baseball cap to cover her face.

"Why don't you go below," Carraro said. She noticed he was careful to place a hand on her back and not her arm, where the t-shirt covered her skin, before he gave her a light push. "There's food and drink in the galley."

Hannah hesitated despite the insistence. She looked back at Star Haven receding behind them. This was it. She was actually going to make it across Mystic Bay to Thunder City. Roger had taken her along the shoreline, but never across. She hadn't considered what would happen if she made it.

"Go ahead." Scott jutted his chin toward the stairs. "I'll join you in a few minutes."

She faced Scott and Carraro before heading down the stairs. "Thank you. For everything."

Carraro nodded, as did Scott. She wanted to say more, but she couldn't quite find the words to convey the depth of her gratitude. She could also see the two men needed time together. Carraro probably knew of Scott's brush with death. As a parent — well, a normal parent — last night's hostage situation must have scared him something fierce. Roger would have been scared for her, had been scared for her, when he last called to warn her. He made her promise to run, to hide, to find safety, so she did the best she could.

Damn, she was tearing up again. Just as well that Carraro had asked her to leave the deck. She needed to figure out what to do next.

***

"You have no idea how scared we've been," Thomas said.

Scott ignored the *we*. He knew how scared Thomas must have been. He didn't give a damn about the rest of the family. He watched Hannah until she disappeared into the yacht's interior. He hoped she wasn't too shy about taking the food and drink Thomas had offered. Her walk still seemed a little shaky, though she looked much better than she had this morning. Her eyes were much clearer. Still bright, but not as glassy. He had to stop thinking about her eyes.

"We knew this was a possibility when I crossed the Bay, even before I entered the police academy," he replied.

"Understanding, accepting, and having to deal with your possible death are three very different emotions."

Thomas's voice lost the honeyed tone he'd used to calm Hannah. Pain leaked with every word. Scott

60

lowered his eyes, but didn't apologize. He needed to keep the blame where it belonged: on the Left Fists.

"It happened so fast," he said. "One moment I'm falling out of the helicopter — I have no idea of where they got one, never mind a pilot — the next, I'm awake, flat on my back, with Hannah fainting on top of me."

Thomas waited a beat. "Sounds as if she risked a lot to save you."

"If everything she says is true, then yes, she did."

Thomas nodded leaning on the nearest handrail, his arms folded. "What has she told you about her situation?"

He might as well get it all out now. Thomas would already have seen the streaming feeds from his second apartment. "Hannah claims her mother killed Roger Dane and all of her previous husbands."

Thomas rubbed his chin while examining the accusation, not looking the least bit surprised. "Interesting. Roger Dane was a good man. He ran an honest business and kept his nose out of politics. From what I understand, Miranda already had money from her previous marriages when she started her climb to the Mayor's seat. I can't imagine she would have risked the scandal to kill him for his fortune. Do you believe Hannah's story?"

"I don't know." Scott joined his father against the rail, his back to the disappearing coastline, his old — new — life. He couldn't bring himself to watch it slip away, maybe forever. "Mayor Dane painted her as a shy, quiet girl suffering from a mild case of teenage rebellion. Everyone in my precinct expected her to show up dancing in one of the clubs, or maybe at a frat party experimenting with newfound freedom. Nothing could have been further from the truth. She built a shelter out of sheets and plywood on the roof of Star Haven Memorial. If she wanted to experience street life, that's not how you do it."

"Do you think she's lying about Miranda?"

Scott stared at the dim glow from the galley. "I believe Hannah believes what she's told me."

Thomas sighed. "For a child to believe her mother desires to harm her...that's a powerful and unnatural concept for any young woman to grasp. Do you believe her mother is capable of harming her?"

He'd only had one direct meeting with Mayor Dane — the day she'd given him a medal for shooting an Alt. Despite the summer sun, he'd been too numb to care for the festive air blowing from the crowd onto the bandstand. From a distance, Miranda had the charisma to challenge an entire city to follow her into battle. Scott had heeded her call. Up close and personal, though — "Miranda Dane is powerful, driven, and doesn't suffer fools lightly. Sound like someone you know?"

"Are you referring to yourself or your mother?" Thomas asked, not rising to the bait.

"Touché," Scott conceded.

Thomas, as usual, let it go. "Do you think Miranda abused Hannah? Physically?"

A tough question he should have expected. "Physically abusing an untrained Alt? Dangerous. On the other hand, Hannah's a healer. Miranda used to be a nurse. Maybe Miranda trained Hannah? Maybe she used emotionally abusive tactics and Hannah didn't think she could escape. Not from an anti-Alt city like Star Haven."

Thomas checked his watch. They still had over an hour before they'd reach the other side of the Bay.

"Your mother wants to speak to both of you after we dock. Do you think Hannah is ready?"

On any other day, Hannah could probably handle an encounter with his mother better than he could. "I think Hannah wants nothing more than to find a hole to jump into for a while."

Thomas pushed off the rail. "Then let's not blindside her with the family business. We'll talk to her now. Warn her about what to expect. I would think that after six months on the run the fewer surprises she has in her life, the better. What about you?"

Scott rubbed the bubble of anger building in his chest. Like it or not, he would have to talk to Catherine about Hannah. If he couldn't avoid the confrontation, he could at least minimize his exposure.

"Do you still have the penthouse downtown?" he asked.

Thomas nodded, his eyes cautious.

"After we drop Hannah off and get her settled, I'll stay there," he said. "It'll give me and Catherine neutral territory if she wants to talk about other things."

"How long will you stay?" Thomas asked.

Until Hannah breaks what she fixed. Until she makes me a Norm again. He wouldn't tell Thomas about his Alt power. Not yet, if ever. If he could control it for a little while longer, everything would be okay and no one would ever have to know what Hannah had done to him.

"Until I can figure out a story to tell Mayor Dane about why I disappeared at the same time as her daughter," Scott said instead, as he pushed away from the rail. "I'll also have to explain to the department why I took an unexcused absence."

63

"Being held hostage by the Left Fists lends itself to all sorts of creative excuses." Thomas clapped his hand on Scott's shoulder. As he did, his hand brushed past Scott's right ear. *Shit!* Scott held his breath and prayed his Alt-power didn't misfire.

"Hannah did this?" Thomas asked, gingerly touching the lobe.

"She calls it bloodsurfing." *Focus. Act normal. Don't make him suspicious.* "I haven't had time to question her about the details. She said I had multiple broken bones, a fractured liver, punctured lungs..."

Thomas dropped his hand. Scott fought his sigh of relief. "Why did she heal your ear, though? After ten years, it's hardly life threatening."

"I don't know. Instinct maybe? She said when she sees something wrong, she fixes it." He shrugged, for lack of any other explanation.

"Your mother's going to have a field day with this. An Alt with a unique ability who also happens to be the daughter of the most powerful anti-Alt politician in both cities combined." He chuckled as he pulled Scott into a tight hug. "I know it's not funny, but damn me if you don't drop the most bizarre situations into my lap."

"It's not my fault this time." Scott returned the hug, grateful he'd kept his jacket on and careful to keep his head tilted to the side. If anything happened to Thomas because of him, he'd never forgive himself.

"None of what happened back then was your fault." Thomas stepped away and placed his hands on Scott's shoulders. "If I had thought so, I never would have adopted you."

The intensity of his father's concern burned him, humbled him. "Right. You adopted me because of my upbeat personality."

Thomas laughed again, then turned serious. "Let's go talk to Hannah. If any part of her story is true, if Miranda Dane is everything Hannah says she is, then bringing Hannah to Thunder City won't save her. This could turn into a long, dangerous fight."

More dangerous than you know. Scott stuffed his hands into his pockets as he followed Thomas toward the galley. *Just a little while longer. Keep it together for a little while longer. Hannah will break your power. She has to. I can't live like this, I can't live as an Alt. I just can't.*

CHAPTER SIX

The lights to the galley flickered on as Hannah descended the stairs. She paused at the bottom and closed her eyes. The colors were wrong; warm cream and brown and burgundy, instead of cool white, dark blue, and stainless steel. Roger had preferred a more businesslike look to his sailboat's interior design, making it a place to bring clients rather than a home away from home. Carraro's yacht had a lived-in look. It was a place to bring friends or the odd Alt he needed to rescue. Except Roger had tried to rescue her, too, and look at what had happened to him.

Panic swirled up briefly, as the yacht increased its speed. Roger was gone, dead. Oddly enough, knowing Miranda had done her worst and couldn't hurt him further soothed Hannah's stomach. Her panic subsided. Carraro wasn't a stupid man. He might even be able to fend off her mother if he didn't get too wrapped up in Hannah's life. Wherever Carraro brought her, she couldn't stick around too long. Not without putting everyone in danger.

What about Scott? a tiny voice whispered. The fluttering in her stomach returned. Thoughts of leaving Scott behind sent her stomach swirling again.

Oh, c'mon. It's not like you have a chance in hell with him. A Norm? A cop? An Alt-killer. Don't let a pretty face distract you from what's really important.

That sounded more like something her mother would say. She'd have to watch out for those thoughts. If she could expunge her mother from her mind, from her soul, she might have a chance to undo some of the damage her mother had inflicted on her over the years. She might even turn out to be a decent alternative human after all.

She had to focus on the concrete present, not on romantic wishfulness. With a parent like Thomas Carraro, a known Neut — neutral — who hired both Alts and Norms for his security business, she could understand why Scott would need to change his name and even afford a second apartment. It didn't explain why he lived in Star Haven, or even needed a job in the first place.

The small refrigerator behind the bar contained several thick sandwiches, sodas, and imported beer. She chose what looked like chicken salad and a diet cola before she hopped onto a bar stool. Too fast. Her head protested. She hoped Scott had brought more of those painkillers with him.

If she'd had the courage, she would have stayed on deck to talk with the Alt Carraro had brought with him. The Alt deserved a thank you for assisting with their escape. In truth, what Hannah really needed to ask was what it was like to live as an Alt in Thunder City.

Before the anti-Alt movement organized, before her mother had started campaigning for a seat on the city council, Star Haven Alts always had to hide behind masks to avoid harassment by anti-Alt Norms if they wanted to use their power in public. Around the same time, Thunder City Alts stopped wearing masks. Somehow Captain Spectacular had convinced her city to let Alts work with the police and the fire department and other rescue services.

The press in Star Haven had made a big deal about all of the Thunder City residents who had moved to Star Haven to get away from the Alts. News reports talked about Alts using their powers to take jobs away from Norms just because they were stronger or faster, using their powers to spy on Norms in their home just because they could see through solid brick, or worse: those sneaky telepaths reading your mind anytime, anywhere. The stories had scared her so much that she obeyed Miranda's orders to never use her power unless she had permission. Which, of course, meant never using her power unless her mother was in the room.

Yet, Hannah also took notice of the half-a-dozen kids who disappeared from her school around the same time. Whispers in the hallway said their families had moved to Thunder City, but no one was allowed to talk about it. Hannah didn't think all the students were Alts, but how could she know for sure?

The sandwich and soda quieted her headache. What little cash Roger had given her before Miranda blocked his accounts, she'd spent on food. If she could score a new identity, she might be able to find a regular job. It would have to keep her behind the scenes, not out in the open like a waitress or a cashier at the mall.

What she needed was a newspaper, a print one. She didn't dare try to use a computer. Who knew what sort of algorithms her mother had woven into the internet?

Her head spun with possibilities, inserting and deleting ideas into a matrix of her own making. Roger had told her a little about Thomas Carraro. Her stepfather could afford the best investigators, but Hannah had no idea how much he'd paid Carraro to review his import records. Still, Carraro might know someone who could create a new identity for her. A new name would get her in the door of a few jobs; a new background with a high school diploma would open a few more.

She would have to ask. If he couldn't, or wouldn't, well...Thunder City had plenty of rooftops she could occupy until she found a way to leave.

Deep voices warned Hannah before Carraro descended the stairs into the galley with Scott following behind. She quickly tucked her hair behind her ears, as if she could improve the rat's nest created by the dye job and ball cap.

Whatever Scott and Carraro had been talking about, they stopped as soon as Scott hit the last step. He brushed past her to toss his windbreaker onto the sofa, exposing the gun holster strapped to his upper body. Each arm also had its own weapon: a taser clung to the well-defined bicep of his left arm, and a knife hugged his right forearm, both of which he loosened and set aside. The second holster remained clipped to his belt. His jeans weren't so tight that he couldn't hide more equipment under there too.

He caught her staring. "Yes, I have more concealed weapons. No, I'm not removing my pants to show you."

Well, she could solve everyone's problems right now by dying of embarrassment. Instead of instant death, she pulled the rim of the ball cap lower to cover her face, which was probably as red as her hair used to be.

Carraro, at least, wasn't paying attention to her. He reached into the refrigerator and pulled out another sandwich, but with a beer this time. He handed both to Scott before settling on a stool opposite her. He folded his hands and watched his son break open the plastic wrap.

"Hannah," Carraro said, after Scott began to eat, "Scott has told me a little about what you've been through, but before we reach Thunder City, I'd like to get to know you a little better."

Ugh. Carraro used the same tone as the principal when he had called her into his office because he needed to clarify who started the fight in the girl's locker room. What did they call this on TV? Good cop/bad cop? Was Carraro the good cop and Scott the bad? She stalled by sipping her soda, but her panic choked on the fizz. "What would you like to know?" she coughed.

"Why don't we start with your expectations." He handed her a napkin.

She took it and wiped the soda from her lips. "Expectations?"

"What do you want from Thunder City?" Carraro continued. "What do you believe the City can provide for you?"

She glanced up just as he smiled, but the smile didn't hold the warmth that it had when he'd first pulled her onto the runabout.

"I'm not sure what you mean." She hoped Scott would explain, but he didn't. He kept his eyes on his food.

"You've made some serious accusations against your mother," Thomas said. "You've indicated she might harm you should you return to Star Haven. I need to know what led you to this belief and why you think Thunder City can help you."

So Scott had told his father about her mother. Except neither of them believed her, judging by Carraro's impersonal tone. "I can't prove any of it, so it doesn't matter. You won't catch her. She's too careful. I think..." She had to be so careful in how she handled these questions.

"Think what?" Carraro prompted.

"I don't think she's working alone. I mean even beyond the men she's hired."

More eye contact between father and son. "What men?"

"I only figured it out after they trashed Scott's apartment...his other apartment. I've been bloodsurfing through the same group these past few years. Sometimes they were dressed as cops, sometimes as Left Fists or another gang, and a couple of times Miranda brought me to them while they wore business suits. It makes sense if she's had them working undercover in all of those different organizations. When I tried to flee Star Haven, I saw them at the marina, dressed as security guards. If I hadn't jumped over the gate and into the Bay, they would have gotten me."

"You jumped into the Bay?" Scott thumped his beer on the countertop.

Oh, good lord, could she possible go five minutes without pissing him off? "Yes. It was either jump or run. I couldn't outrun them, but I'm a strong swimmer. I would have made the swim team if mom had let me..." *Idiot. Who cares about the swim team?* "I swam between the boats and had to tread water for the rest of the day. Once the sun set, I crawled onto one of the

71

ramps and slammed my knee against the boards. Which is why I went to the hospital in the first place. After I snuck in and found out how easily I could get cold packs and bandages, I stayed."

Neither of them said anything, so Hannah nibbled a little more of her food. Maybe they wouldn't ask her again about who her mother worked for because she really had no answer.

"So you can't heal yourself?" Carraro asked.

Her mother knew she couldn't and it gave her an advantage. Just how much of her personal details should she share? How much should she risk, based on a man who was more interested in rescuing his son than her. On the other hand, the answer was fairly obvious and it wasn't her worst secret. Not by a long shot. "No, sir."

He considered the information for a moment. "Let's get back to your expectations. What do you think you'll do once we arrive in Thunder City? How do you expect to live, knowing your mother is chasing you?"

"I don't know. I never really expected to get this far." She toyed with the plastic sandwich wrap. She'd gotten complacent on the hospital roof — tucked away in her misery, figuring she'd just stay there forever. She should have been thinking ahead, figuring out how to get across the Bay, how to survive once she got there. Now she was at the mercy of the unknown, with no plan.

"With my power, I always thought I could help people who were sick or wounded. With my mother after me, though, it won't work. I need a quiet job, something out of sight. Either that or I'd have to wear a mask. Since Thunder City Alts don't wear masks, wearing one would only make me stand out more. I haven't had time to think too much beyond getting out of Star Haven."

She kept her head down, but glanced again at Carraro from under her bangs as she found a smidgen of courage. "Regardless of where I end up or what I do to earn a living, I'll need a new identity."

"Of course," Thomas said, with a shadow of his smile. "Lucky for you, our family has a history of changing identities. Right, Scott?"

Ah-ha. Scott *had* changed his name, from Scott Carraro to Scott Grey, so he could join the police force. His father had probably made the arrangements.

Scott reached toward her. For a split second she thought he was going to take her hands into his. Instead, he pulled the plastic wrap from under her fingers, swept the crumbs off the counter. He was cleaning up, nothing more.

You are such an idiot. He's a Alt-killer. Never forget that. It was her mother speaking again, but the thought still crushed her heart. *Hormones. It's just hormones. A biological response you can't control. Just like she trained you.* It still hurt like hell.

"There's nothing wrong with wanting to help people," Scott said, as he dropped the trash into the garbage. "I wouldn't have become a cop if I believed otherwise. Even in Star Haven, you don't join the force unless you believe in justice."

"Even if the person you're helping is an Alt?" she asked, with more indignation than she intended. Hey, he's the Alt-killer who dared to talk about justice.

His dark brows knit together as he returned to his stool. "I owe you my life. The least I could do is make sure you crossed the Bay safely."

73

The least he could do. Paying off a debt. Why would she think helping her would change his mind about Alts?

"The only expectation I have is to remain safe." If she said it loud enough, strong enough, maybe she'd believe it. "I don't need much and I'm willing to earn my keep, but I won't put anyone in danger. I know that limits my opportunities, but after what my mother did to Roger...I'll leave Thunder City before I let her hurt someone else because of me."

The timbre of the engine changed as the yacht slowed. Scott's whole body language changed. His easy, relaxed posture turned into a tightly wound spring. He snapped up the knife and strapped it back onto his arm.

"We're almost there," Carraro said. "We'll talk more about Miranda and Roger later."

She wasn't ready. Oh, hell no, she wasn't even close to ready. The whole game would change once she stepped off the yacht. She'd gotten soft living on the roof, forgotten how to keep up her guard. What was wrong with her? "What happens now? I don't even know where we're landing."

"We're taking you home," Carraro said. "Our home."

"Your home," Scott interrupted, slipping on his windbreaker. "I'll bring her inside, get her settled, but I'm staying downtown."

Defiance threaded through his words, a challenge to his father to disagree. He'd fulfilled whatever obligation he felt toward her by finding her safe passage. She'd half-expected this, but his confirmation nevertheless brought with it a sense of abandonment. Well, screw him and his anti-Alt attitude.

"Oh, she'll be just fine with us." Carraro stood with a stretch. "Your mother and I will keep her snug. Of course, we'll also have all of your brothers to back us up if she gets out of hand."

If it wasn't for the wink he tossed in her direction, Hannah might have thought Carraro was serious about the *getting out of hand* part.

Scott sputtered. "What the hell are they doing at the house?"

"Your brothers? Why, they all came together to search for you, of course." Carraro leaned on the countertop, his focus entirely on Scott, as if she'd disappeared from the room. "All three of them followed your mother across the Bay while I scoured the networks searching for clues to your whereabouts. Captain Spectacular, Rumble, Ghost, Roar, and Hack-Man. The Blackwood Family all gathered together in a time of crisis."

The *Blackwood* Family? *The* Blackwood Family. As in Blackwood Enterprises? Catherine Blackwood was Captain Spectacular, the most powerful Alt in existence. She had pulled Blackwood Enterprises out of Star Haven before the ban because she openly employed other Alts. Carraro said Scott's mother and his brothers had crossed the Bay to find him which could only mean, Scott wasn't a Carraro. He was a Blackwood. *Oh, God!* Captain Spectacular was Scott's mother.

Stars appeared in her mind's eye before she fell to the floor.

***

Scott grabbed Hannah before her head could hit the bar. What the hell had Thomas been thinking by dropping the Blackwood bombshell like that?

"Careful," Thomas said as he rounded the counter, but Scott had Hannah tucked against his chest. "Don't touch her — "

"Skin? It's a little late for that, don't you think?"

"I think you overestimate my abilities," Thomas said. "It's been awhile since I've had the power to make a woman faint at my feet. Bring her over here."

Scott moved to scoop Hannah back into his arms, but she wiggled out of his grip. She hadn't completely lost consciousness. She pushed against his chest to get herself back onto her feet.

"Stop. I didn't faint. I just...I mean... I was surprised."

Scott stalled, half bent over, one arm still around her shoulders. Her breath, short and shallow, hit the pulse point on his neck.

"Do you want me to let go?" he asked. He fought the urge to pull her closer, cradle her, keep her in his arms.

She hesitated, but said, "Yes. Let go. I need space."

Thomas was watching, so Scott pulled away as she wrapped her arms around herself. He'd have laughed at the comical look on her face, caught between anger, outrage, and shock, but there was nothing amusing about bringing her to a home filled with Blackwoods. She wasn't ready to talk, so he vented his ire at Thomas.

"Call them. Now. Tell my brothers we don't need them. *I* don't need them. They can go back to...wherever in hell they live. Hannah will be fine with you and Catherine."

"Do you think they would listen?" Thomas asked, as he stooped to recover the baseball cap that had fallen off Hannah's head. He handed it to her, but didn't look at her. "Your mother and I have kept the Blackwood estate open to any Alt in need of refuge. Your brothers, and you, will always be welcome there. I can't ask them to leave any more than I could force you to stay."

The standard Blackwood speech. Thomas was right, though. His brothers wouldn't listen. Nik would stay because he'd want to back up Catherine when the inevitable fight began. Evan and Alek would stay just to torture him. At least Thomas would be there to balance the power struggle.

Poor Hannah looked less angry and more confused by the minute. He didn't blame her. You'd need a flow chart to track all the players in the Blackwood family drama. Thomas had won this round. Scott would stay at the house for a couple of days at least. For Hannah's sake.

The yacht's engine shifted and the boat slowed even further as it approached the Blackwood's private dock.

"Could you give me and Hannah a few minutes alone, please?"

Thomas nodded and headed to the deck.

No sooner had he left than Hannah demanded, "Why didn't you tell me your mother was Captain Spec?"

Her eyes appeared larger with her outrage than when she was scared. He wanted to hug her all of a sudden, tell her it would be okay. Instead, he stuffed his hands into his pockets, because really, it wasn't okay. None of this would end well. And Hannah was still an Alt.

"I've been a little busy smuggling you out of Star Haven," he said.

"How am I supposed to meet her like this?" She tugged at her hair and his t-shirt.

She was worried about her wardrobe? "What's wrong with my t-shirt? It's the same brand I'm wearing now."

She growled at him in the way women did when men pointed out how illogical they were acting. Good. If she could growl at him, then she wasn't scared. He didn't want her to be scared. You should never show a Blackwood your fear. "If you want, you could check the closet in the master bedroom. Catherine might have stashed some clothes there."

"Wear Captain Spec's clothes?" Her voice rose two octaves. "That's even worse." She clapped her hands over her eyes at the horror of it all.

"Hannah, listen to me..."

"No, you don't understand." She dropped her hands. "Your mother is the Alt I aspired to become. She's the greatest Alt in existence. I tried to collect articles about her, but my mother threw them out. Whenever I could, I would listen to the news reports out of Thunder City instead of Star Haven. I tried to memorize every stat, map every location, take notes on every good deed she ever did. I had to read between the lines of the Star Haven reports because they never reported about all the good Alts do. She's about as perfect an Alt as you can get. To meet her in this condition..."

Same old, same old. He'd given up trying to understand the near worship, or in some cases actual worship, some folks had for his mother. Yes, she'd performed some astounding feats to keep Thunder City safe, but she wasn't the paragon of virtue everyone thought she was.

Hannah started to pace. He could tell her strength had returned. Her walk was firm, controlled, deliberate even though she only traveled to the wall and back. Her long hair swished just above her backside with every step.

And why are you looking at her backside? It wasn't as if the shapeless scrubs and his oversized shirt did her any favors. Or that he couldn't get laid if he really wanted to. He just hadn't had time since the Alt-ban went into effect. Overtime kept him busy, but it didn't help in the relationship department.

As she made her next pass, he stepped into her path. He started to take her hands, but then reminded himself, yet again, that he shouldn't. "Hannah, my mother, Catherine, is many things, but one thing she isn't is a snob. The crew has kept her apprised of our progress out of Star Haven. Thomas will tell her what you've been through in the past twenty-four hours. Showing up barefoot in an oversized t-shirt and scrubs is not going to shock her."

Hannah's posture sagged as he talked, allowing his t-shirt to slide off one pale shoulder.

"Think about it. Would my mother expect every person she rescued to be dressed for a banquet?"

Tousled hair shook back and forth.

"What makes you think you're any different? You've been on the run for half a year. You saved my life. Do you think Catherine is going to care about you wearing my clothes? Or hers for that matter?" He stepped closer to her and carefully slid his shirt back onto her shoulder. So much bare skin distracted him.

"My mother has had three husbands and four sons. She'll be thrilled to have another woman in the house."

He waited until Hannah could meet his eyes again. "Everything okay?" he asked.

She nodded. "Yeah."

The final clunk of the yacht's plank hitting the dock signaled their arrival. From outside, Scott could hear Thomas asking a crew member to escort Tasha, the Neut Thomas had hired, back to her apartment. Good. Tasha was another complication he didn't need hanging around Hannah. A minute later his father appeared in the doorway.

"We're all set. Are you two ready?"

Scott looked at Hannah. She nodded.

"We're ready," Scott answered. Sure, he'd managed to calm Hannah, but what about himself? His speech about Catherine had been for Hannah. The old fears and hatred he'd left behind in Thunder City came flooding back. His weapons, tucked close, gave him comfort. He might not be calm, but he was ready for anything.

CHAPTER SEVEN

Each plank along the long, wooden dock lined up perfectly with its neighbor. All of them were sanded to such a smoothness that not one of them would dare stick a sliver into Hannah's bare feet. Beyond the dock, a shadowy tangle of foliage decorated the border of a small beach.

A railing offered her support as she descended from the dock onto a boardwalk that was just as meticulously maintained. Scott waited for her at the bottom of the stairs. He held out his forearm so she wouldn't miss the last step in the low light, forcing her to grasp his sleeve instead of his hand. Right. No touching his skin. She could feel the knife holster flex inside the smooth nylon, locked into place, ready to slide into Scott's hand with a twitch of his wrist.

Why did he strap his weapons back on? Isn't this his home, too? Was he expecting her mother to attack her here? At the home of Captain Spec? It would be a stupid move, and her mother wasn't stupid. Something else had Scott spooked about coming home. Not comfortable at touching the knife, even through the nylon barrier, she let go of his arm as soon as she hit the boardwalk.

The shadows grew thicker under the bright lights shining over the top of a brick wall. A trellis covered in vines beckoned. Underneath the trellis, not bothered by the vines, a man stepped out to meet them.

"Welcome home, sir. The family is waiting for you in the parlor."

Carraro nodded, but didn't stop. "Thank you, Garrett."

"You're welcome, sir."

She looked back at Scott, who nodded her forward. She gave a small smile to the butler as she walked past him. He gave her an uninterested nod before turning his attention to Scott.

"Welcome home, Mr. Blackwood."

"Thanks, Garrett."

"I understand you will be staying with us, sir?"

Hannah hitched her step, listening.

"Thomas called that one right. Yes, I'll be staying."

"Very good, sir. Your room is already prepared."

Scott didn't reply, so Hannah continued to walk. Behind the trellis, the wooden boardwalk eased into a flat stone path winding its way around a courtyard ringed with flowers and low bushes. Several stone benches circled a fountain at the center, but no water flowed in the moonlight.

Carraro waited for them at the edge of a screened porch. Beyond the porch Hannah could see a mudroom with a coat rack. In the distance, fine tile covered the floor. She scrubbed her feet as best she could on the mat.

Carraro looked amused, but didn't stop her. She didn't dare turn around to see what Scott thought. She'd be damned if she was going to trek the last twenty-four hours of her life across Captain Spec's immaculate home.

Two rights and a left later, Carraro opened the polished doors to the parlor. Hannah hesitated at the threshold, her heart in her mouth.

"It's okay," Scott whispered, coming up from behind her. "She won't bite."

Hannah gathered her dignity as best she could and walked inside. Carraro had already crossed the room to the oversized fireplace to kiss his wife. His broad shoulders blocked Hannah's view of Captain Spec. Since she didn't want to get caught staring, she looked around instead.

Another man stood by the picture window to the right. His stiff posture lessened as he looked her over, but he didn't say anything. With his dark hair and high cheekbones, he resembled an older version of Scott, if Scott ever dressed to work in an office.

Opposite the window, two other men in jeans and t-shirts sprawled across a sofa. Twins, she realized, with the same messy, light-brown hair. One held a game console, fingers flying over the controls, while the other one dangled a string above a couple of kittens. The game player shut down the console as soon as he spotted her. The other scooped up a kitten to cuddle.

Scott pushed his way past her into the room, partially blocking her view. Faster than Hannah could blink, Catherine Blackwood stood in front of her son.

Hannah stumbled back, slapped by the waves of tension rolling off mother and son.

"Catherine," Scott said.

"Cory," Catherine answered.

After several long seconds, Catherine raised her arms up so she could pull Scott into an awkward hug while he snaked his hands around her waist. After a beat, he raised a hand and patted her on the back.

Cory Blackwood. An anti-Alt cop who was the son of the most powerful Alt in Thunder City. She would have changed her name, too.

Mother and son broke their embrace, but before the Captain backed away, she lifted her hand to stroke Scott — Cory's — earlobe. The one Hannah had rebuilt.

Uh-oh.

But the Captain said nothing and dropped her hand. Only then did Scott gesture toward Hannah.

"This is Hannah Quinn. Hannah, this is my mother, Catherine Blackwood."

Cool, hazel eyes pinned Hannah in place before she could flee.

"You saved my son's life."

A simple declarative statement — or did she need confirmation? "Yes, ma'am. And he saved mine."

Captain Spec — Mrs. Blackwood — Hannah wasn't sure how to think of her, so she settled on "the Captain", gave her a smile just wide enough to erase the worry lines across her brow. Hannah stood so close she could see the top of the Captain's head, which shocked her not because she recognized the familiar bob, but because she was taller than her hero by at least half an inch. On television the Captain appeared so much bigger, larger than life, her uniform fitted to emphasize her strength rather than her height.

"I understand your reasons for leaving Star Haven, but even in Thunder City, living as an Alt isn't as easy as some Newcomers — Star Haven Alts specifically — think when they first arrive."

Hannah nodded. What else could she do? She couldn't go back home. "I understand."

"Really?" the Captain looked at Scott then back at her. "Has my son explained how you will have to undergo a strict training regimen before you'll be allowed to stay?"

"No, ma'am, but I've been bloodsurfing since...well, for as long as I can remember. I know how to control my ability."

The Captain frowned. "Control isn't always the issue with Alts, especially those who've used their power since childhood. Ethics is an issue. How, when, and where it would be appropriate for you to heal someone. We've never had anyone with your particular skills in Thunder City. How do we train you?"

Good questions, ones she never had to think about before now. Her mother had always told her what to do.

"I'll need time to think about this," the Captain continued. "Until then, I'm going to have to ask you not to use your power under any circumstances."

What? "Any circumstances?"

"Correct."

Was this a test? A way for the Captain to discover if Hannah could be trained? What if she said no?

"All right," she agreed, despite how wrong it sounded. "No bloodsurfing."

"Good." The Captain seemed pleased, but Hannah had doubts. Her decision to heal Scott had been spur of the moment. Could she look the other way if someone needed her help? Especially now? In a city that was supposed to be less hostile to Alts?

The Captain stepped closer to Hannah and looked her over with a critical eye, just as her husband had done. "For the moment, we won't worry about your training. You need sleep and a new wardrobe. I've had a room prepared for you on the second floor. I'll see what I have in my closet. I must own an outfit or two that'll fit until we can get you to a store."

Her tone sounded like a dismissal, but Hannah couldn't leave just yet. "I really appreciate your help, but I need you to understand how much danger you've put yourselves in by helping me. My mother..."

"Miranda Dane," the Captain said.

Of course she would know who Hannah's mother was. "Yes. She killed Roger Dane six months ago. He was trying to bring me to Thunder City. She murdered him rather than lose me. Or rather, lose access to my power. It won't matter to Miranda if I'm living in Thunder City with Cap...with all of you. She'll do whatever it takes to get me back."

"She'll try," said one of the twins, but Hannah didn't dare look away from the Captain to see which one.

"It's not a joke." Her throat tightened. If she couldn't get them to take her warnings seriously, then she might as well leave Thunder City tonight.

"Evan, leave her alone," the Captain ordered. "We'll take precautions. Your mother isn't an unknown threat. We were monitoring her long before she proposed the Alt-ban. If it makes you feel better, my husband will assemble a specialized team to watch Star Haven for any unusual activity."

"I'm not sure how much you'll be able to find." She bit her lip, uncertain if she should keep talking. Carraro didn't seem the type to hide his employment by Roger from his wife, but you never knew. If he didn't want the Captain to know, he could always accuse her of lying. "Roger hired your husband to help discover who hacked his business computers two years ago, but he couldn't figure it out."

"Which tells us more than you think," Carraro said from where he stood next to the fireplace, a drink in his hand. No accusation of lying, so she was still in safe territory. "A newcomer in my field won't stop after one job. If they're good, they'll up the ante each time they take a job, but it isn't always about the money. It's about the challenge. The more challenging the job, the more determined it makes people like me. The more this person works, the more traces and patterns they'll leave behind. Don't worry, my dear. I'll figure out who they are and if they're connected to your mother."

Hannah wished she could borrow some of his confidence.

"We'll talk more about Miranda and why she's so determined to keep you in Star Haven in the morning," the Captain continued. "Evan, please show Ms. Quinn to her room."

There was no mistaking the dismissal this time. Evan rolled off the sofa and placed the kitten back on the floor. He headed in her direction, but before he got close, Scott grabbed his brother's arm.

"Mess with her and I'll kill you."

His words cut deeper than the knife he slid from under his sleeve. The absolute certainty of the threat spiked the tension in the room a hundred fold. The man at the window took a step forward, while the other twin shoved off the couch. The Captain stayed rooted in place, as did Carraro. Hannah hadn't felt so exposed since she ran from her mother's thugs at the marina. An unconscious need to protect, or maybe it was to be protected, shuffled her closer to Scott.

Evan jerked his arm, but Scott's grip remained firm.

"So I still exist in your world," Evan said.

Scott didn't blink, didn't budge. "You exist only as long as I allow it. I'll warn you once: Anything happens to her," he jerked his chin over his shoulder, "I'll peel off your skin layer by layer and watch you die screaming."

Evan's jaw shifted around, as if he were going to say one thing, then another, but decided against it. He ended with a sigh. "I won't allow anything to happen to her. I promise."

Scott's stance never shifted, but he let his brother go. The knife slipped back up his sleeve.

This was supposed to make her feel safer? Did Scott mean what he said, or was this just schoolyard posturing heightened by the threat of Alt powers? She tried to get Scott's attention, but he'd already turned his back to her.

Evan opened the door, so she followed more confused than ever.

***

Scott sucked back the bile in his throat. At this angle, he could see every target in the room, with the north wall at his back. While Hannah stood behind him, the threats seemed manageable. Not even the twin bastards his mother had birthed would try anything with an outside Alt present. Even though Catherine had sent Evan out of the room, probably in hopes of lessening the antagonism, the base fear of being outgunned and outnumbered heightened his instinct to fight his way out of the house.

"She looks sweet," Nik, his oldest brother said, "and sounds naive, but if she's survived this long in Star Haven with Dane for a mother, she's probably tougher than she looks. I can see why you like her."

Of course Nik would try to play peacemaker. The conversation about Hannah meant that Scott would have to talk to them. Across the room, Thomas swirled the drink in his glass. It wasn't fair, forcing Thomas to choose between his son and his wife, so Scott would try to keep his father out of this. And what did Nik mean by *I can see why you like her?* "Appearances can be deceiving."

The sharp words shut up Nik. Catherine sighed and backed up too, heading closer to Thomas.

"Cory, please," she said. "I know how hard this is for you."

"You know nothing." How could she? They hadn't talked in over a decade, not since she relinquished custody of him to Thomas. Yet, he still hugged her when she reached for him, damn it to hell. Had he given in because she'd crossed Mystic Bay to find him? Did breaking the law for him wipe out years of animosity? It shouldn't — it couldn't be that easy. "I'm here only because of the threat against Hannah. As soon as the threat's neutralized, I'll leave."

"Then let's discuss Hannah," Catherine said. She returned to her husband's side. "We've never been able to pin down a clear motive for Miranda Dane's unyielding support for the Alt-ban. Having and hiding an Alt child for all of these years muddles our assumptions. Thomas has already reported what you told him, but I'd like to hear it from you, Cory. What happened to you? What happened when Hannah saved your life?"

89

Where was her concern when he was thirteen? When he *wanted* to tell his side of the story? Before he had Thomas to protect him? Why did it take his second near-death for his mother to finally find the value in her Norm son? Why did all his anger have to melt into a useless puddle at his feet just because he had her attention now?

He told her everything he had told Thomas. As long as he talked, no one else in the room existed.

"Wait, stop."

Alek in particular didn't exist, so Scott talked over him.

"I mean it, Cor. Hold up."

Alek got in his face. Out of the corner of his eye, Scott could see Thomas push off the mantle, but Catherine held him back with a touch of her hand.

"You hit the roof? For real? This isn't one of your exaggerations?" Alek said, not really a question, but daring Scott to confirm it as true.

Maybe Thomas hadn't told them everything. From behind his back, Scott drew out the knife again, the firmness of the hilt filled his palm. Before he could use it, Nik jerked his brother away.

"Back off. Give him room."

Alek didn't fight Nik, but instead turned on Thomas.

"Why didn't you tell us?" he demanded.

Thomas took a sip of his drink. "I told your mother. Telling you was her prerogative, not mine."

"Mom?"

Catherine stepped between the three of them, easy for a woman who didn't have to worry about flying fists or knives. "I didn't tell you because Thomas promised me Cory was alive and unharmed. I needed time to

90

come to terms with how close I came to losing him again and I couldn't do that with the rest of you hovering over me."

Neither brother questioned her decision, and they returned to their respective corners.

"Cory, please continue."

His mother paced the floor while he finished his story, ending with their arrival at the back dock. Catherine didn't break her stride.

"When she bloodsurfed through you, was she physically inside your body? Or does she mentally transverse the circulatory system and heal through telekinesis?" she asked.

"I don't know. I was unconscious until she finished. She passed out the second I woke up."

"We'll ask her tomorrow," Catherine said, more to herself than to anyone in the room. "Do we know why she fainted at that moment?"

Scott shook his head. Catherine looked at Thomas.

"I'll access her medical records." He drained his glass and set it on the mantel.

"Get her school records too," Nik suggested. "We can look for patterns. If she gets sick every time she heals someone, her absences might give us a clue as to what her mother is up to. Even her class schedule might help."

"Do we know her mother is up to something?" Scott asked. He'd seen no evidence that Hannah's suspicions of her mother were correct, no proof that the thugs in his apartment worked for Mayor Dane. He knew nothing of Hannah other than the fact that she was an Alt and a runaway.

"Yes." Nik, Alek, and Thomas all answered at the same time. Nik snorted while Alek glared at Thomas.

"I didn't tell Hannah the whole truth when she mentioned meeting me at Roger Dane's warehouse," Thomas said. "I didn't recognize the work of whoever hacked his system. I did, however, copy the import/export records to examine later. I had a unique opportunity to learn more about the powerhouse behind the anti-Alt movement, so I took advantage of the situation. Someone used Roger Dane's import business to smuggle construction materials into the city without paying taxes or duty fees."

"Did you tell Roger?" Scott asked.

"No, I didn't," Thomas said, his answer laced with regret.

"What happened, Carraro?" Alek asked. "Did old Roger not pay you enough to give him the information you picked up from the records you stole?"

"I didn't tell him because for all I knew, Roger might inadvertently alert whoever was changing the records. If I'd suggested it might have been his wife, he could have become offended and let Miranda know she was under suspicion," Thomas said. "Obviously, I was wrong."

"So you don't know if Miranda is actually up to something," Scott reiterated. "All you have are suspicions because Miranda used her political clout to create a Alt-free city."

"Isn't that enough?" Nik asked.

"Some people don't want to live with Alts, if you haven't noticed," Scott answered.

"Oh, we noticed, all right," Alek said.

"Can you blame them?" Scott's voice rose. *Back down, asshole. You can't win this argument.* But he didn't, couldn't. "Who'd want to live in a city with Alts harassing them every day?"

"We don't harass people," Alek said. "We never have. It's the Norms who harassed us."

"Enough!" Catherine raised her voice. "Don't make me have to start handing out concussions."

Thomas placed a hand on his wife's shoulder. She reached up and gave it a gentle squeeze. Scott didn't understand the attraction, much less the marriage, but he also didn't have a say in the matter.

"Let's get back to the original problem," Catherine said. "We have an adult, untrained Alt with an ability we've never seen before. She's the daughter of a powerful anti-Alt politician who may or may not have designs to expand her anti-Alt zone across Mystic Bay. I have worked too long and too hard for too many years to build a peaceful co-existence between Alts and Norms in Thunder City. I won't let anyone's fear or ambition destroy that."

Nik cleared his throat. "We should take Hannah to the hospital tomorrow. See what she can do."

"No," Catherine said, with a shake of her head. "People are not lab rats to be experimented on unless we have a controlled trial and get approval from the medical community."

"That'll take forever," Nik said. "How about we take her to the animal shelter?"

"Hey." Alek scooped one of the kittens off the floor. "Animals are people too. If you're not going to experiment on people, Evan sure as hell isn't going to let you near any of his animals."

"You can experiment on me," Scott said.

Thomas opened his mouth as if to object, but Scott plowed forward, not certain he really wanted to volunteer for this, but the bickering scraped against his nerves like sandpaper. "She's already healed me once so this won't be new territory. We'll start small, a paper cut, and work our way from there. We should also have a doctor present in case she passes out again."

"Are you sure you want to do this?" Nik asked.

No. "It's either this or we set up a formal clinical trial."

"I don't like it," Catherine said. "There has to be another way."

"You're not the one who's going to be hurt." Scott pointed out. "It's not your choice to make."

Silence, until Thomas cleared his throat. "I'll contact Doctor Rao and see when he's available. The sooner we do this, the sooner it'll be over with and we can figure out how to train her."

Scott couldn't agree more. He'd have to talk to Hannah ahead of time. This would be a perfect opportunity for her to break his Alt power with no one the wiser. He wanted to go home. He had to get away from his family.

Away from Hannah. Because that's what he really wanted, wasn't it?

CHAPTER EIGHT

The last of Hannah's energy abandoned her halfway up the staircase. "I'm sorry," she said, when Evan turned to find her lagging behind. "I need a minute.

"Take your time." He walked back down to stand next to her, close, but not too close. "You've had a long day."

Whatever he thought he knew about her day couldn't come close to reality. Scott's distrust of his brother bothered her. If he didn't trust any brother, how could she? Yet Evan was an Alt, either Rumble or Roar, she couldn't remember which. Six months ago she wouldn't have had to think of which Alt he was. Standing right in front of her though, he looked no different from a regular human and not like one of the Thunder City heroes.

"I'm ready," she said after a minute. In all honesty, she should have waited another minute or two, but she'd spent enough time as a damsel in distress.

When they finally reached the top of the stairs, Evan opened the first door on the left and motioned her inside while he flipped on an overhead light. Dark panels lined the walls of a room that was fitted out with a floor-length mirror, a six-door wardrobe, an oak desk, and an adjoining shower. Someone, probably the butler, had already draped a full-length nightgown and robe across the king-sized bed.

"I'll give you a quick tour," Evan said. "If there's anything you need, say so. Don't be...Eight-ball, how did you get in here?"

Hannah couldn't see what was bothering him until he lifted a coal-black, fuzzy lump off one of the huge pillows.

"They say there is no such thing as an Alt cat, or any sort of Alt animal, but I don't believe it." The cat meowed a protest, but didn't bite or scratch. "This one walks through walls. Are you allergic to cats, Hannah? I can have Garret prep the room next door."

"Oh, no. I'm fine. You can leave him here if you don't mind." She reached out to scratch the cat behind the ears. She'd never had a pet. Her mother wouldn't tolerate them. "Is he the father of the kittens?"

Evan flipped Eight-ball over for a belly rub. Eight-ball blinked, clearly used to the manhandling. "No. The kittens are rescues from a kitty mill I shut down last month. The mother died right after. My apartment allows pets, but I'd be pushing my luck with eight kittens. Mom said it was okay to bring them here until I found homes for all of them."

"How sad." Hannah held out her arms and Evan draped the cat over them. Eight-ball's long body drooped over her elbow. He purred, so she guessed she was doing something right. Careful to keep the cat balanced, she sat on the edge of the bed.

Evan sat next to her, and Hannah was glad he wasn't leaving right away despite Scott's distrust. The hospital had offered the worst temptation: so many people around, but no one she could talk to. She'd said more in the past twenty-four hours than she had since she ran away. She'd said more to Scott than she ever intended. Her trust in him held, but the thread was frayed. Why had he pulled a knife on his own brother? Would she have to arm herself the same way to live here? Evan didn't appear threatening, but her judgement was skewed. She'd trusted her mother until she killed Roger. How could Hannah trust her own judgement now?

"May I ask you a question?"

"Sure," Evan said, playing catch with Eight-ball's tail.

"What do you do when you're not rescuing kittens?"

"You mean other than flying around Thunder City as Rumble?"

At least now she knew which twin he was. "Yeah. Do you have a regular job?"

He nodded. "I work part time as a vet tech. I started volunteering for an animal shelter when I was sixteen — well, it was more like volun-told — and decided to become a vet tech after high school. The hours are flexible enough so I can still work for the city."

"As Rumble?"

He nodded. "Both paychecks cover rent and groceries. I don't need much else."

Not with the Blackwood fortune as backup, she assumed, but didn't say so. "I'll need to get a job at some point, but one where I'm away from the public."

Evan let go of Eight-ball's tail one last time. "I heard a little bit about your power. Can you also heal animals?"

Maybe he would offer her a job with the veterinarian? That would be cool. "Yes, but only once, a long time ago. It was the first time I actively used my Alt power. I was five. A puppy — or maybe it was a small dog, a terrier I think — had run into the middle of the street and been hit by a car. The car took off. I had been sitting on the steps of our apartment building, drawing pictures. I ran over to comfort the puppy, but when I touched its nose I wound up bloodsurfing. I operated on instinct. Next thing I knew, the puppy jumped up and knocked me out of its body. It barked, licked my face a couple of times, then ran away. I was so sick afterward, I just lay down right there in the street until another car came along. At least this one stopped."

"Where was your mother?" he asked.

"Inside. We lived in the Swamp, Southern Point, in those days. The guy in the car called an ambulance. Miranda almost lost me to social services. I wish she had." She'd gotten too chatty again, but was too tired to care.

"Can't say I favor your mother's policies," Evan said. "But having an Alt daughter makes her Alt-ban even stranger."

He looked at her as if he expected her to explain, but how could she? The more she said, the closer she came to admitting her own crimes. How fast would Captain Spec get her on the ferry back to Star Haven if she found out the whole truth? Pretty damn fast, Hannah figured. "Yeah, she's got strange notions about Alts. I'm wondering, though — why did Scott think you were going to hurt me?"

Damn her tongue. In her rush to change the topic, she picked the wrong one. Evan didn't say anything for a long time while he stroked Eight-ball's fur again. She'd backed him into a corner, made him think he had to answer. But before she could apologize, he asked, "Has Cory already told you about what happened to him ten years ago?"

"No. I don't know anything about him." *Except that he's an Alt-killer.*

Evan nodded. "It's his story, so he should be the one to give you the extended edition, but when I was sixteen I pulled a prank and almost killed him. I've tried to apologize, but what happened downstairs was the first time he's acknowledged my existence since...it happened. Cory isn't the forgiving sort."

Good to know.

"That's why Mom forced me to volunteer for the animal clinic. She said I needed to learn compassion." Evan stood up to leave. Had she driven him off? "I meant what I said though. Nothing is going to happen to you while you're in Thunder City. The Blackwoods won't allow it."

He left her alone with the cat. Scott — to her, Cory Blackwood would always be Scott Grey — was a man of many secrets, something they both had in common.

"I do hate to be rude," she whispered into a soft as velvet feline ear. "But I think I'm going to take a shower. Your keepers seem to have a plan for me, but I'm not sure it's the best plan. I need to think on this. You won't tell them, will you?"

The cat rubbed his face against her chin demanding more affection, but Hannah rolled him back onto the bed instead. The shower had all the basics to scrub her clean of sweat and sea salt. What little she knew about Thunder City Alts didn't include how they were trained. Did it take weeks? Months? Years? She didn't have years.

However she lived in Thunder City, it would have to be done quietly, under her mother's radar. "Karen Smith" had been a fluke, a spare identity card she'd filched from a volunteer. As long as no one actually looked at the card and Hannah didn't try to access any restricted areas, she had been safe.

The shower spray massaged her tense muscles and she closed her eyes to enjoy the warmth, her thoughts drifting. She'd also have to change her appearance again. The quick and dirty dye job wouldn't cut it much longer. If...no, when...her mother's henchmen crossed the Bay to hunt for her, she'd have to have completed her makeover.

She'd never cut her hair, more out of fear of asking Miranda for money to get it styled than anything else. Most girls her age had been using credit cards for years. Her mother had slapped that idea, and her cheek, the one time she'd asked.

Hannah poured shampoo into her hand and smeared it around the mass of tangles. She could cut her own hair, not fancy, but at least make it shorter. Maybe she should try make-up? She'd never worn any before and some women looked completely different wearing it.

What else could change her appearance? She faced into the spray to rinse off the soap. Maybe colored contact lenses — blue eyes instead of green? Brown might look more muted. Did they even make brown lenses?

Make-up could hide the dusting of freckles across her nose, but a plastic surgeon could make the nose smaller. No, make it bigger. She needed to fade into the background, not draw attention to herself. A bigger nose, droopier eyes, maybe have her ears stick out more. Then no one would recognize her.

Of course, all of this cost money and she didn't have any yet. If Evan could get her a job with the veterinarian, she could work behind the scenes cleaning cages or equipment and heal the animals in secret. No one would have to know except Evan and maybe the vet.

It wasn't much of a plan, but it was a start. She'd talk to Evan about it tomorrow.

Eight-ball had returned to his place on the pillow by the time she'd dried off. The butler had also come in and replaced her scrubs and Scott's t-shirt with a pair of jeans, a blouse, socks, and sneakers. The baseball cap was also missing.

She checked the label on the jeans, which said size six. She hadn't been a size six since middle school. The sneakers looked okay though. Maybe the butler only intended to clean the baseball cap and return it to her. If she couldn't keep Scott's t-shirt, she'd at least like to wear his cap for a while longer. Maybe he would let her keep it. It would become a keepsake, something of his she could hold onto after he left. He could always get another Star Haven Saber cap, but when would she ever have a chance?

The idea of Scott disappearing from her life bothered her more than it should. Scott didn't like Alts, had killed one. She needed to remember that. Right now, she had a warm bed to sleep in and her mother was far away. Her last thought before falling asleep was how much more comfortable Scott's t-shirt was than the nightgown.

Scott checked his watch. By all rights he should get some sleep, but he needed to contact his precinct and let them know he would be out for a few days at least. He'd take a chance and call Juan first. If his luck held, his partner might have volunteered to work a double shift to help clean up the mess left behind by the Left Fists. If not...well, Juan would understand why Scott might call him at two in the morning after a hostage crisis.

Before he opened the front door, he paused at the bottom of the stairwell and listened. He didn't know what he expected to hear, but there was no noise from the guest suite. He hoped Hannah slept. Everyone else had wandered off to their own rooms.

His hand no sooner turned the doorknob when Nik emerged through the wall.

"Going somewhere, Cor?" his brother asked.

"Outside," he snapped. Instinct had him on high alert for any sort of attack, even verbal.

Nik held up his hands to surrender. "Don't get hostile. I just wanted to know if you were leaving us."

Nik lowered himself to sit on the bottom stair. Scott matched his oldest brother in height and hair color, but they shared nothing else. The twins resembled their mother as much as Nik resembled his father. Many folks mistook him for Thomas's son because of his blue eyes, until they took a closer look.

Scott released the doorknob. "If I was heading home, I'd do it in broad daylight. I don't have to sneak out of the house if I want to leave."

"Well, you don't smoke, so you must be making a phone call you don't want the rest of us to hear."

How would Nik know he didn't smoke? Maybe he just assumed? Ghost might work for Thunder City Alt Support Services, but Thomas had told Scott long ago that Nik also held a private investigator license. He had contacts on both side of the Bay, though how many of those contacts dried up after the ban, Scott had no way of knowing.

"I'm just going to call my partner and my precinct," Scott said. "Let them know I won't be in for a few days."

"Is that wise?"

"It's not a secret I grew up in Thunder City," Scott said. "Juan knows I have family here, just not who."

"What if Dane is monitoring your phone calls?"

Something he should have thought of. "So you believe Hannah's story? The part about her mother murdering her husbands?"

"Don't you?"

What did he believe? "She has no evidence. Nothing I can use to start an investigation."

"Forget police procedures. Do *you* believe her?"

She had no obligation to save his life, and every reason to keep her secret buried. Yet, she'd risked her freedom, maybe even her own life to save his.

"Yes, I believe her."

Nik pulled out his phone and tossed it at Scott, who caught it. "Use my phone to call the precinct. Thomas installed new software this morning. Route your call through the operator at the front desk. Keep your phone off. In fact, give it to me and I'll destroy it. We'll get you another one tomorrow."

Good advice. He handed Nik his phone. "Since when do you accept anything from Thomas?"

His brother yawned. "Even Neuts have their uses once in a while."

Nik stepped into the wall and disappeared.

"Nik," Scott called.

The wall quivered.

"Thanks," Scott said, and held up the phone.

"You're welcome." The wall added a surround sound effect to his voice before it shivered, then stilled.

Scott made it outside this time. He walked away from the external light above the door. He felt like he had a target painted over his head. He dialed the operator and asked her to connect him with the Lieutenant's office. He left Pearson a message, another bullshit story about needing to recover from the beating. By the time he made it halfway to the front gate, he was ready to call Juan.

"Costenaro."

His partner sounded wide-awake. "What the hell are you doing up at two in the morning?"

"What the fuck, man? Do you have any idea how much trouble you've caused?"

Scott pulled the phone away from his ear and turned down the volume. "I guess I don't. Fill me in."

"The Commish discovers you found Dane's daughter, which, by the way, you didn't bother to tell me. Then she disappears, then you disappear. I get worried, so I stop by your apartment and no one answers. I talk the super into letting me inside and it's completely trashed, so I call it in as a break-in, but Becksom finds out and tells the Lieutenant not send anyone to investigate. Then Internal Affairs shows up and goes through your locker. They haul me in and start grilling me about you — where are you? How come I don't know? Where would you go if you were in trouble? All this shit that I don't have answers for and even the ones I have are bullshit 'cuz no one can find you..."

"Juan...Juan...JUAN!"

Juan shut up.

"I am so sorry, man. I didn't mean for all this crap to land on your head." Scott paused, thinking fast. He really hated to lie to his partner, but most of his life was a lie anyway. "I did find the Mayor's daughter. I didn't tell you because I didn't think Dane would want anyone to know until she was home safe and away from the press.

"The hostage situation was bad. They tried to push me out of the helicopter, but a fight broke out, so the pilot landed on the hospital roof and I managed to get away. That's where I found Hannah, at the hospital.

"She fainted when I took her into custody, then disappeared when I took a few minutes to use the men's room. I knew how much trouble I was in and I just cracked. You know what it's like to stare death in the face? I went home and trashed my own apartment. I don't know why. It happened and I couldn't fix it, so I left. I had to get away for a while, get my head on straight before I came back to face Becksom and Dane."

Juan cut in again. "Okay, okay. Relax. I got your back. It's cool. It's just when a partner of mine is in trouble, it becomes personal. Know what I mean? You do what you got to do, but don't take too long. Keep me in the loop. Got it?"

"Yeah, I got it. Thanks, man, for everything." He knew he could count on his partner. He closed the connection.

Now what? He circled around and headed back toward the house. Had he placed his partner in danger by bringing Hannah here? Had Becksom or Dane traced his number? Thomas had placed counter-measures in the software to protect Scott, but if Hannah's story was true, then Dane might have a hacker just as good as Thomas working for her. How stupid of him to not have destroyed the phone the moment he decided to help Hannah.

But what did Dane want with Hannah? Why keep an Alt daughter under wraps while creating an Alt-free zone? What was the old saying about a one-eyed man in the kingdom of the blind? Well, if the one-eyed woman was Hannah and she was the only Alt in Star Haven, Miranda Dane might have set the ban in place to better exploit Hannah's ability. If word leaked about Hannah's power, any Norm with an incurable disease or other irreparable condition would sell their own soul and the souls of their children to get access to her. Dane could create a city enslaved to her under the right conditions.

Pure speculation at this point, but taken to a logical conclusion and hell, Star Haven could become an underground oligarchy. Is that what he wanted to return to? He didn't have much time to figure out the answer.

***

Miranda grabbed her phone off the nightstand the second it buzzed.

"What do you have?" she demanded, snapping on a light.

"A hit," Becksom said, his voice rough. "Grey's partner just received a call from an unlisted number with a private phone service. No identification at this time. We tried to track it, but lost the signal."

"Do you have a general location?"

"Yes, ma'am. Thunder City."

It could be Grey calling his partner, which meant Hannah had managed to sweet talk the cop into smuggling her out of Star Haven. Grey was smart enough to have used a clean phone instead of his own.

On the other hand, Juan Costenaro had a few ties to Thunder City himself. The Alt-ban didn't prevent Norms from visiting Thunder City. It only prevented Alts from entering Star Haven. Costenaro had a few friends who had thrown in their lot with the Alts just before the ban and had left Star Haven. It was possible one of them had called.

At two in the morning it would have to have been one hell of an emergency. Miranda disconnected the call and speed dialed another.

"Coreville."

"Pack your bags. You're leaving for Thunder City. I'll meet you at the airport with further instructions."

She disconnected the phone a second time and slid it back into its dock. The Court of Blood would arrive in less than two days. If she didn't get Hannah back, she wouldn't live long enough to see The Project through to the end. It was time to pursue more aggressive tactics.

CHAPTER NINE

"Ummm, no." Hannah flopped onto her stomach to escape the bright beam of sunlight when it hit her eyes. She reached for Eight-ball, a soft cuddle buddy during the night, but her wandering hand couldn't find the fuzzy, black cat.

She cracked open an eye. "It can't be morning yet." The digital clock on the nightstand read nine o'clock. Oh, great. The Captain would probably think she was a layabout.

After she washed, she held up the Captain's jeans. Size six, huh. She slipped them over her legs. Surprise, surprise — they fit. A little too tight at the hips, but at least she didn't have to ask for another pair. She still had to suck in her gut and the hems brushed her ankles, but they were clean. The sneakers, on the other hand, were a half size too big. Walking wouldn't be a problem, but if she had to run...it would be best if she didn't have to. At least the blue and white blouse fit.

Scott's baseball cap hadn't magically reappeared while she slept. If Garrett had returned it to Scott or if it was being cleaned, she'd request another one. A house with so many men had to have a spare sports cap lying around. She wouldn't go outside without one. For the moment, though, she wound her hair into a single braid down her back, a style she could count on to make her look like a six-year-old.

Only a death grip on the handrail kept her on her feet on the stairs. The first floor looked so different in daylight, the dark wood not so ominous, but she didn't see anyone around. The closed parlor doors didn't help. Voices echoed through the hallway. She followed the sounds but ended up in the garage.

"Lost?"

Holy hell! The older brother jumped right out of the wall.

"Sorry, I didn't mean to scare you," he said.

What was his name?

"Nikolaos," he said as if he'd read her mind. Maybe he had. In a family of Alts anything was possible. "We weren't properly introduced last night."

"Hannah," she replied, noting he didn't offer to shake her hand. Already she could feel her mother breathing down her neck, reminding her to introduce herself, then stay out of the conversation. Except her mother wasn't here, was she? So why shouldn't she want to make conversation with this handsome older man dressed for a morning run? "Pleased to meet you, Nikolaos. Have you seen Scott this morning?"

"He and Thomas are locked in the office back there." He jerked his thumb behind him. "I'll let them know you're awake. In the meantime, you should have breakfast."

"Uh, okay." She looked past his shoulder, hoping he'd take the hint.

"Go right, past the bathroom." He pointed in the other direction. "You'll see a video room. Turn left and walk through the kitchen to the other side. You'll see

109

Evangelos and Alekos in the sunroom. They'll make you breakfast if Garrett isn't around."

Greek, much? "Got it. Thanks." She expected him to walk away. Instead, he backed up until he disappeared into the wall.

"This way is faster." The faint pattern blurred and sharpened as if the wall breathed.

Entranced, Hannah walked closer. "You can still see me?"

"I can see and hear everything in the house from here." His voice surrounded her from all corners. "I could pull you through right to the sunroom, but perhaps you should walk there the first time."

No wonder they called him Ghost. Hannah laughed as she reached out and touched the wall, her fingers sliding over the painted surface.

"Hey, that tickles."

Shit! She yanked her hand back.

"Just kidding."

He laughed with her this time.

"Go ahead and get something to eat. I'll be back."

The pattern sharpened and she knew Nikolaos had left the hallway.

She started to skip down the hallway, but slipped, so she slowed to a fast walk. Garrett wasn't in the kitchen so she continued through to the wide-open screen doors. The twins still sprawled, this time in wicker chairs. She recognized Evan only because he had a kitten in his lap instead of a video console.

"Morning, Sunshine." He waved her over.

"Hi." Sudden shyness. She wasn't used to dealing with so many strangers by herself. Except Evan wasn't really a stranger anymore, was he? "Um, Nikolaos sent me here. He said I could get breakfast."

110

"Sure thing. What would you like? We have everything from cereal to pancakes." He pulled his legs off the chair arm and stood up, but kept the kitten with him. He motioned for her to sit in his place.

"I'm not picky."

He retreated into the kitchen, so Hannah took the seat he'd offered. This left her alone with the other twin. She should say something. Say anything.

"Is she Cue-ball?" Hannah nodded her head toward an all-white cat dozing in the splash of sun near the screen door.

He turned off his console and placed it on the glass table. His smile had an air of trained politeness. "Yeah. You can call me Alek, by the way. Don't let Nik's use of our full names scare you into being all formal and stuff."

"Hi," Hannah said. "I met Eight-ball last night."

"You saw him?" Alek looked around. "I don't think I've seen him in a year. I'm not out here as often as Evan, and Eight-ball only comes out at night to hunt. Of course, he doesn't eat what he catches. His palate is far more refined."

Hannah noticed the morning paper folded on the table.

"May I?"

"Go right ahead." Alek looked relieved she'd found something to do other than talk to him.

As she unfolded it, the front page displayed: BLACKWOOD FAMILY SAVES TWELVE FROM BURNING BUILDING. The headline was accompanied by a picture of Captain Spectacular, Ghost, Rumble, and Roar dressed in black uniforms and walking toward the camera, the shambles of a building blurred behind them. She scanned the article as

111

fast as she could. Amazing. They all looked so powerful, united, unstoppable.

"Powershot," Alek said, his focus back on his game. "The photographers around here are getting better at catching our photogenic side."

"Does it bother you that the headline says 'Blackwood' but they still use your monikers in the article?" Hannah asked. Using the Alt names seemed silly if everyone knew who the Blackwood family was.

Alek shrugged, but didn't pause his game. "We don't choose our monikers. The media chooses them for us. It's more of a game the public plays when a new Alt is added to the roster. Sort of like earning an aviator call sign. 'Name that Alt' is a huge contest, big prizes. Mom says it gives the Norms an investment in us, a reason to care."

She glanced up as Evan returned to the sunroom. At first she thought he carried a breakfast tray, but then she noticed he still had the kitten in his arms. The tray levitated in front of him. Hannah refolded the newspaper. A breeze blew through her hair as the tray lowered.

"We don't really have control over what they call us," Evan said. "Most folks know me and Alek for creating thunder and lightning, hence Rumble and Roar."

"But you made the tray float by creating a cushion of air?" Hannah picked up her spoon and poked at her cereal. Rumble and Roar, rescuing people one day, serving her breakfast like it was no big deal the next.

"It's safe to eat. Promise."

Startled, she saw both brothers smirking at her. "Sorry, I was just thinking."

"I have that effect on women," Alek said, as he leaned back in his chair, pulling up his shirt to expose well-formed abs.

She ducked her head and stuffed a spoonful of cereal in her mouth. Evan saved her from more embarrassment by snatching the paper and smacking his brother's head with it.

"Jerk," Alek said. He made a grab for the newspaper.

Evan pulled back. "Hey, watch the kitten."

"You've been hiding behind those kittens for three days."

"And you've been hiding behind the console."

"At least I put the console down once in a while."

"Gentlemen."

Oh, thank heavens. Carraro stepped into the sunroom with Scott right behind him. "Not in front of our guest, if you don't mind."

The difference in the twins' reaction was vast. Alek's smile melted into a frown. Evan, on the other hand, paid no attention to Carraro. He froze in place, his eyes on Scott, with the same look of nervous anticipation he'd had the night before.

Scott didn't look at either of his brothers. Instead, he walked over and knelt next to her, one hand on the tabletop, the other on the back of her chair. "You okay?"

No Left Fists nipped at her heels, but her heart still raced — whether it was because of the twin's bickering or because Scott leaned closer than necessary to talk to her, she wasn't sure. Yesterday, he had been her patient in a bloody police uniform turned knight in shining armor. Today he dressed in jeans and an oxford shirt — like any other Norm on a lazy morning.

"Yes, I'm fine," she replied, and quickly scooped up cereal.

"How do you feel about shopping?"

Hannah forced the cereal down her throat. "For clothes?"

"I didn't bring any with me, and you're going to need outfits to get you through your training regimen."

The idea of a training regimen sounded so severe. "I don't have any money. Not to sound greedy, but I'll need interview clothes before I start training."

His dark brows knitted. "Interview clothes?"

"I need a job. I can't live off the charity of others forever." He didn't say anything, so she plowed ahead. "Evan told me about how he works part-time for a veterinarian as well as for the City. Even after I'm trained to control my powers, which shouldn't take long because I already know how, I'll need to make a living somehow."

A brief twitch of his eyes told her he fought the instinct to look at his brother. "We'll meet my mother downtown. You can explain the situation to her. She designed the training program and knows where people fit. She'll figure something out."

"What about you?"

He shrugged. "I'm not an Alt. I was never allowed to train with them, so I know nothing about how it works."

Bitterness laced his voice, kept low and just between the two of them.

"What about the Thunder City police department? You can't go back to Star Haven, but maybe you could join..."

"I killed an Alt, Hannah." His voice rose, but he hushed it again before he caught the attention of the

114

twins who at least pretended not to listen to them. "The TC police work with the Alts of this city; they protect each other. They won't want me either."

He stalked back into the house, pausing only to take the key ring Carraro handed him. He could never return to Star Haven and he blamed her for it. Hannah turned to Evan, who wore the disappointment she felt.

"I'm so sorry," she said, for lack of anything else to offer.

He shrugged, but he pulled the kitten closer to his heart and scratched its ears. "I wasn't really expecting him to change."

There was nothing else she could do to ease his pain or hers. She couldn't heal what wasn't physical.

Carraro placed a hand on Evan's shoulder. "He's been here for less than a day. Give him more time."

"He's had ten years," Alek said.

"No one asked you," Carraro replied.

Alek's glare turned black.

She scooped another spoonful of cereal into her mouth and then another, chewing as fast as she could, reluctant to leave good food behind even though she wanted to flee.

"I'll repeat myself," Carraro said. "We have a guest. Let's not make this any more uncomfortable for her. Can we agree on this?"

Alek mumbled something like "sorry" before he hunched over the console again.

Carraro looked across at her. "Is there anything you need before you go shopping?"

She didn't want to ask for anything, but safety won out over inter-family arguments. "I think Garrett took Scott's baseball cap last night. I'd like it back, please.

And if you have a pair of sunglasses, I'd like to borrow them while I'm out."

"I haven't seen Garrett this morning," Carraro said. "Catherine has some sunglasses you could use. Stop by the parlor when you're ready. I'll leave a pair for you in there." He turned to walk back inside.

Evan called him back.

"If you go into the video room, I left a ball cap on the entertainment center. She can use that one."

Carraro nodded and left.

"Thanks," Hannah said to Evan as she finished her cereal. "Every little bit helps."

"Anything for a friend," he said.

***

"If I wasn't a good driver, Thomas would never have given me the keys to the Porsche," Scott shouted over the wind rushing through the convertible. Poor Hannah had scrunched down so far in the passenger seat, she couldn't see over the dashboard. Only stray strands of her hair still whipped above the seat.

"It's not your driving," she yelled back at him. "I don't want anyone to see me."

For a second he started to reach out to touch her, comfort her, but pulled back and placed his hand on the steering wheel. Rules. When had keeping her safe extended to a desire to touch her?

At least she didn't look scared anymore. They'd both be fools to think her mother wouldn't be searching for her, assuming her mother was guilty in the first place, but getting a good night's sleep had erased the dark circles under her eyes.

He forced his focus back to the rear view mirror, just in case someone had followed them. He didn't see anything suspicious until his mother landed in the back seat.

"Hello, Cory, Hannah."

Hannah yelped.

"Sorry to scare you. Thought I would drop in before we hit the stores."

Even after ten years, his mother's sense of humor hadn't improved. "Not cool, Catherine. And put on your seat belt. You're setting a bad example."

"Ooo, the big, bad police officer ordering his mother around." She flashed a smile at Hannah, but secured the seat belt before the light turned green. His mother was trying to have a normal conversation with him. If she could put in the effort, then so could he. For Hannah's sake, if nothing else.

"Where've you been?" he asked.

"Police headquarters," she said. "Hannah, be a dear and hand me the spare sunglasses from the glove compartment."

Out of the corner of his eye, he could see Hannah stared for a moment, then realize the great Captain Spectacular had asked her to do something mundane. Catherine really didn't need the glasses, but she wore them for effect. They made her seem more approachable, less superhuman. Hannah opened the compartment and pulled out the case. She handed it Catherine with unabashed reverence.

"Thank you." His mother slipped them on. "The police commissioner asked to meet with me about the reports of missing Alts that have been trickling in from the Newcomers."

Newcomers must mean Star Haven Alts who had arrived before the ban. "How do you know they're missing?"

"No one can find them," his mother shouted, as he accelerated. "They never arrived in Thunder City."

"Wait, Thunder City has been keeping track of Star Haven Alts? Before they've crossed the Bay?" His defenses crawled up his neck.

"No," Catherine said. "*Star Haven* has kept track of everyone: Alts and Norms. Who stayed and who left. Why do you think they have those biometric scanners at the marina and the airport?"

"How did you get those reports?" he asked.

"Do you really want to know?" His mother gave him her best *are you kidding me* look.

Thomas. Scott buried his irritation. "Who's submitting the missing persons reports?"

His mother waited until he swung into the parking garage.

"Relatives who thought the missing had crossed the Bay on their own," she said. "There was also a social worker — a Norm — who had a couple of Alt clients. She thought all of her Alt clients had crossed the Bay before she decided to join them. We checked their names against the list of Alts registered in the most recent training group. No matches. We also can't find them in the public arrest records from Star Haven. The social worker told us her clients lived on the fringe, either homeless or just anti-social. The families of the others said the same."

"No one would miss them if they disappeared," Hannah said before Scott could. Good, she caught on fast.

"People are missing them though." He pulled into the first available parking space and stepped out of the car to hold the door open for his mother. Hannah got out on her own, her hand on the brim of her borrowed baseball cap, her face turned down, away from the security cameras. Something he should have told her to do, but she already knew.

Together, the three of them walked toward the elevator alcove, Scott and Catherine keeping Hannah in the middle. "There are only six missing Alts reported so far. There could be more. The commissioner ordered three undercover detectives across the Bay. Norm detectives," she added, before Scott could protest. "Just to scout the territory and see if they could find those six. The detectives returned last night. They couldn't find any of them."

"They went underground." Like Hannah had. He pushed the call button for the elevator.

"They looked underground." His mother handed him her phone, which had a list of names on it. "Do you recognize any names?"

He checked the list as they entered the elevator and his mother selected the third floor. None of them sounded familiar. On impulse he handed the phone to Hannah.

"How about you?"

The way she bit her lip made him think she might know something, so he was surprised when she handed the phone back. "No, I'm sorry, I don't."

Catherine took her phone. "Don't be sorry. It never hurts to ask."

The elevator chimed and they all stepped out on the top floor of *Roberto & Vaughn*, the only clothes store where his mother shopped. Before she had surrendered custody of him to Thomas, Catherine would drag him here every time he grew half an inch. Perfume still clogged the air, making his nose itch with memories of arguments about what clothes he had to wear for school, for play, for pretty much everything. Like Hannah, he kept his head down as Catherine guided them over to the concierge desk.

"Catherine Blackwood." An older, skinny woman with thinning brown hair and thick makeup stepped out from behind the desk. "I haven't seen you all summer. Why just the other day your husband stopped by and I said to him, 'Where is your wife? She never goes this long without a visit.'" She gaily took both Catherine's hands in hers.

"I know, Alice. I've been so busy lately."

Alice stepped back. "Oh, of course. I read the headlines every morning. That fire...such a tragedy."

"Yes, it was," Catherine agreed.

"And who are your guests?"

"This is Scott and...

"Carrie," Hannah said. "Carrie Jones."

Catherine didn't even pause to digest the new name Hannah gave herself. "Carrie Jones. We're here to give Carrie a complete makeover."

"Oh, how fun."

Alice eyed Scott, though, as if she was trying to place him. Few people remembered Catherine's son from her second, very brief, marriage. He glanced at Hannah, her head still down, face obscured by the baseball hat. He understood how she felt. An Alt-killer in a city trying to welcome Star Haven Alts was asking for trouble, but if anyone connected Scott Grey to Cory Blackwood, the entire Thunder City Alt community — no, the entire city itself — would splinter: those who would support Catherine Blackwood's right to keep her family life private, and those who believed Scott Grey should still pay for killing an Alt. If he lost control of his own Alt power before Hannah could break it...

Scott looked down at his hands. Empty. He hadn't translocated anything in almost twenty-four hours. He just needed a little more time. "I'm going downstairs to hit the racks. I'll meet you back up here in an hour?"

Catherine gave him another *are you kidding me* look. "Make it two."

Right. Even the fastest woman alive couldn't shop for clothes in under an hour. He backed away and headed for the escalator.

***

Hannah lifted her cap just a smidge as Scott retreated. The conflict of wanting him to stay warred with her guilt. Did he suspect she'd lied about the names on the list? She'd lost track of the number of times her mother had gotten her released from school early. The Alts would be lying on the couch in her mother's office with all sorts of wounds. She'd fix whatever was broken and didn't ask how they'd gotten hurt. Maybe someday she'd gather her courage to tell the truth. Not yet, though. Not today. Not until she had a foothold here. She needed a chance to prove she wasn't a bad person. To Scott. To his family. Maybe to herself?

"Carrie's my new trainee," the Captain said, "and she lost everything in yesterday's fire, so we need a little bit of everything. Why don't we start with casual and work our way up to..."

"Interview suits." When did she get so ballsy that she would interrupt the Captain and tell the woman what to buy her?

The Captain raised an eyebrow, but didn't disagree.

"Well, I'll get both of you something to drink first, then we'll get started. The usual?" Alice asked Catherine.

"One for each of us." Catherine picked up the end of Hannah's braid. "And if you don't mind, could you make an appointment with Joyce? I'd like to do something with Carrie's hair before she starts... interviewing."

Hannah winced. This was going to be one hell of a shopping trip.

CHAPTER TEN

"What do you think?" the Captain asked, as the salon seat twirled to face the huge mirror. Hannah squinted against a burst of hair spray.

"I don't know what to think," she said. The stylist had stripped the brown dye and added subtle blonde highlights to her natural red. With the heavy dye gone, her hair gently curled along her neck and shoulders.

"It's me, but it's not me. Is it enough to fool my mother?" she asked.

Catherine hunched next to her to look in the mirror. "Too drastic a change will look unnatural and draw even more attention to you. Everything you said while you tried on clothes focused on hiding yourself, fading into the background. It's a legitimate tactic, one we'll refine over time. We'll keep you away from the public as much as possible, but you can't stay indoors all the time. Not if you're determined to have a job."

There was no sarcasm in the Captain's voice. She'd said nothing about Hannah's selection of interview clothes, but they hadn't been alone long enough to discuss details.

The stylist unfastened Hannah's cape. Good God, the wall clock said it was after two o'clock. Four hours had passed since Scott had left them. He must think her some sort of spoiled clothes horse.

Hannah collected the overstuffed bags of clothes and made her way to the front of the salon while the Captain settled the bill. In the reflection of a chrome shelf, she saw a dark head bent over a magazine.

Scott spotted her at the same time and started to stand, but stopped before he reached his full height. His storm-gray eyes swept from her breasts down to her hips and finally back up to her face. Her instinct to flee hit a crescendo except she'd have to push past him to get to the door.

It wasn't the light green capris or the asymmetrical coral top that flowed from her shoulders and flared at her waist that caught his attention. Or maybe it was, because her new clothes revealed a lot more than the scrubs.

After years of doing everything possible to not draw attention to herself, to not upset her mother, Hannah loosened her fear and let her pride keep her in place. Let him look at her, let him enjoy what he saw. Let him see the new Hannah, or maybe this was the Hannah she was supposed to be all along.

"You look nice." His eyes lingered. "Pretty. I'm glad they didn't cut your hair too short."

Her toes curled in her gold sandals at that word, *pretty*.

"Typical male understatement," the Captain called over from the register. "She looks gorgeous."

Maybe she should ask if Alts could be trained not to blush so damn much. The Captain left the register to face her son. "Well, don't stand there staring. Take her bags."

Scott blinked, then added Hannah's bags to his own small one. "Aren't you the one with super strength? Not to mention, you can fly."

"True," the Captain said, as she brushed past both of them to open the door connecting the salon with *Roberto & Vaughn*. "But Thomas taught you better manners."

Hannah surrendered her bags rather than get into the middle of another argument. The Captain took the lead, so Hannah followed with Scott right beside her.

"I mean it." He bent his head to whisper in her ear, the warmth tickling her ear, churning her blood from a low sizzle to full boil. "You really do look great. Different."

"You're not so bad yourself." Her turn for an understatement. He'd changed out of the oxford, which she suspected was Carraro's shirt, and into another t-shirt, forest green this time with a jean jacket. The casual material was still loose enough to give him easy access to the arsenal he carried around, but hid none of his confidence. Now that she had relaxed, now that she had the time, she could appreciate the solid wall of muscle hidden, barely, by Scott's clothes. She could remember the feel of those rolling muscles when he'd cradled her in his arms, carrying her away from the hell of the hospital. She'd outmaneuvered her share of doughnut-filled security guards at Star Haven Memorial. Scott's broad shoulders and flat abs had more in common with her mother's personal security detail, or with the Left Fists she'd healed over the years.

Don't you dare compare Scott to those bastards. They almost beat him to death. Forget them. You're safe. Scott will keep you safe. He promised.

They reached the top floor as the lovely dream of Scott carrying her away from all of her problems faded to black. The Captain waved good-bye to Alice before sweeping over to the elevators. "Yes, my son is very handsome," she said. "But it wouldn't have killed him to buy a blazer."

"Where am I going that I'd need a blazer?" Scott asked.

Was this what normal mothers and sons bickered about? If so, why was Scott armed to the teeth? It couldn't be because of Miranda. He didn't believe her story, at least not entirely. There was something weird about the Blackwood family that she didn't understand, and it wasn't her place to ask.

The elevator doors opened and deposited the three of them back where they had started. Shouting greeted them. A crowd had gathered near their car. A sudden breeze disheveled her hair — the Captain had moved so fast that Hannah hadn't seen her run. Scott shoved all of their bags into Hannah's arms and took off to join his mother.

Damn the bags. She hobbled as fast as she could to the car. By the time she reached the crowd, the Captain had started to beat them back with her voice.

"An ambulance is on the way. This isn't a spectator sport. I mean it, people. Move. Put the camera phone away. Don't make me fry it."

The Captain's threat galvanized the crowd to back off. As they receded, Hannah could see an older, chubby man lying on the ground. Scott had knelt next to the unconscious man and had already begun rhythmed chest compressions.

"You're going to lose him," Hannah said, dropping the bags and squatting next to Scott.

126

"No, I'm not."

Hannah looked beyond Scott, toward Catherine, Captain Spectacular. The Captain had herded most of the crowd away, but one woman was trying to get around the Captain, hysterical, with a boy of maybe eight clutching her hand. The Captain took the woman by the shoulders and spoke to her face-to-face. Hannah couldn't hear the words, but she knew the Captain was telling the woman to keep back, to let Scott work to try and save her husband. The Captain couldn't heal the man, but she could comfort his family. That's what heroes did when they couldn't save the day. Wasn't it? Hannah looked at the little boy, wide-eyed and scared, half-hiding behind his mother.

Who are you, Hannah? Are you a hero? Like Captain Spec? Or are you your mother?

"Move your hands." She reached out to touch the victim's chest.

"Don't do it, Hannah. I mean it." Scott continued to pump.

"You're losing him." She shoved his hands just far enough off the victim's body that she could place her own hand over the man's heart.

Inside. First circle the heart to give it a charge. One beat, two, three. Good, except it did the patient no good if the blood couldn't get through the arteries. So much plaque to break down and she had to make sure the bits were small enough to not build up somewhere else. After she cleared the arteries, she zipped through the veins, then made one complete circuit of the body. She could do more, she should do more, but she pulled out instead.

The ambulance siren greeted her as she floated back into herself. Her head pounded and she fell back, catching herself on her elbows. How long had she been inside?

She looked around, but Scott no longer sat next to her. Without warning, the Captain hauled her up by her shirt collar. A yip of pain escaped as she was marched toward the Porsche. The Captain released her to lean on the trunk.

"I don't care," the Captain barked into her phone. "Get him off the golf course. I have an untrained Alt here who needs medical attention."

She disconnected the line.

"I'm sorry," Hannah said, but her voice sounded weak even to her own ears. "I know I wasn't supposed to bloodsurf, but he would have died if I didn't."

"You don't know that," Catherine said.

"Yes, I do." The Captain could criticize her fashion sense all she wanted, but Hannah knew how to treat a heart attack. "All of his arteries were blocked. No blood was getting through. You could have performed CPR for an hour and it wouldn't have changed anything. He'd have died before the ambulance arrived."

"She's probably right." Scott reappeared from behind the ambulance. He slipped his arm around her waist, and firmly pulled her out of the Captain's grip, taking control away from his mother.

The Captain's face didn't change. All Hannah had accomplished was to make her own headache worse. Her frustration was interrupted by another shrill alarm. The Captain plucked her phone from her hip, scanned the screen, then clipped it back to her belt.

"Take her to the clinic," the Captain said. "Protesters at the harbor are threatening to riot. I have to go."

Without further warning, she flew away, right over the ambulance toward the garage's entrance. A flash, then she was gone.

"I don't understand why she's so angry."

Scott didn't answer as he opened the car door. She managed to seat herself, but the second her head hit the backrest, she was done. His hands reached around to tug her seat belt into place. She didn't even have the energy to thank him, so she kept her eyes closed while he collected their belongings. A minute later, he sat next to her and revved the engine.

"You disappeared, Hannah. The second you touched his skin, your whole body turned translucent. Like a spirit or a ghost."

"I didn't know," she managed to whisper. "No one ever told me. My mother never tells me anything."

He pulled out of the parking slot. "I guess there was no way for you to have figured it out on your own. But, Hannah, you're the one who keeps telling us your mother is after you, that you have to stay out of sight. This doesn't help."

He was right. The Captain was right. And yet, they were both wrong. She'd had to act, and if she had to run because of her actions, if she had to leave Thunder City, she would. You don't leave people to die to save yourself. Her mother would have. Hannah knew this in her heart. She wouldn't become her mother. Even if it meant disobeying Captain Spec. Even if it meant disappointing Scott.

"If any one of those gawkers..." Scott stopped the car and jerked his chin toward a few people still lingering near the elevators. "...had taken a picture, or worse a video...Do you know how fast images of Alts spread? Especially the ones of Catherine?"

Yeah, she knew. She'd seen them on the internet. Looked for them because the Captain was her hero. Was still her hero. "Did they?" she asked. "Did they get a picture of me?"

"I don't think so." Scott steered the Porsche toward the exit, faster than necessary. "Catherine and I kept you covered. I doubt it, but you never know."

No, she didn't know. She could only hope, just as she'd been doing for the past six months. How much longer would her hope hold out?

***

Scott paced outside the exam room while Doctor Rao examined Hannah, but as soon as the doctor had finished, Scott joined both of them in the exam room. He leaned against the cabinets while the doctor snapped off his gloves.

"You're dehydrated. We're going to keep you on the IV while we wait for your bloodwork." The doctor spoke to Hannah, but he addressed Scott as well. "We can keep you overnight if you'd like, or I can discharge you as soon as the bloodwork comes back, assuming there's nothing else wrong."

"I'd like to leave as soon as possible, but..." Her fingers curled around her sheets.

"If you want to leave, we'll leave," Scott said. Keeping her here would only delay her confrontation with Catherine. The sterile environment would make the inevitable fight more difficult. Once home, he could defend her — at the top of his lungs if necessary. Someone had to take Hannah's side. He had a shiny resumé of run-ins with Catherine's inflexibility. His qualifications to take on Captain Spec outranked those of anyone else in Thunder City.

"I'll get the paperwork started." Doctor Rao left them alone.

"Could you turn the lights off?" Hannah asked. She raised a hand to cover her eyes.

He did, but left the door open so they would still have the light from the hallway. "How do you feel?"

"Much better." She sighed and lowered her hand. "Dehydration. All this time, I thought it was exhaustion. I would try to sleep away the pain. Instead, I made it worse."

He walked back over to the bed and pushed the IV pole out of his way while he hooked his foot around a small stool to roll it closer to the bed.

"Do you think the Capt...your mother will still be angry with me when she gets back?" she asked. She still had a death grip on the sheets.

"Don't worry about my mother right now. I'll handle her later."

"Another example of good intentions biting me in the ass."

Her bitterness wrapped around him like a familiar blanket. This trip home had proven just how much anger still fueled him. The temptation to comfort her brought his hands close to hers. He stopped short, his fingers blocked by a thin wrinkle in the sheet. God help him, he didn't agree with Catherine about a lot of things, but this was about more than just obeying rules. The sight of Hannah turning translucent had scared him. She had disappeared into a world where he couldn't follow — not just inside that man's body, but into the Alt community. Seeing her in action left no doubt he'd made the right choice in bringing her to

Thunder City, but he couldn't, wouldn't follow her here. He had to make her break his power before it broke him, his world, his life. He had to keep himself from touching her, no matter the temptation.

"The first lesson you have to learn about Catherine Blackwood is that Thunder City comes first. It always has, it always will. The second lesson is no matter how hard you try to change lesson number one, you'll always fail."

"Sounds familiar," she sighed, and scootched up farther on the pillow, forcing him to pull his hands away. "Back home, Miranda is number one. The second you forget...".

She stopped short. He'd taken his share of domestic violence calls and knew the look. Thomas had called this one right too. His rage rose close to the surface, but Hannah didn't need to see it. "You frightened me, Hannah. When you disappeared, I couldn't protect you. When you use your power, you're vulnerable, helpless from the outside."

"I'm sorry," she said.

"Don't apologize." He leaned in closer. "I'm not telling you because I want you to feel bad, I'm telling you because there's so much I don't know about you. Your power — it's the antithesis of every Alt ability known to us. What we don't know about you, what you don't know about yourself, is dangerous."

She smiled weakly. "You can leave. I know you want to. Why are you still here? Why did you come shopping with us? It's like you're planning to stay. You could have dropped me off and taken the first ferry back to Star Haven this morning."

Now wasn't the time to tell her about his Alt power and how he wanted her to break it. For a moment, the idea of leaving her sounded as crazy as staying. Crazier, in fact.

"I need a favor." He held up a hand to stop her from asking questions. "Not right now. Not even tomorrow. I have some leave time I can burn before I have to report back to work. But soon."

"Does it involve bloodsurfing?"

Scott nodded.

"Your mother..."

He sighed. His mother didn't even know how to train Hannah yet and he couldn't wait too long. "Doesn't have to know. It'll be our secret."

Hannah rolled onto her side, her lips right next to his. "Who needs my help? What's wrong with them?"

So close. Temptation roared again, his desire to pull her head off the flimsy hospital pillow and hold her against him. He leaned closer, but the IV tube swung in the way and hit his nose. He jerked back.

What they hell was he thinking? She was an Alt. Alts represented everything he hated about Thunder City and his family. Too many obstacles, too many Blackwoods stood between them.

He pushed the stool further from the bed. His heart damn near exploded in disappointment, his soul screamed at his cowardice. Neither he nor Hannah deserved what would happen to them if he pursued her. Not to mention she was barely eighteen.

Yeah, and you're a crotchety old fart at twenty-two.

She rolled onto her back. Some day he would convince himself that this was the best choice for them both.

"What happens now?" she asked, her voice a tight rasp.

"Nothing's changed." He hoped his own voice didn't betray his emotionally bent equilibrium. "We stick to Catherine's plan: Get you trained and find you a job."

"Everyone says I need to train if I'm going to live here but no one has told me what that means." She tried to sit up, but lay back with a grimace. Scott saw the problem: the IV needle had dug deep into her elbow.

"It's not as bad as it sounds." He wracked his memory trying to remember what little he knew of Alt training. "Most of the physical training is reserved for Alts who decide to work for Thunder City Alt Support Services. T-CASS for short. Before I left for Star Haven, there were always two or three T-CASS teams working with emergency services in shifts around the clock. They need to learn how to work together to maximize their abilities. The rest of it is just classes on laws, ethics, basic physics. It's designed to make sure you don't hurt yourself or anyone else by accident."

He could tell she was thinking over his words by the way she scrunched her face. "Evan said he works a part-time as a veterinary technician to help pay for rent and groceries. How much do T-CASS members make working for Thunder City? Will I have to work two jobs to make ends meet?"

Evan worked as a vet tech? Why? It wasn't like his brother needed the money. Did Alek hold a job outside of T-CASS, too? He knew Nik worked as a private investigator, but Thomas had never said anything about what the twins did with their free time. Then again, Scott had never asked. He didn't care enough to ask. Why should he care about them when they'd proven they cared nothing for him?

"I don't know," he said. "Joining T-CASS was never a job option for me, so I never looked into how much the city pays T-CASS Alts."

"If all T-CASS members work in teams, I would have to work with others." Her fists clenched the sheet. "I'll be exposed. My mother will find out and come after me. My only hope is to keep as low a profile as I can manage. Joining T-CASS isn't a career option for me, either."

The pure disappointment squeezed tears from the corners of her eyes. She smashed her hand against her temple to wipe them away before Scott could do it for her.

"Hey, hey, it'll be okay." He risked pulling the sheet up further to cover her shoulders. "There are other options for Alts. Neuts — Neutrals like Thomas — own their own businesses, offering to use their powers for whoever hires them. We'll work this out somehow. I promise."

"You shouldn't make promises you can't keep." She fixed her gaze on the ceiling.

"I never make promises I can't keep."

"Never?"

"Look at me, Hannah."

She did, her face tight with suspicion and hope.

"I never make a promise I can't keep," he repeated.

The sheet rose as she took a deep breath. "I believe you."

Good. He needed her to believe him because he wasn't sure if he believed himself. "Now, why don't I track down a nurse? We'll get this IV yanked, and I'll get us the hell out of here."

She nodded, but the worried look remained. He didn't blame her. He'd just promised her everything would be okay. If he remained in Thunder City, he'd have to stay in contact with his family, stay in contact with Hannah. Pleasure and dread mixed in a tsunami of emotions tugging him toward choices he didn't want to make, shouldn't have to make. He'd stay in Thunder City. He promised to protect Hannah for now, but he never promised her he'd be there for her in the future.

CHAPTER ELEVEN

"What's your status?" Miranda grabbed her phone and turned off the volume to the streaming news feed.

"We found the house. Grey's parents," Coreville clarified, over the sound of passing cars in the background. "It's located in the Fargrounds neighborhood. Working class, mostly small single-family homes mixed with mom and pop shops. We're still setting up surveillance. They have a stronger than usual security system. Your hacker said she could crack the Wi-Fi code and see what we can access without breaking inside."

"Do what you have to do," Miranda said. "Is there any sign of him?"

"No, but it's early in the day and there are no vehicles in the driveway. I can send one of my men to knock on the door and confirm."

"Do it. I'll wait." She only had two days left to get the girl back. "What other contingency plans have you made?"

"We're checking Grey's phone record, but there's not much beyond his partner, pizza, and a couple of girls. I left one of my men behind to press the girls for information. If Grey's not on this side of the Bay we'll know before tonight. We couldn't find any record of him on the more popular social media networks. He's a privacy nut."

Not surprising for a cop with ambition. If it turned out he hadn't fallen victim to her daughter's machinations, and his trip to Thunder City was just a coincidence, she would consider recruiting him into her network. She couldn't afford to let good resources go to waste.

"We're also looking at his high school records. There might be someone from his past he would tap if he needed to hide."

Another voice interrupted Coreville's report. Miranda heard a rumble of concern before Coreville muted his phone. He returned a moment later. "One of my men knocked on the door. No one answered."

Miranda glanced at the television. "Which could mean anything. They're either helping their son hide my daughter elsewhere or they simply took him to lunch." Across the television screen Catherine Blackwood flew into the heart of the Alts protesting on the other side of the Bay, her uniform a sleek, dark dot among the colorful signs held by the protesters.

The Star Haven Alts wanted to come home, wanted to fight for their right to live wherever they chose. If any of them actually attempted to cross the Bay, she would have to eliminate them and risk stirring up the Thunder City Alts.

Blackwood had made many a pretty speech when the Star Haven Alts first fled. She would train them, find them homes and jobs. So damn helpful, but then she could afford to be. Miranda pulled the phone from her ear as two of Captain Spectacular's sons joined her in the sky over the protesters. Catherine Blackwood could afford to help any Alt who crossed her path. Even Hannah.

"Pull the list of every Alt in Thunder City. Natives and Newcomers," she told Coreville. "Compare it against a list of the protesters or any Alt involved in the protest movement."

"You think the girl is hiding out with them?" Coreville asked.

"Hardly. I think my daughter is smart enough to stay as far away from the protesters as she can get. The comparison should narrow the list of possible Alts who might be protecting her. Focus on any Alts who have a connection to Scott Grey, no matter how tenuous. Also, put a tail on Catherine Blackwood. She might also have my daughter. Once you have confirmation, regardless of whether it's Blackwood or not, do not attempt to capture Hannah. Contact me first."

"You have a plan?"

Miranda hung up without answering. Of course she had a plan, but she needed concrete evidence first. Not only might she have the brat back in under twenty-four hours, but she might also have the pleasure of getting the better of Captain Spectacular.

***

Hannah shifted around on the leather bar stool while she sliced through another chunk of beef. There was nothing more satisfying in the world then a steaming bowl of stew and all of the sparkling water she could drink. Doctor Rao had been right about the dehydration. This was the fastest she'd ever recovered from bloodsurfing. She should have figured it out before now. Hell, her mother should have figured it out.

Maybe Miranda did know and kept it to herself. How much easier to keep you under control, keep you dependent, if you were constantly sick, always in need of her care. How many times did you plan to run, but didn't because you were afraid of needing her too much? She never even told you how you disappear when you bloodsurf. All those years of watching you heal people and she never said a thing.

Beside her, Scott flipped from one television station to another, so he didn't notice her drop her spoon into the near-empty bowl. Hannah's increased distance from her mother didn't make her suspicions easier to swallow. And they were just suspicions. If she told Scott, he would demand proof. He still didn't completely believe her story — or if he did, he couldn't do anything until she could prove it.

This time her headache wasn't caused by bloodsurfing. She rubbed her temples until the ache dulled, then picked up her spoon again.

Scott had asked if she minded eating in the video room rather than at the formal dining table, since they were the only two in the house. She understood why Scott would want to keep an eye on the news tonight. All of the local coverage showed endless shots of the Star Haven Alts demanding their right to cross the Bay.

Why they would want to go back to a city where they had to hide their identities and their powers baffled her. She had come to Thunder City where Alts lived free, except now she had to hide her face among Alts who didn't hide theirs.

She swallowed the remaining hurt along with the stew. If she had eaten lunch, or at least had drunk more while at *Roberto & Vaughn*, she wouldn't have landed in the clinic.

But if she hadn't gone to the clinic, Scott wouldn't have almost kissed her. She might never have kissed a man before, but she could recognize desire when she saw it. The way he'd looked at her in the salon...he'd thought her attractive now that she didn't resemble a sewer rat.

So she was attractive enough to kiss, maybe even pretty enough for him to stick around Thunder City for a few days. He wouldn't stay here, though. Whatever Evan had done ten years ago had driven Scott to Star Haven. He had his life there and she wouldn't blame him if he wanted to rebuild it. He had access to the Blackwood money and the Carraro talent to help put the pieces of his life back together.

She speared a soft chunk of potato while Scott changed the channel one more time. Another repeat of Captain Spec flying around the harbor. The protesters would have their say, but not at the expense of safety. No one tried to abuse the police lined up to protect the disembarking ferry passengers.

"Scott?"

He didn't hear her.

"Scott?" she said a little louder.

"Huh? Oh, sorry." He turned down the volume.

"I just wanted to know if all of the protesters have already trained to work with T-CASS? I mean, none of them are using their powers. You would think they would use their powers to, I don't know, make a stronger statement?"

She'd caught him off guard. Maybe he really was worried about his family? Could his anger at his

141

brothers have cracked a little in the past twenty-four hours?

"They can't use their powers until they're trained and can prove they have control, regardless of whether or not they join T-CASS. That's the law and part of the agreement Catherine negotiated with Thunder City back when Alts started to remove their masks." He spun the stool around to face her instead of the screen. "I doubt they're all trained at this point. They'd be stupid to jeopardize their safety by challenging T-CASS or the police. Since there are so many Newcomers, they would have to be broken up into smaller groups. Unless things have changed, they'd use the lecture halls at Thunder City University for classroom work, and the sports fields for the physical training. Though I've heard they sometimes use Thunder City Arena."

"Where the Tornadoes play?" Made sense with all of the fields for different types of sports. "I've seen the Arena on TV. Roger was a huge Sabers fan. The actual sport didn't matter. He just wanted Star Haven to win."

"You miss him a lot, don't you?"

Only after he asked did she realize she was rubbing her heart. It would be a long time before Roger's death didn't sting. The last game she and her stepfather had watched together had been a football game, not even the championship. The Sabers trashed the Tornadoes, but it had been a hard fought win. She and Roger celebrated with ice cream. Strawberry, her favorite, with whipped cream and rainbow sprinkles.

"I'm sorry," Scott said. "I didn't mean to..."

"Tell me more about the physical training," she interrupted. She didn't want to travel down memory lane. She was tired of remembering what she'd lost to her mother. Someday, she'd able to mourn Roger, without the memory of her mother's vileness. "If I can't train out in the open at the University or the Arena, do you think I can still train somewhere else? Someplace more private?"

Scott clicked off the television. "I don't know. Any information I have is a decade out of date. I would imagine the physical training isn't all that different from police training. You'd have to learn to coordinate your ability with the other Alts. Like with what they're doing down at the harbor. The Thunder City Alts and the police have to work together or there will be chaos. It's a safety issue."

That made sense. "So Captain Spec knows what everyone's capability is so that she can tell them where to go and what to do."

He shook his head. "It sure does seem that way, doesn't it? Except Catherine can't be on call twenty-four seven, though God knows, she tries."

More bitterness.

"Think of it this way," he continued, a napkin crumpled in his hand. "A raging fire breaks out in an apartment building downtown."

"Like the one before we arrived. It was in the paper."

"Right, but let's say we have one T-CASS team on call and neither of them are a Blackwood. Let's say it's Spritz, who controls water, and Blockhead, a shifter who can turn his fists into blocks that can punch through almost anything. Who takes the lead for the call?"

Easiest answer ever. "Spritz."

"Why?"

"He..."

"She," Scott corrected.

"She could help the fire department put out the fire," Hannah answered.

"Okay," he said. "But what do you do about the Alt on the fifteenth floor who's high on so much blitz that he's telekinetically tossing his furniture all over his apartment? Big stuff like the sofa and the lamps. Maybe sharp stuff, like a broken mirror or a kitchen knife. He's so far gone, he doesn't even know the building's on fire. For all you know, he started the fire. Now what do you do?"

Easy again. "Well you send Blockhead up there to get him. Blockhead can use his fists to break down the door and deflect the debris."

Scott's stupid little smirk meant the obvious answer was the wrong one. She had missed something. "Good thought, except Blockhead isn't fireproof and he still needs oxygen to breathe. How's he supposed to get up to the fifteenth floor? Also, he can't put on a firefighter's protective gear because he needs to have his forearms exposed to turn his fists into blocks."

Of course there had to be complications. "So you would have to send both Spritz and Blockhead into the building. Spritz first to put the fire out ahead of Blockhead so they could get to the floor where the other Alt is going crazy."

"Better, but you also have all the other apartment residents to think about too. Not to mention the building itself. You have to make sure that the fire doesn't spread to the building next door."

Hannah tossed her napkin onto the table. "Oh, good grief."

"Not as easy as you thought," he said, with a full grin this time. "It's a huge responsibility. Not everyone has what it takes. Some Alts burn out after a couple of

144

years. It's not because they don't want to help or contribute, but not everyone has the stamina to join T-CASS, at least in emergency situations. They'd rather not use their abilities at all than do what my family does on a regular basis."

He said *my family*. Not *the Blackwoods*, as if he wasn't a part of them. She would keep that observation to herself for now. "Or they become Neuts?" she asked, instead.

Scott shook his head, his smile disappearing. "Even Neuts take risks in their line of work. It's more hazardous and you have to screen your clients very carefully. If you take on a client with a less than legal assignment, you risk getting caught or having the client skip out on you, or worse, blackmail you. A lot of Neuts play in the gray areas of the law. Just ask Thomas. He did it for years and he's not even an Alt. He'll tell you the same thing he told me: it's a thrill so long as you can get away with it, but eventually the odds will catch up with you. A lot of Neuts turned two-shoe when Thomas did because they were tired of the risk of dealing with the less than savory side of Alt life."

"Two-shoe?"

Scott grimaced. "Goody two-shoe. Derogatory for T-CASS Alts, or anyone who fights the good fight."

"Like Thomas, who plays in the dark gray areas, like hacking into the Star Haven biometric database," she said. "Or you, a cop?"

Scott nodded, scraping his spoon around a near-empty bowl. "Yeah, but now Thomas has Catherine to watch his back. And he watches hers."

But who would watch Scott's back? Carraro would, but how often could a man call on his father to pull him out of trouble? Hannah reached over to grab the remote and turn on the television again, but muted the sound.

Captain Spec flashed onto the screen. She was flying with a man lying prone on her back, his arms wrapped around her waist. The news scrawl said Captain Spec carried the president of the ferry service, who had agreed to talk to the protesters.

Flying had to be the best Alt power. Maybe not the most powerful, or even the most practical, but to soar into the sky any time you wanted? Even just to get away from your problems for a while. "Did your mother ever take you flying? When you were younger, I mean?"

Scott shook his head. "Nope. As Catherine would say — she's not a pack mule or taxi service. Unless you have a damn good reason, no free rides. Getting the president of the ferry service to the harbor to stop a riot is a good reason."

The camera changed its angle so the protesters came into view. Overhead, Rumble hovered, as he expanded a cloud to hide the brutal late afternoon sun. She couldn't see Roar, but she liked to think he had something to do with the breeze. Other colorful costumes appeared around the edges of the crowd, keeping a respectful distance, but still close enough to intervene.

All those Newcomers, protesting out in the open where everyone could see their faces. They honestly thought they could return to Star Haven and change the city, force the Norms to accept them. It would never happen. Even if every Norm in Star Haven had a change of heart, her mother would sabotage any challenge to the Alt-ban.

"Scott?"

He looked back at her. "Yeah."

"Could we go down there?"

"Where? To the harbor?"

She nodded.

"Why?"

"I'd to see the Alts in action. I'd like to know how all this works."

He drummed his fingers on the bar a few times. "We can't drive down there. I doubt the police would let us near the harbor unless we were actually going to use the ferry. My badge won't even get us through. Plus, we wouldn't want you to accidentally end up on the news."

It was a stupid idea. She should have kept her mouth shut.

"Still," he said. "We could drive along the coast. Silvergrass Pier is less than a half mile from the harbor and you can see the entire boardwalk. There's probably a pair of binoculars around here we could use."

"Really? I mean, I bought a hoodie this afternoon, so I could hide my face, at least until sundown."

Scott pushed back his chair. "Sounds like that would work."

"Yes!" She threw her arms around him, her cheek next to his. The rough stubble jerked her back almost as fast as she'd hugged him.

"I'm sorry. I'm so sorry. I broke the rules." Panic overrode the fierce, brief thrill of holding him in her arms instead of the other way around. Would she ever learn?

Scott touched his the side of his face where she had pressed her cheek to his. For a wild moment, Hannah though he would yell at her. He'd have every right. Instead, a slow, mischievous smile tugged at his lips. "I won't say anything if you won't."

Hannah relaxed, but not too much. Scott wouldn't say anything because he'd told her he'd never break his promise. In little more than a day she'd come to place her trust in an Alt-killer, but even with all Scott had done for her, she had to hold back on some of that trust. He still wanted her to use her powers on someone, to break the rules again, but under more careful circumstances. He had a reason for not ratting her out that had nothing to do with his attraction to her. It was a subtle form of manipulation she had learned to recognize over the years.

Hannah backed away from Scott, careful to keep a grateful smile on her face and hide her doubts as she ran out of the video room and up the stairs to her guest room. Let Scott play whatever game he was playing. She'd spent her life being manipulated by those she loved and who were supposed to love her back. Right now her desire for Scott Grey pushed her into dangerous, exciting, and new emotional territory. For tonight, she would embrace the danger and damn the consequences.

For just once in her life, she wanted to be the manipulator.

CHAPTER TWELVE

"Did you see? Did you see? It's Hopper! She jumped all the way from the terminal to the police line."

Scott almost dropped his beer as Hannah knocked his arm in her excitement. He switched the half-empty bottle to his left hand to avoid an accident.

"Oh, oh, oh, Spritz is helping her. In the white and blue uniform? Oh my God, it's Blockhead. He looks just like he does on the 'net, a tank with blocks for fists. Tangling with him has got to hurt."

She bumped his arm again, so he put down the beer and raised his binoculars. Yep, she'd named the Thunder City Alts three for three: Blockhead, Spritz, and Hopper were handling the crowd. Overhead, Rumble and Roar flew in tandem, patrolling the harbor now that the sun had set. He doubted they saw him sitting on the edge of the Pier halfway between the point and the parking lot. His brothers had to make sure the gawkers in the Bay kept a safe distance while ensuring the media got whatever coverage they needed. He hadn't seen Ghost yet, but more than likely the police had asked him to stay hidden. He'd be their ace in the hole in case something went wrong.

"Look, there's Captain Spec...I mean your mother...I mean Catherine."

What had he gotten himself into? Back at the clinic he'd promised himself to keep his distance from Hannah. An hour later, she was giving him puppy dog eyes over dinner and his resolve weakened. She'd looked so forlorn, he spoke before he could think through the consequences of bringing her out here. Then she hugged him. Now, it was all he could do to watch the boardwalk instead of her. Her enthusiasm was so over-the-top. Why did she have to sound so damn happy and look so damn cute at the same time? Fucking hell, he needed to get laid. Soon.

He lowered the binocs and increased the volume of the streaming news station from Nik's phone hooked to his belt. The commentary wasn't as colorful as the television broadcast, but the reporters kept them updated well enough, confirming that the president of the ferry company was still in negotiations with a representative of the Newcomers.

"What do you think is going to happen next?" Hannah asked. She leaned on him without realizing it, her eyes fixed on the action. In the sunset, with no one close enough to see her, she'd pulled back her hoodie so that her hair, only partially tied back, whipped around in the breeze.

"Nothing." He pulled the wayward strands away from his face. "The ferry service can't take them across. The Star Haven Police won't let the Alts off the boat, never mind into the marina. They can't go back, not ever. They'll be stuck on the ferry riding back and forth across the Bay. The ferry will have to kick them off in favor of paying passengers."

Her sigh sounded so wistful. "It's not fair."

A lump formed in his throat. "Some would argue it's not fair to force people to live with Alts. It's not right when Norms lose their jobs and their privacy to Alts who can lift ocean liners and read minds..."

He hadn't meant to upset her, but by the way she stilled he could see he had, so he stopped his rant mid-sentence. He shut off the radio.

"What about you?" she asked, her head down, eyes on her lap. "Is that why you moved to Star Haven? Why you became a cop in a city where it's illegal for Alts to live?"

"I left Thunder City to become my own man. I became a cop because I want to help people." It was the answer he would give on both sides of the Bay, no matter who asked. He wanted to ease her fear, but he wouldn't lie to her either. How far down into the emotional pit of his childhood did he have to plunge in order to convince her he wasn't the ogre in the family? "If you haven't noticed, my family earns its reputation by helping people. We're born two-shoes. It's a trait."

He tried to laugh, to make it sound funny, but even to his ears the attempt fell flat. Hannah still wouldn't look at him.

"Hannah..." He stopped before he began. No, he wouldn't complain, but he had to make her understand the Blackwood family. "We were never the 'sit around the dinner table and share your day' sort of family. And my mother never coddled her kids. My grandfather trained my brothers, but when it became clear I wasn't an Alt, he left me with Garrett. For a short while I thought Garrett was my dad, but Catherine sent him on a long vacation when she found out. She sat me down and listed the facts: My dad was dead, he wasn't coming back, she didn't have time for my tears, there's a prison break, bank robbery, fire, gang fight, or fill in the blank that's far more important than any of my problems."

He had to stop because his throat closed around his anger.

"I knew you had difficulties with her." Hannah tossed her braid over her shoulder. "Maybe it's like having a politician for a mother. Everyone expects you to agree with her policies even if you don't understand them half the time."

"Except in my family..." His voice trailed off as a van pulled into the parking lot of the Pier, tires crunching gravel. An entire TV camera crew spilled onto the walkway and headed right in their direction.

"Put your hood back on." He capped the beer bottle. Keeping his body between Hannah and the news crew, he tucked her under the crook of his harm. He should have figured one of the news channels would have set up shop here. He'd been out of Thunder City so long, he'd forgotten how often the media filmed the boardwalk from this angle.

Hannah's breath tickled his neck. There was nothing they could do but wait. If the crew passed behind them and set up closer to the point of the Pier, he could get Hannah back to the car with no one the wiser.

The TV crew didn't get his telepathic message. Instead, they set up their equipment not ten feet from where he and Hannah sat.

"Now what? Should we move further toward the end?" she whispered.

"We could be here all night if we do that." His pulse raced with the thought. Quiet, dark, and alone with Hannah curled against him.

The bright light from the camera crew arced their way. Hannah flinched closer, her hands snaking around his waist.

"Relax," he said. "If we stay put, they'll ignore us. Making out on the Pier is hardly news."

The reporter started her spiel, how the Star Haven Alts came to Thunder City before they organized and decided to fight for the right to live in Star Haven. The camera light swung their way twice as she talked, but Scott didn't dare raise his head.

"Should we?" Hannah whispered.

"Should we what?"

"Make out."

Good thing he'd put down his beer. "That's a joke, right?"

She shrugged, her shoulders rubbing against his chest. "Just thought we should make it look good. I promise — no bloodsurfing."

His reaction had sounded far more harsh than he had intended. "The plan is to stay off camera, not attract their attention."

"If you insist." She tucked her chin onto his chest.

Never let it be said impulsiveness wasn't also a family trait.

"Hannah."

She tilted her head back just as Scott lowered his to place the most gentle kiss he could manage on her lips.

"Oh..." She didn't say anything further. Instead, she slipped her arm around his neck and pulled his head down toward hers. His plan to keep it slow and short flew across the Bay with the breeze. He slid his arm down from her shoulders to her waist.

"I think we should move," he said, when she pulled back to catch her breath.

"Good idea."

They stood up, pressed together since neither of them was willing to let go of the other. She giggled.

"Do you want me to pick you up again?"

"That would be romantic."

He curled his left arm around her legs. In the next instant, without warning, a familiar series of staccato pops erupted. One instinct overrode another. He shoved Hannah to the ground and covered her body with his.

"Ow, Scott, not so fast..."

"Gunfire. Stay down."

"What? Who..."

Damn it. His arm was crushed under her body. He couldn't reach the phone on his belt. "Shhhh. Listen."

Behind them the reporter shouted into her microphone. Faint screams of panic carried over the water. What the hell had gone wrong?

"Arch your back," he said. "I need my arm."

Hannah pressed her body into his and he slid his arm free.

"Can we stand up?" she asked.

"Not yet." The phone vibrated. He pulled it out. Thomas's name appeared on the screen.

"Ghost, where the hell are you? Everything is pandemonium over here and the GPS shows you at the Pier."

Crap.

"It's Scott," he said. "Nik let me borrow his phone last night. I'm over at the Pier with Hannah. What's happening? Where are you?"

"One moment."

He heard Thomas shout at someone, probably Catherine, that he couldn't locate Ghost. At the same time, Hannah shoved at Scott's shoulders. "I'm sorry. You're too heavy."

He rolled off of her. A police boat skimmed past the Pier, followed by a second, then a third. Overhead, a helicopter buzzed low to the water, the searchlight blinding him to the fishermen who raced toward them from the point. No one was in immediate danger of getting shot, so he sat up, his brush with desire a thing of the past.

"I'm at the ferry terminal," Thomas said. "I can locate everyone except Ghost. The Star Haven Alt representative didn't like the president's excuses for barring them from ferry service. He took a swing, and the president pulled a gun and started firing."

"He killed an Alt?"

"No. Electrocyte, the Star Haven Alt, deflected the bullet and took Kavenaugh, the president, hostage. Catherine couldn't risk making a grab for Kavenaugh before Electrocyte pulled Kavenaugh onto the ferry. Electrocyte has his power and the gun."

Electrocyte. Scott had never heard of him, but that wasn't a surprise. He hadn't kept up to date with all of the Alts who'd left Star Haven. As long as they weren't in his city, they weren't his problem. "Let me guess. He's an electricity manipulator."

Hannah grabbed her binocs to watch the action as Thomas described it to him.

"I see something," she said. "On the ferry. There are two shadows."

Scott took up his own binocs so he could confirm what Hannah saw. This particular ferry, a twin hulled catamaran, carried passengers only. Electrocyte had dragged Kavenaugh to the sundeck, keeping the bridge between himself and anyone who might take a shot at him from the boardwalk.

"I can see the Alt and Kavenaugh," Scott said.

"At this point, you're probably the only one who can," Thomas replied. "SWAT's here. Stay put. Let me know if Electrocyte moves. I'm going to put you on the line with the Incident Commander as soon as she's set. And for God's sake, keep an eye out for Ghost."

Thomas disconnected.

"What did he say?" Hannah asked.

"No one can find Nik because he loaned me his phone." The phone weighed heavy in his pocket. "Thomas is going to have me talk to the Incident Commander, since we're the only ones who can see Electrocyte."

The sun had set and all the lights on the boardwalk put the ferry's stern into shadow. The Incident Commander must have warned off the copters because none of them tried a flyover with their searchlights. Beyond the ferry, Scott could see a SWAT sniper crossing the irregular rooftops of the boardwalk's shops. Another pair of SWAT team members ran along the jetty adjacent to the boardwalk, parallel to the Pier.

"What are we going to do?"

She stood close to him, her hands clutching his jacket, as if she expected him to have a clue as to how to make this right. Scott lifted the binocs again. One of the shadows on the ferry's sundeck moved back and forth, the other leaned against the railing. He half listened to the reporter yammer in the background. The news crew didn't have any information Thomas hadn't already given him. If only he could get his hands on a sniper rifle.

"Scott..."

"There's nothing we can do, Hannah," he said, his frustration boiling. "Just sit tight. My guess is they'll try

156

to get a negotiator to talk Electrocyte into letting Kavenaugh go."

"No, look down."

What? He looked at his feet. Even in the low light of the Pier's lanterns he could identify the sniper rifle lying there.

"How did it get here?"

She reached for the gun, but he knocked her hand away just in case it was loaded. He picked it up and checked. Loaded and ready to fire. *Fuck, fuck, fuck.* His Alt power. He must have grabbed it from one of the SWAT officers by accident.

Nik's phone vibrated. "Yeah."

"I found Ghost," Thomas said, his relief obvious.

"Where is he?" Scott asked, his thoughts on automatic, the rest of him numb.

"The IC asked if he could sneak onto the boat. We're going to isolate Electrocyte and Kavenaugh. If Ghost can close and lock all of the doors leading into the ferry, they'll be forced to remain on deck where you can keep them in view. But we have another problem."

Scott already knew what Thomas was going to say.

"An Alt, we're not sure who, managed to translocate a sniper rifle. We don't know where it is or who has it. Hopper is trying to search the protesters, but they scattered when Kavenaugh started firing. Some want to leave, others are ready to fight. If they start using their powers, then T-CASS can handle it, but if one of them has a gun..."

"I have it." The situation was out of control. He couldn't keep his Alt power hidden any longer. "I have the gun."

"How did you get it? Hannah? Did she grab it?"

"Hang on." He had to keep Hannah out of this. All of it. He yanked out his car keys and shoved them into her hand. "Pull your hood over your head and sneak past the camera crew. When you get to the car, start the engine, then get in the passenger seat and wait for me. Don't turn the engine off no matter how long you have to wait. Don't open the door for anyone except me or Thomas and keep the hood over your head, understand?"

"What are you going to do? Where did the rifle come from?" she stuttered with fear.

"I promise, I'll tell you, but not now."

She bit her lip. "You're going to shoot him, the Alt, aren't you?"

"Maybe. I'm the only one who can see him. Unless the IC has a better idea, or an Alt who can get the gun away from Electrocyte without putting the Norm at risk."

He sure as hell wasn't going to try and translocate another gun. If he did so he might trigger Electrocyte's rage and the Alt might kill Kavenaugh.

She hesitated, undecided, but he couldn't wait. Thomas was holding the line for him.

"Go. Now. Don't look back."

For a moment, he didn't think she'd leave, but she pushed past him with the hood slipping over her hair. He watched, holding his breath, as she kept close to the safety rail. The camera lights shone on the reporter whose never ending broadcast kept the crew facing the boardwalk. Hannah didn't stop, not even to say 'excuse me', and barreled between the equipment, crew, and the railing, her fingers tugging the hood far past her forehead. No one noticed her.

Scott put the phone to his ear as he headed farther down the Pier. "I sent Hannah back to the car."

"You didn't tell me she had translocation abilities."

"She doesn't." Thomas wasn't stupid. He'd figure it out. "Right now I have the gun and I can see Electrocyte and Kavenaugh. What I need is enough light."

If Thomas realized the implications of what Scott hadn't told him, he put it aside. "You can't do this, Scott. You're not part of the Thunder City police. You're not even SWAT trained. The IC won't authorize you to shoot someone. What if you miss?"

"What if we wait and Electrocyte shoots Kavenaugh? Or worse, electrocutes him to death?"

"Let the negotiator do his job. The IC has a SWAT team on its way to the Pier."

Scott stopped walking. He could see the target better without the ambient light of the camera crew. He lay down flat and tucked the rifle into position. He'd practiced a lot with this model. Juan hadn't laughed at him when he let it slip during one of their first patrols that he planned to apply to SWAT. Instead, his partner had invited him to the range so they could prepare together.

"We called in Highlight," Thomas continued. "She'll create a couple of light spheres that Roar will float out to the boat."

"Not too bright. You'll spook them."

"They're looking for searchlights, not spheres."

Scott checked the night sight. He could see both men now, even in the shadow of the bridge, but couldn't tell one from the other. He watched and waited. If he had more faith in his Alt power, he might try making a grab for Kavenaugh. As quickly as he thought it, he banished it. He couldn't...wouldn't risk translocating a person. Not unless he knew for sure it wouldn't kill them in the process. The only thing Scott had faith in at the moment was his marksmanship.

One of the shadows held out his arms and sparks jolted the other shadow. Now he knew which one was Electrocyte.

"Thomas, Electrocyte just electrocuted Kavenaugh. What do you want me to do?"

"I can't authorize you to shoot, Scott. Just wait. Ghost is on his way."

More sparks. Scott swore he heard a scream, but he couldn't be sure. Highlight's light spheres had reached the boat's stern, floating above the water. Scott used the scope to see Electrocyte grab Kavenaugh and haul the wounded man toward the bridge. The door wouldn't open. Frustrated, Electrocyte shoved Kavenaugh away and yanked on the door's handle.

"He's trying to get back inside. The door is locked."

"Good," Thomas said. "Once Rumble gets a phone out there, we'll open communication..."

Sparks shot out of Electrocyte's fingers and struck Kavenaugh again.

"Too late. I'm sorry, Thomas. I'm so sorry."

Scott dropped the phone, checked the sight. The light from Electrocyte's power spread across the deck. Scott let out his breath and fired just as Ghost emerged from the door to the bridge.

Blood splattered from Electrolyte's chest a half second before he dropped onto the deck. Ghost...Nik...his brother... staggered, blood spilling over his hands as he clutched the wound in his own chest, then fell on top of Electrocyte.

Light blinded him, but Scott didn't move. The reporter and her crew surrounded him now but he stayed prone. Farther down, heavy footfalls rattled the planks, the vibrations becoming stronger as the SWAT team approached.

Scott picked up the phone. Nik's phone. "Someone needs to pick up Hannah. She's waiting in the car." He lay the gun and the phone down and placed his hands behind his head. He followed instructions as the camera crew broadcasted his arrest to all of Thunder City.

CHAPTER THIRTEEN

Hannah jumped at the single gunshot, louder than the others. Had Scott fired the mysterious rifle? Had he killed the Alt? This was worse than being on the roof of the hospital. Her instincts scrunched her down farther in the car seat, tugging her hood all the way down to her nose. The light from the news crew flashed over the Porsche. A monstrous armored truck with the initials SWAT plastered along its side lurched to a stop not ten feet away. Doors slammed open, then closed. Big men with big guns hit the sandy parking lot, a wall of black blocking the light from the TV cameras.

The men shouted, but Hannah couldn't understand the words over her panic. She couldn't think, all her trust lay in Scott's orders to stay in the car. Sweat dripped down her forehead into her eyes. A few minutes more and everything would be okay. Scott would appear and drive her back to the house. She'd find Eight-ball and cuddle with the cat in her comfortable bed and sleep the nightmare away.

This was all her fault. She never should have asked Scott to bring her here. What had she been thinking? That she could fit in? That she could be safe? That she wouldn't be putting others at risk? How stupid to think so.

She turned on the car radio. The announcer shouted as the events across the water unfolded. Scott had hit an Alt called Electrocyte. The Alt was dead. She wanted to believe Scott had no choice. He claimed he'd had no choice the first time he killed an Alt. No one in Star Haven cared much about why he had killed, just that he had done so successfully.

But where had the gun come from?

Her logic scattered with more shouts from the radio. Captain Spectacular was flying two paramedics to the ferry, Rumble right next to her with two more, while Roar carried their equipment.

More yelling from outside. The SWAT team returned. Scott was with them, his arms awkwardly pulled behind his back. Oh, God, they'd arrested him. Why?

The news crew blocked the SWAT team in their efforts to broadcast the action, but the SWAT team swept them aside like bothersome flies.

Hannah reached for the door latch, but caution stayed her hand. Scott didn't look at the Porsche. He didn't fight or shout or try to signal her in any way. The SWAT team bundled him into their truck, with the camera crew recording every humiliating moment, damn them.

Then it was over. The truck pulled out of the lot at high speed. The news crew clambered into their own van to follow.

Hannah's tears mixed with her sweat. What should she do? Should she follow them? She didn't have a driver's license or a phone to call for help. She didn't know which station they were taking him to. What would happen to Scott once they got him to the police station? Thunder City loved their Alts and Scott had just shot a second one.

A fist banged on the driver's side window.

"Hannah, it's Thomas. Open the door."

She leaned over and punched the button. Carraro slid into the driver's seat.

"Are you hurt?" He yanked the Porsche into gear and backed out of the parking space before she could answer.

"No. I'm okay."

The screech of tires on asphalt drowned out whatever Carraro muttered under his breath.

"I'm sorry, I didn't hear you," Hannah said. "What happened?"

"Later. I need to know what happened on the Pier. Everything you saw, felt, smelled..."

Hannah stuttered but managed to relay everything as she remembered it. Everything except Scott's kiss.

"The gun just appeared? Did you call it to you?"

Hannah shook her head.

"Have you ever had the ability to translocate an object? Bring an object to you from a distance?"

"No. I swear. I've never done anything like that. Please, what's happening? Why did they arrest Scott? He did nothing wrong."

Carraro took another turn, too tight. Her shoulders hit the door and only her quick defensive reflexes kept her head from slamming into the window.

"When you healed Scott, did you see anything unusual? Heal something you've never encountered before?"

Yesterday seemed a million years ago, but she knew exactly what Carraro was asking for. The mysterious black thread she'd fixed in Scott's brain. She

164

hadn't known what it was. The black thread she'd reattached had been broken a long time. No one else could have fixed it but her. No one else would have even known to look for it.

If she was right, Miranda would kill for this information. So would a lot of other people. Of all of her secrets, this one was the most valuable — and the most deadly.

"I don't know what you're talking about," she answered.

Carraro took a deep breath and slowed just long enough to check the intersection for cars before blasting through the red light. "Nik reported to the Incident Commander. She sent him onto the ferry to block Electrocyte's access to the bridge. The bullet passed right through Electrocyte just as Nik emerged from the door to stop him from killing Kavenaugh. Nik didn't have time to phase back into the door or the bullet would have passed right through him."

Scott's bullet had hit Nikolaos. Hannah felt sick. "You're taking me to the hospital, aren't you?"

Carraro didn't look at her. His voice cracked, hardly above a whisper as if he wasn't speaking to her but to himself. "I shouldn't. Catherine wouldn't want me to...won't let you...she's such a stickler for training. There have been accidents, horrible accidents before..."

"You want to quote rules while Nik dies?" How had she come to care so much in so little time?

"He may already be dead."

The lump in her throat bobbed. "Take me there anyway."

The car didn't change course. Carraro had planned to take her to the hospital all along.

"What's going to happen to Scott?"

165

"I put a call in to my lawyer. She's heading over to the police station now."

By tomorrow, Scott's face would be a fixture on TV. Everyone would see him, including Miranda and whoever she sent to find her daughter. While Carraro pulled into the parking garage attached to the hospital, Hannah compiled a mental list of all the items she'd need to get before she ran.

Not tonight, though. Carraro put his hand on her back as he escorted her through Harbor Regional's main entrance. The sweet mix of alcohol, soap, and air fresheners smelled the same as Star Haven Memorial. At least at the main entrance she didn't have to hear the screams of the desperate trying to get inside.

Carraro spoke to the woman behind the information desk. She checked her computer and frowned.

"One moment," she said, and picked up her handset.

Impatient, Hannah stepped away from the desk. A security officer stood behind another desk at the opposite corner, alone. At Star Haven Memorial, there had been no fewer than two guards stationed at the front entrance and double that number in the emergency room. She would have no difficulties losing herself here if she was forced to.

"Your son is already in the OR," the receptionist said. She waved them through a set of doors behind her. They followed the signs through the extra wide corridors until Carraro shoved open another set of doors. Groups of people clumped together in different corners of the colorful lounge. All of them had the look of tense expectation as they clutched cups of coffee.

One young woman clasped a fussing baby in her arms. Ghost wasn't the only one needing surgery this evening.

"Over here."

Evan waved to them from behind another door. Hannah followed Carraro into what looked like a break room, with more coffee, a refrigerator, a small table, and plastic chairs.

"The charge nurse allowed us to sit back here. It's more private, so we don't create a circus outside. It's just not as comfortable," Evan said.

Carraro pushed past Evan to sweep his wife into a deep hug.

"How is he?" Hannah asked.

Alek pulled out a chair and motioned for Hannah to sit down, but she shook her head and walked over to the refrigerator.

"Alive, last we heard," he said. Alek didn't ask what happened at the Pier. No one asked about Scott.

Inside the door, behind bottles of soda, was a carton of juice. She knew what she was going to do and juice was better than soda. She gulped right from the carton.

"Can you do it?" Evan asked as she drank. "Can you heal him?"

She lowered the carton so she could see the Captain. "Yes."

The Captain pulled away from Carraro. They exchanged a silent message, the only way two people who shared everything in their lives could.

"I can't," the Captain said, but the catch in her voice stopped whatever she was going to say next.

"She's already saved one son." Carraro's fingers brushed his wife's bangs off her forehead. "Let her save the other."

"How will I justify this?" She pulled away from her husband. "There are at least four other surgeries in progress as we speak. Kavanaugh is in the burn unit. How can I explain to another family that my son is more important than theirs? How can I tell them I let Hannah heal my son, but no one else's?"

"I say we let her heal Nik and deal with the consequences later," Evan said.

"Consequences like this could destroy everything we've built in Thunder City." The Captain dropped her hands to her hips. "We have a safe zone here, but if the people of Thunder City lose faith in my objectivity, if they think I'd favor the life of an Alt over a Norm. You boys don't remember what it used to be like. The suspicion, the hatred, the attacks."

"We're not talking about just any Alt, mom," Alek said. "We're talking about Nik."

Silence. Absolute silence except for the hum from the refrigerator.

"You don't get a say in this," Hannah said, because she had to say something. Every moment they wasted made her job all the harder. "I'm not an employee of Thunder City. I'm not a member of T-CASS. I'm the only one who gets a say in who I heal and who I don't. I lived for six months in a hospital and I healed no one because my own survival demanded I stay hidden. Then Scott fell out of the sky, I did what I had to do to keep him alive for no other reason than..." Than what? Why had she made an exception? Because she thought she could get away with it? She thought she could change his mind about Alts if she healed him? Because she wasn't her mother and couldn't continue to look the other way? Her throat tightened. "...than I had met him once. If that's not the height of selfishness, I don't know what is."

She gulped the rest of the juice to hide her shame. Alek handed her a paper towel to mop up the mess on her chin. She couldn't wait any longer, so she tossed the wad into the trash as she headed for the door. "I'm going to go heal Nik. If you want me to heal all the others who are in surgery tonight, including Kavenaugh, bring me more juice or water, but stay out of my way."

She managed three steps out of the lounge before the Captain appeared at her side. Together they entered the operating suite. They blew past the sinks, the spare equipment, the rosters, and the computers. They peeked inside three operating rooms before they found the one with Nik. Hannah pushed her way in before the Captain had second thoughts.

No one noticed them at first. The doctors and nurses huddled around Nik, his face obscured by the oxygen mask. Tubes hooked into his body, and wires connected him to stacks of equipment monitoring every aspect of his life. At least the cardiac support unit still beeped.

The Captain stopped and stared. Hannah couldn't afford to lose her now. "I can force out the bullet if it's still inside him, but I can't remove the clamps. You have to talk them into disconnecting all of the equipment. Don't let them touch me once I'm inside."

The Captain didn't respond, still absorbed by the sight of her son on the operating table and all the blood.

"Captain!"

The Captain blinked. "Yes, of course."

Hannah's voice also got the attention of the medical staff.

"Get them out of here."

Hannah assumed the surgeon gave the order. A nurse left the table. "You can't stay."

Hannah had to trust the Captain to take care of her end of things. She skirted past the nurse as the Captain blocked the woman. Only Nik's open wound was exposed and she couldn't reach around the surgeon, the second nurse, and over the forest of clamps and sponges to touch him there. She'd have to enter through his head, which meant getting around the anesthesiologist.

"Move," she ordered.

"What the fuck do you think you're doing?" He made a grab for her arm, but she sent her elbow into his nose, not hard enough to break the bone, but sufficient to distract him long enough for her to get inside Nik. She hoped her disappearing act and the Captain's authority would take care of the rest.

Hannah laid a forefinger on Nik's eyelid.

Inside. She hit one of the conjunctival vessels, a very tight squeeze. She fought the claustrophobic sensation and surfed faster. If the doctor refused to remove all of the operating equipment she'd have to work around it.

She found chaos in the chest cavity. The bullet had torn through the chest wall and created a sucking wound, one too large to seal itself. It had also nicked the right side carotid artery before lodging next to the heart. The blood meant for Nik's brain was draining into his chest. His heart still beat strongly, so Hannah left the bullet alone and sealed the artery instead.

170

Not a moment too soon. The clamp on the artery released, sending the blood back into circulation, washing Hannah along with it. She fought the riptide effect and jumped into the nearest vein that would bring her back to the chest cavity, blasting any blood clots she found along the way.

She waited until after she'd stitched together the punctured lung and the pleural sac to tackle the skin around the wound, leaving just enough of an opening so all the free air in the cavity could escape. Damn, if she could communicate with either Rumble or Roar, they could probably manipulate the air molecules and force the air out faster than she could.

Her energy level faltered, but she refused to give in. It's not exhaustion, just dehydration, she repeated to herself. Fix his muscles and bones first, then handle the bullet. Damn thing loomed like a monolith, but at least it didn't fight back like the white blood cells scurrying around. She pushed and pulled until it popped through the small opening she'd left in Nik's chest. Then she sealed the hole.

Everything was working properly, but what about brain damage? A quick hop into the artery she had sealed brought her to the cerebral arterial circle. She picked an artery to begin with and carefully checked every inch of the brain, but didn't see any damage.

As she floated in the cerebro-spinal fluid near the frontal lobe, she thought about the black thread. She needed to confirm her suspicions, so she dived through the gray matter until she hit the midline. Yes. There it was, just as tiny and fragile as the thread she'd found in Scott, except Scott's had been broken. Nik's had held firm throughout the trauma.

171

The gun Scott had used to shoot Electrocyte and Nik had appeared out of nowhere. Carraro had asked if she'd ever called an object to her. She hadn't, so it must have been Scott.

Which could only mean Scott was an Alt, and she'd given him his power. A power he didn't want. No wonder he'd been so angry with her. He didn't leave Star Haven to protect her. He'd left to protect himself. He must have known before they met in the alley otherwise he would have turned her over to his mother. *Son-of-a-bitch.* And to think she'd kissed him just because he thought she was pretty.

Her world shifted as Nik tilted his head. The chemically induced paralysis was wearing off as a part of her healing. She had to get out. A moment later she drifted back into her body and stepped away from the operating table.

The Captain leaned over her son, one hand on his shoulder, presumably to keep him still. The ET tube had been removed, and all of the equipment shut down. Only an oxygen mask remained over Nik's nose. The surgical team had left the room.

"Let me help you remove this." Hannah pulled the mask away. The Captain caught him in her arms as he pushed himself to sit with his legs dangling over the edge of the operating table. His mother held him tight, though Nik looked confused.

Hannah backed out of the operating room to give them privacy. The doctors and nurses waited by the door.

"He'll be fine," she said. "I would appreciate it if you kept this quiet."

"There'll be questions," one of them said, probably the surgeon. "I have to file a report, include what I witnessed or I could be held liable for any post-op complications."

She couldn't stop him from reporting her actions. "Just don't broadcast it. I can't stay in Thunder City, so this won't happen again. If anyone has questions, they can talk to Captain Spec later."

Outside the surgical suit, Carraro and the twins waited. Evan handed her a bottle of water as soon as she emerged, the cap already twisted open. "The Captain is with Nik now. They need some time alone."

She gulped down all the water in the bottle. Her head throbbed a mild pulse in rhythm from her heartbeat, but she was nowhere near as sick as she'd become after healing Scott. Another victory.

"I should take you back home." Carraro pulled the keys out of his pants pocket. No one said anything about her healing anyone else.

"Let's wait," Hannah said.

A few minutes later, the Captain emerged with Nik bundled in clean scrubs and sitting in a wheelchair. Her emergency healing didn't include replacing the blood he'd lost. He'd need time to get all of his energy back. His brothers surrounded him, touching him, but the Captain's voice rose over their concerned chatter.

"Let's get him home."

"Hang on." Nik grabbed Hannah's hand. "Thank you."

She almost forgot to squeeze back, stung by the intensity of his gratitude. No one had ever thanked her before. Not even Scott.

The moment passed. He dropped her hand as the Captain pushed his chair forward. They wheeled him down the corridor as a group. Carraro made phone calls assuring others Ghost would make a rapid recovery. He didn't specify how rapid.

She wanted to join them. What she had witnessed from the Pier — coordination, cooperation, organization — that's what Captain Spec had meant by training, what Scott had tried to explain to her. Her own haphazard way of healing whoever happened to be in front of her wasn't good enough.

Yet all of their training wouldn't protect the Thunder City Alts from Miranda. As powerful as the Alts were, they could still fall to a hail of bullets — except for Captain Spec, but even she couldn't protect everyone. Miranda understood weapons and power, and she wielded both with ruthless intensity. She would never give up until she got what she wanted, and what she wanted was Hannah.

"Hannah, are you coming?"

Evan had noticed she'd fallen back. She jogged a few steps to catch up. He threw his arm around her shoulder. "Can't leave you behind."

They wouldn't, but she would have to leave them behind. No matter what, she had to run.

CHAPTER FOURTEEN

Thirty-six hours after he'd returned to Thunder City, Scott was back in the same spot where he had started — the parlor. Thanks to Thomas's attorney, the police had been forced to let him go just before dawn, but not without a warning: don't leave town. Scott made another call to his Lieutenant, who, of course, had seen the news. So had Juan and all of Star Haven. At least his reputation as a defender of Norms remained intact. He'd still have friends to welcome him when he returned home.

For the first time, he realized just how many of his current friendships were based on his Alt-killer status. He'd thought he'd moved beyond his reputation, had earned respect because he was a good cop, not just because he was a good shot. Now he wasn't so sure.

None of the news reports so far had mentioned Hannah, though there was speculation as to who had been with Scott on the Pier. The police had asked, over and over again, but Scott had refused to answer. Thomas's fake ID held up. As far as the Thunder City police were concerned, Scott Grey was nothing more than a Star Haven, Alt-killing Norm.

Now he watched Catherine pace and Thomas drink. This time, though, Evan and Alek had given up their place on the sofa so Nik could lie down. Nik's tan complexion had a pasty cast and he kept his eyes closed, though he spoke quietly to Hannah, who sat next to him with perfect posture on the ottoman. She only looked at Scott once, then turned her attention back to Nik. Thomas had filled him in on what she had done, saving Nik's life. He didn't blame her for turning her back on him. If she had to choose between trusting him or trusting his family, she'd have to trust his family. They had the power to protect her. Whatever he had — power, influence, tactics — paled in comparison.

"I've received word from Kavenaugh's wife," Catherine said, after she'd paced the room a few times. "She asked me to express her gratitude to Cory for saving her husband's life. Her husband has a long recovery in front of him, but he will recover."

He still couldn't believe Catherine had allowed Hannah to heal Nik, but not Kavenaugh. It was completely unlike his mother to put family before anyone else. Trained or not, if Catherine had witnessed Hannah's power, then she knew what Hannah was capable of. What had held her back?

"The police commissioner," Catherine continued, "has asked to meet with me later this afternoon. By then she'll have completed a review of the Newcomers' records. She'll learn what we already know: None of the Star Haven Alts have translocation abilities. None of the protesters could have deliberately or accidentally ripped a rifle from the SWAT sniper on the jetty and sent it to Cory.

"Unfortunately, our own translocation specialist died last year. After reviewing his records, we have found nothing to indicate he could send an object from its origin to a destination other than himself."

Another pause.

"Scott?" She didn't have to elaborate.

"What would you want me to say that you haven't already figured out? I translocated the rifle. I didn't plan it. It just happened."

No one in the room reacted. They'd known what he'd done, had talked about it behind his back.

"How long have you had this ability?" Catherine asked.

"Three days."

"Since Hannah healed you?"

"Yes."

"When did you first realize you had this ability?"

Scott recounted his experience with his phone at the hospital and how he discounted it, but couldn't ignore the packet of peanuts when it appeared in his hand. He also told them about the Left Fist's lighter he'd acquired during the evac from his apartment. He still had the damn lighter in his pocket.

Catherine resumed pacing. "Hannah, do you have anything to add?"

"No," she said, her eyes on Catherine, not him. "I don't."

"Really?" Catherine changed her trajectory so she drifted over to where Hannah sat. "You turned a Norm into a Alt and you don't know how you did it?"

"Leave her alone." Scott stepped away from the wall. If Catherine wanted to bully him, fine. He could take it. "She's not the one in trouble here."

"I didn't say she was in trouble," Catherine said. "I'm asking for her input."

Hannah cut him off before he could lash out further. "Scott was never a Norm, Captain..."

177

"Catherine," his mother interrupted with a raised hand. "I dislike being called Captain. It's a rank bestowed upon me by the media. It's not a rank I earned."

"Okay, Catherine," Hannah said. "Scott was never a Norm. He's an Alt. He always was. What makes him an Alt broke. I don't know when or how. I fixed the problem, and in doing so, activated his power."

"You're saying you found a physical defect in Cory?" Catherine asked.

"I wouldn't use the word defect." Hannah scrunched her nose. "Scott's tie to his Alt power was broken. I repaired it. If it breaks again, his power goes away. If it breaks in any of you, you will no longer have alternative powers."

Silence, while everyone considered the implications.

"Have you told anyone about this 'tie'? Where it's located? What it looks like?" Catherine asked.

"No."

"Not even your mother?"

"I didn't know about the tie until I healed Scott. I confirmed my findings in Nik. He has the same tie." Hannah swiveled around so she could face all of them at once. "Miranda would want this information if she knew it existed. For all I know it's a part of her agenda, but she hasn't shared her plans with me. She killed Roger because he found out what those plans were."

Alek swore softly. Scott could imagine how unpleasant it was to learn that everything you thought made you so powerful could be taken away so easily. The wrong word to the wrong person and every Norm in Star Haven would know how destroy Alts.

178

Except Scott was an Alt now. He'd used his power. No one outside this room knew it yet, but they would eventually. Hannah was now the most important Alt in Thunder City. He'd bet she didn't even know it.

"It all comes back down to Miranda Dane, who we can't do anything about so long as she remains in Star Haven," Catherine said.

"Her men are here. They have to be," Hannah said.

"If you saw them, could you recognize them?"

Scott knew where Catherine was going with this, but Nik spoke up before he could. "They wouldn't have used the ferry or the airport to get here. There'd be no visual record for Hannah to look at."

Catherine started to pace again. "For the moment, then, all we can do is keep Hannah with us. This house is the safest compound in the city short of the Arena. We'll try not to make it too much of a prison, but I don't know what else we can do without more information. Thomas, hon..."

Thomas stopped twirling his drink as his wife stopped in front of him.

"I'd like you to take another look at those records you didn't download from Roger Dane two years ago. I'm going to guess Miranda had something to do with altering his import records. Let's see if we can figure out why."

Thomas kissed the tip of Catherine's nose. "I'll have a non-existent report ready by tonight."

Catherine grinned before turning toward the twins. "Evan and Alek, keep doing what you usually do: go out there and be visible. The media is going to demand answers about Nik. They love you two more than the

179

rest of us. Give them what they need instead of what they want."

Of course, she saved Scott for last.

"We'll get you started training tomorrow. Since you've graduated from the police academy, you can skip a few of the introductory classes. What we need to focus on is getting your power under your control..."

"No."

Catherine stopped. "This isn't an option, Cory. If you're going to stay here in Thunder City, you have to meet the minimum requirements of the training agreement I signed with the City. You know I can't make an exception for you."

"I'm not staying here. I'm going back to Star Haven. As soon as the ferry service starts again." No one said anything, no one protested his decision. No one understood. Thomas would try to talk him out of it privately; Alek wouldn't care if he left. The others...what did he care about the others, except for Hannah, but he'd kept his word to her. He'd found her safe harbor. Judging by her interaction with Catherine, she seemed perfectly capable of handling the Blackwood powerhouse known as Captain Spectacular.

Catherine sighed. "Did you learn nothing from what happened last night? You have no control over your Alt powers. You've already killed one person and hurt another. You could hurt yourself."

"Only if I'm still an Alt, which I won't be. I intend to have Hannah bloodsurf through my body again and break the tie she fixed. Once it's broken, my powers will disappear. I'll be the same Norm I've been my entire life."

Catherine scrubbed her face. "I don't know what to say."

"It's what I want."

"I can't promise you the police won't suspect that you translocated that gun." Catherine started to pace again. "And what about Miranda Dane? We know she suspects you're the one responsible for bringing Hannah here."

"What if she does? I found Hannah on the roof of the hospital three days after she turned eighteen. I had no legal obligation to turn her over to her mother. As far as Miranda is aware, I still don't know about Hannah's Alt powers. If we're lucky, she'll think I did what I thought was the right thing. As for the gun?" He shrugged. "Alt powers are mysterious. Anything could have happened. Leave it as a mystery and folks will speculate all they want. No proof of my powers exists and it'll never happen again."

"What about your apartment?" Thomas asked. "Miranda's hired men."

Scott shrugged. "I brought Hannah back to my apartment so I could get changed and grab an extra set of keys. We noticed the door lock to my apartment was broken and the burglars were inside, so we ran."

He hadn't expected resounding support for his decision, so he played his last card. "Besides, it can only help to have someone over there keeping an eye on Miranda, anyway."

"Cory, try to understand," Catherine said, her voice heavy. "I can only solve the problems here in Thunder City. If Dane crosses the Bay to cause trouble, we'll deal with it. Thunder City Alts have poked enough at Star Haven these past few days. Don't bring me another problem."

He was still nothing but a problem in Catherine's world. No wonder she'd relinquished custody to

Thomas so easily. With his Alt powers activated, she figured she could just toss him into the pool of Alts she used to defend Thunder City. She expected him to obey without a fight. Just because he was an Alt and she was Catherine goddamn Blackwood.

"Fine, consider this problem solved."

He didn't wait to see how Hannah or Thomas reacted. He swung open the parlor room doors and slammed them shut behind him.

***

"Scott? Are you in there?" Stupid question. Hannah could hear drawers opening and closing through the door.

She knocked again. "Please, Scott. Let me in."

The door clicked. Hannah waited, but Scott hadn't opened the door for her to enter. If she wanted to see him, she had to open the door herself, so she did.

The bedroom looked like it belonged to a teenage boy, from the old rock band posters to the small desk set. On the other side of the bed, Scott was folding his clothes with military precision.

"You're really leaving."

He nodded, but didn't look at her.

"Even though you're an Alt, you're going to return to a city hell-bent on destroying you?"

He didn't stop packing. "That depends on you."

"Don't do this to me, Scott. What you're asking me to do is exactly what Miranda would want me do."

Now she had his attention.

"Miranda wants you to destroy Alts by bloodsurfing?" He dropped a folded shirt and put his hands on his hips.

"She would, if she knew what I do now about Alts and their power."

"Would you, if she asked you to?"

Did he really think she was that kind of person? "Not voluntarily. Scott, I don't know what Miranda is up to. All I know is what she's had me do in the past — keep the men she's hired alive and healthy."

She said nothing about healing other Alts. Alts hurt by Miranda. Scott picked up a package of socks and stuffed them into a gym bag.

"Do you think this is part of what she's up to? Trying to find the source of Alt power?" he asked.

"Like I said, I have no proof. Even if I did, what could I do about it? It's not illegal in Star Haven — or Thunder City, for that matter — to search for the secret to Alt power and theorize about how to destroy it."

She waited as Scott shoved more clothes into the bag.

"It sounds like eugenics," he said.

"I know, and that's what scares me," she said. "No one has to die or be incarcerated because of what I do. It doesn't hurt. I touch your skin and a few seconds later...poof, no alternative power."

"You could do it that quickly?" he asked, with more hope in his voice than disdain. Damn it. She hadn't meant to encourage him.

"Do you really want me to do this?"

"I want my old life back. The life I had before..."

"Before you fell out of the helicopter and almost died," she said for him.

He punched the last of his carefully folded clothes into the bag. Her sympathy wormed its way past her defenses. One kiss didn't mean anything if he still planned to leave. She couldn't rescue him again if he returned to Star Haven. He'd go back to his life as an Alt-killing Norm and she'd find a quiet life in Thunder City. They'd forget about each other eventually. Or he'd forget about her. You never forgot your first kiss, or so she'd read in more than one book.

The clothes packed, he dropped the bag to the floor. "Come with me. I want to show you something."

Suspicious, she didn't take his outstretched hand. "Where are we going?"

"Falling out of the helicopter wasn't the first time I almost died."

He grabbed her arm and pulled her along beside him. "Scott, slow down."

Three long hallways and a two-story staircase later, Scott stopped in the middle of another hall.

"It's gone," he said, crestfallen.

What was gone? The light beige paint covered an empty wall. No paintings or light sconces or vents marred its surface. The hallway itself was dark, its musty odor overpowering. One corner hosted a huge cobweb. No one had visited this floor in a very long time.

Scott flattened his free hand against the wall and pushed.

"She must have filled it in. Gotten rid of the evidence." He gripped her hand harder.

"Filled in what? A room?"

He nodded. "Our time-out room."

"You mean like a room to punish children?"

"Yes, but one designed for Alt children."

She shivered. Evan said he'd pulled a prank and almost killed his brother. "Designed how?"

He touched the wall with his fingertips. "Time-out rooms are supposed to protect the parents of Alt children, especially when they're toddlers and can't control their powers. They're individually designed depending on which powers manifest."

She followed Scott's fingers as he traced an outline. Now she could see a slight difference in the texture of the wall where a door had been.

"What was this room supposed to do?" she asked.

"It would drop the temperature to thirty-two degrees in less than a minute."

Holy hell. "Evan froze you?"

"He told you?" He looked at her, but only for a second.

"A little bit. He didn't go into details."

He stepped back as if to consider his options. "The room hadn't been used in years when Evan tossed me in there. You're not supposed to use it for longer than ten minutes. Long enough to disrupt an Alt's thoughts, have the kid focus on how cold they are, stop them from triggering their power."

"How long were you in there?" she asked.

"Over an hour. I was a block of ice huddled in the corner when they finally pulled me out. Evan kept saying how sorry he was, he didn't mean for me to be in there for so long, how Catherine's father had ambushed them for a training session and they couldn't tell him where I was. Or maybe they did and he didn't care. Evan and Alek wrapped me in blankets and warmed me up as fast as they could. It felt like knives slicing through my muscles, my bones."

Hannah slipped her hand into his and squeezed. She'd run away in the winter. The hospital roof had offered no protection from the temperature. Her first night up there, before she stole the badge, before she figured out when the guards changed shifts...she knew

185

something of the cold Scott experienced. "What happened afterwards?"

"Alek threatened to toss me in there again if I tattled, but I tried to tell Catherine anyway. Time, as usual, was not on my side. A dozen or so Chaos Alts had escaped from Rocklin prison the night before. T-CASS worked through the next four days to recapture them. When I tried to talk to her, she was too busy to listen."

"The Chaos Alts were an immediate danger," she asked. "And you weren't dying right then and there."

"Yeah, I got that. What no one else gets is that I was thirteen and tired of being on the tail-end of a list of problems Catherine needed to worry about. Evan might not have killed me, but when Catherine told me to stop pestering her, I said fuck this shit. I stuffed a few belongings into my backpack and ran...right into the arms of a couple of the escaped Chaos Alts."

"They're the ones who cut off your ear?"

He squeezed his eyes shut, rubbed the bridge of his nose. "Yeah, and mailed it to Catherine hoping for a ransom." Scott opened his eyes again and stepped back from the wall, his face tight, his lips pulled back in a snarl. "Would you believe she didn't open the package until three days later?"

"Didn't anyone else notice you were missing?"

He shoved his free hand into his back pocket. "Who was around to notice? It wasn't Garrett's job to keep track of me, Catherine's father didn't care, Nik worked with Catherine, and Alek and Evan...I don't know what they thought. I don't care about what they thought."

Hannah pulled her thumb loose and stroked his fingers with it. His grip lessened, but he didn't let go.

She stepped into his line of sight so he'd have to look at her and not the wall. "She did ransom you though, right?"

Scott blinked a couple of times. "I don't know if she did or she didn't. I don't want to know. I only know my side of the story."

Of all the stubborn, thick-headed men on the planet. And yet, Scott had the courage to run away, something she'd been wanting to do since she was thirteen. Hell, since she was eight. But, she hadn't had the courage. Which one of them was better off? At least he had tried. She waited until Roger gave her no choice. Roger had to tell her to run before she would do it. "Tell me your story, Scott. I want to know. How did she get you back?"

"She didn't." He looked over her head again at the wall, but Hannah didn't pull away. "The kidnappers gave me a computer with games on it to pacify me. They didn't think I'd have the skills to break the security on the files they'd locked down. I did and found the electronic receipt from the guy who sold the computer. I was pissed and in pain, so I sent the seller an email telling him what an asshole he was."

"You didn't try to contact your family? Or the police?"

Scott shrugged. "Days had passed by the time I sent the email. The kidnappers had us holed up in a cabin out on one of the islands in the Bay. One that had a satellite TV. The national news detailed every move the T-CASS made helping the police capture the escaped Chaos Alts. Thunder City was a mess. Who had time to rescue a runaway? Without my ear, I couldn't even give Catherine a good-looking corpse at my funeral."

187

"Oh, Scott..." She pressed herself into his arms and he pulled her closer. "How did you escape?"

"Thomas was the asshole."

She pulled back, surprised, though she shouldn't have been. "You're kidding?"

"I wasn't thinking clearly. The kidnappers had stolen the computer from the prison, one of Thomas's biggest clients. Thomas got the shock of his life when he received a profanity-laced email from an angry teenager," Scott said.

"So Thomas tracked you down? Through the computer. He rescued you."

"Yeah, he tracked me down, and hired a couple of Neuts to pull me out of there alive."

"Oh." She didn't know what other resolution she was expecting. Thomas was a Norm. He'd have been stupid to try and rescue Scott on his own.

"We hit it off, Thomas and I. He sat with me the entire time I had my ear stitched. Then he took me back to his place and made me a burger and shake. Can you imagine Thomas making burgers and shakes? Himself? Not his chef? Then we played video games until he managed to do the one thing I never could: get Catherine's attention."

Hannah's heart softened. "He took good care of you."

"He tried to reunite us, me and Catherine, but it didn't end well, so he adopted me. Much later I found out Thomas had brokered a deal with Catherine: He'd keep me safe, educated, and still within her reach — if she took care of some Chaos Alts who were threatening him." His smile turned wry. "Thomas would say he got the better end of the deal."

"But I lost a brother."

188

Hannah jumped out of Scott's arms. Evan stood at the end of the hallway, leaning around the corner, his shadow swallowed by the gloom.

"One I never really knew," he said, keeping his distance. "Mom was beside herself the entire time you were gone."

"You mean once she realized I was missing in the first place."

Hannah held her breath. Scott had spoken directly to Evan, though he kept his eyes fixed on the wall.

"At first, I thought you were just avoiding me," Evan continued as if Scott had said nothing, "I didn't blame you. After two days, I forced your bedroom door open, so I could talk to you face-to-face. The picture of Cole was missing from the night stand..."

Scott dropped Hannah. The suddenness made her stagger as Scott took a single threatening step toward his brother. "Don't you talk about him. Don't even say his name."

Evan pushed off the wall, his eyes flicking in her direction. Would Scott attack his brother? Here? How would she stop him? What could she possibly say to make this better? Who was Cole? She laid a hand on Scott's arm. "Scott, let him finish. You can't go on this way. Let him apologize. You can decide later if you want to accept it."

Scott covered her hand with his. Maybe he saw wisdom in her words, or maybe he just decided to keep her out of the toxic mix. Either way, he didn't move any closer to his brother.

Evan tried again. "I knew how much you treasured that picture of your real dad. The only way it would disappear is if you took it with you and you weren't coming back. I went to mom and told her you had run away. I also told her why. She hadn't opened the package yet. She went ballistic, took her anger out on Grandpa. Blamed him for teaching us to hate Norms. She threw him out of the house. We haven't seen him since. Later, once the custody issue was settled, Mom sent me to work at the animal shelter and Alek to the medical clinic. She said we needed to learn compassion and acceptance for those who are different."

Scott snorted. "Blames everyone else except herself."

Evan shook his head, as if surrendering to Scott's inflexibility. "You don't know how much she blamed herself. You just kept pouring on the hate until she gave up."

Evan paused, waiting to see if Scott would respond. Scott said nothing, his face like stone, his muscles flexing under her touch. The police had returned all of his weapons. How long did she have before the knife would be in his hand?

"I just wanted to tell you again how sorry I am," Evan said. "If I could go back in time and stop myself from being a jerk, I would. I've changed a lot since then, but you never gave me a chance to prove it. I'll prove it to you someday. You have my word, for what it's worth."

Evan disappeared. Hannah heard no footsteps. Her whole world consisted of Scott. He looked exactly as he did the day he was awarded the commendation — lost and alone. She stepped back into his arms and held him close. As tall as she was, she still had to stand on tiptoe to get her arms around his shoulders. He let go of her hand so he could wrap his arms around her waist and bury his face in her neck.

"I thought Miranda was bad," she whispered. "All she wants is to turn me into a monster."

"I don't believe you could ever become a monster," he said. He slipped his hands up her back to stroke her hair, looking down at her now. Maybe it was easier to look at her than the empty space where his brother had stood. Better to see her than at the empty hallway where he had suffered so much.

How little he really knew about her if he thought she couldn't become a monster. She lowered her hands to his chest, so strong after years of pushing away his demons. "You know nothing about what I'm capable of, the extent of my ability."

"I know enough." His hands cupped her cheeks, his fingers strong against her temples.

"But you don't know everything. Stay here, Scott," she begged. "Stay with me. We could train together, work together as a team. We can keep each other's secrets."

Indecision crossed his face and he looked back up at the wall. "You don't know what you're asking of me. You don't understand what I'd be giving up."

She understood more than he thought. One last time she stood on tiptoe and pulled his face to hers. Last night had been her first kiss ever, so she improvised. She bypassed his lips and teeth to stick her tongue into his mouth. Nothing. No reaction, no return kiss, his eyes uncertain. When she pulled away, he didn't pursue her.

"Stay with me," she repeated, her hands exploring the muscles stretched across his back. "If you leave me here, it'll be forever. Is that what you want? Forever?"

His growl rumbled from his chest before he lifted her into his arms, perhaps for the last time. "I'll show you forever."

CHAPTER FIFTEEN

Hannah had no illusions about where Scott was bringing her or why. This wasn't love, it wasn't even lust. Release, maybe? A chance to drop-kick caution across the Bay? A chance to make her own choices? Miranda wasn't here to dictate her every move. Catherine wasn't here to plan her entire future down to every minute detail. It was just her and Scott and for the first time in years the voices of worry and reason fell silent. This moment was her decision, her choice. Damn the consequences.

He never took his eyes off of her as he laid her down on the bed. It was almost comical watching him discard his jacket along with the shoulder holster, hip holster, ankle holster, two knives, and the taser. Not content to wait, Hannah toed off her new sandals. She'd started this and she'd finish it, before the frightened, good-little-Hannah re-emerged.

Scott lay down, partially covering her body with his. With her arms trapped, she had little leverage, so she dug her heels into the sheets and squirmed her body higher, rubbing her chest against his until they were face-to-face. Her arms freed, she pressed the heels of her hands into his shoulder and rolled him onto his back. Before he could protest, she leaned over and kissed him again.

"Hannah," he whispered.

He tried to push her off, but she had the advantage on top. "Shut up. If you're not going to stay with me, at least give me this to remember you by."

He started to say something else, but she silenced him with her mouth. This time she kept it slow, exploring the different parts of his face, not just his lips. His rough stubble scratched, but didn't stop her from nipping his chin. Her tongue licked a trail up to his new ear lobe which she sucked into her mouth.

He groaned before his hands crushed her closer and he rolled her all the way on top while his hands found their way up her shirt to massage her breasts. The fine, dark hair on his chest twined around her fingers as she mimicked his motions. He groaned, then changed tactics to skim one hand down her pants.

Just as he reached between her legs she realized she had a problem. No protection. She already knew he had no diseases, but pregnancy? Under other circumstances she wouldn't care, but the thought of Miranda getting her hands on another child, another Alt, scared Hannah cold. *Shit.* She pressed her lips to his ear.

"Do you want me to stop?" she asked. "If you want me to stop, tell me now."

"Fuck no. Keep going. You feel so good."

He might have condoms in his wallet. No doubt a good-looking guy like Scott would have a roster of women at his beck and call. Older, far more experienced women who didn't have to worry if a man wore a condom or not.

Well, there was another way to resolve her dilemma, but it would mean breaking the rules again.

She unzipped his jeans, and slid her hand under his briefs.

He hissed as her fingers wrapped around his penis. She waited a beat, then surfed, entering through the dorsal artery. Now what? She reached out to touch the pliable tissue. It shimmered as she stroked upward. His blood rush pushed her toward the tip. She kept herself in full contact as she surfed back down again. Up and down, dorsal, then ventral. The blood vessels expanded, which gave her more room in which to work.

His respiration increased, so she slowed down even further. It took her a moment to glide down to his testicles. When she healed someone, she never thought beyond the clinical side of the human body. Parts were parts, and if they broke, she stitched them as needed. A loud rumble added to the cacophony of a healthy, aroused body. Scott was moaning. The sound gave her the most gleeful, powerful, wicked pleasure.

Would Scott appreciate what she was doing to his body? Was it really so different from touching him on the outside? Would he hate her for using her Alt ability at all?

She couldn't stop, though. More muscles spasmed. Her world tilted as Scott rolled to the side and the pressure against his skin increased. He must have grabbed himself. Oh, no, no, no. No coming allowed until she was ready to let him go. She beat back the nerve signals to slow down the action.

Once she was sure he would stay right on the edge of ecstasy, she returned to her regular rhythm - up, down, dorsal, ventral, slow and steady.

She kept the rhythm as long as she dared. How much time had passed? Scott's body rocked again, so

195

she quickened her movement to stimulate the blood around her.

The bloodrush washed her back to the tip as everything contracted in rapid succession. Scott heaved in time to the contractions, over and over again. She'd done it and kept herself safe. Time to leave.

She drifted back into her body. Scott had returned to his supine position with her on top. She laid her head on his chest. His heartbeat was rapid, but normal.

She started to slide off, but he wrapped his arms around her waist and pinned her in place above him. He was sweaty and sticky, and his breath blew her bangs off her forehead in gusts.

"Do you have any idea what you did to me?" he asked.

Panic twisted her. Had she screwed up? "You didn't enjoy it?"

He smiled, languid, satisfied. He reached up to caress her face. "You kept me on the edge for almost twenty minutes. I thought my heart would explode."

Relief eased her tension. She hadn't hurt him.

"Now it's your turn," he said.

"Oh, you don't have to. I mean, this was enough..."

"Shhhh..." He ran his hands under her waistband before he unzipped her fly.

She closed her eyes so he wouldn't see her fear. It's not as if she didn't understand the mechanics. She'd figured she had enough information to carry her through until she met someone special. Someone who could stand up to her mother, who'd driven off the few boys who dared to ask her out on a date. After she'd run away, consensual sex became the least of her worries.

Scott's finger returned to its place between her legs and oh so gently touched her. Her whole body twitched, but she kept her eyes closed.

"Open your eyes, Hannah," he whispered.

She did as he asked, but focused on the hollow of his throat. She couldn't watch him watch her. It was a good strategy until his finger stroked her again. Oh, the textbooks didn't even come close to describing what it felt like.

"Don't you dare close your eyes," he said.

She widened her knees so she could lift her hips and give him better access. She should have taken off her jeans. The material tightened as Scott's hand moved lower.

Her first moan caught her unawares, but his finger didn't increase its speed.

"How do you feel?" he asked, his voice low.

How the hell did he expect her to answer? She could hardly think.

"So good," was all she could manage.

He chuckled as he brought his thumb into play. She gasped.

"Tell me what you want."

Her hips lifted higher, and his finger moved faster, but only slightly. Want? What did she want? No one had ever asked her. No one had ever cared enough. No, she didn't want. She needed. That was the real question. What did she need?

"You," she said before a moan escaped. "Just you. I only want you. No one else. Oh, Scott."

His rhythm increased. Her body soared as her hips pressed against his finger, and she cried out with the wave of pleasure that spilled up her spine to disperse through every nerve ending. Even as she rode her orgasm over Scott's body he never stopped touching her until she had nothing left to give.

Only then did he pull his hand away. She stared down at him and wondered what she should do next.

***

He'd fucked up again. As soon as Hannah pulled him into a kiss, he should have pushed her away, told her it was wrong. What had he been thinking? She was everything he didn't want: An Alt, a runaway, his mother's new trainee. The list went on, but he'd thrown every security protocol out the door because he needed to feel something other than the brutal cold of the time-out room freezing the life out of him.

"Now what?" she asked, her hands massaging his chest again. Half an hour ago, her body had faded into a vague outline of a disheveled goddess with bright green eyes looking at him like the Cheshire cat spying its prey. He didn't want to leave her, but he couldn't stay with her either. Not if he wanted to go home. Not if he wanted to pick up the pieces of his life in Star Haven. It would never work.

"I don't know." He trapped a tail of her silky red hair between his fingers.

She huffed and climbed off of him. Great, he'd offended her. *Smooth, Grey, real smooth.*

She disappeared into the bathroom. He took the time to clean himself up and change. When she reappeared, she stepped into his personal space, all challenge.

"It's a simple question: are you staying or are you leaving?"

"If it were simple I'd have an answer for you." He swung his old desk chair around so he could straddle it. It creaked, unused to holding the weight of a full grown man. "In the past three days, I've become the one thing I hate most in this world, and I've discovered that the sweet, shy Norm girl I thought you were is actually an aggressive, self-assured woman who can make me howl when she's only half there. I mean...look at this place..."

He waved his hands at the walls of his childhood bedroom. Nothing had changed because he'd grown up elsewhere. Only the bed had changed from a twin to a queen, borrowed from a guest room.

"I left home to get away from Alts, from this house, from the people who live here. You're a member of a community I want no part of."

"If you're implying I tried to trap you..."

"I'm not saying that at all."

Hannah leaned against his dresser, her arms crossed. "People run away so they can feel safe. I did. It doesn't mean I haven't changed. God knows how much I changed while I was sitting all alone on that roof day after day. I know you've changed, too, Scott. It's not possible for you to not have over the past ten years. You're a man now."

Yeah, but what kind of man? A liar for sure. He'd hidden his Alt power, and would have kept it hidden if he could have. A judgmental man, too. He'd sure had everyone pegged wrong since he'd returned, especially Evan. How about selfish? All he had thought about for these past three days was how he could talk Hannah into breaking his Alt power instead of helping her adjust to this new life.

No Alt could possess those three qualities if they hoped to work for Thunder City either as a cop or with

T-CASS. And since he was branded as an Alt-killer, it was unlikely Thunder City would hire him for either regardless.

"You can't go back to Star Haven," she said. "Even if you could convince Miranda that you honestly thought you were doing the right thing and she let you keep your job, she would have you watched."

He knew she was right. The rest of his family did, too. He had to face the fact that he was stuck here. He'd also have to train until he could wrestle his Alt power under control, which meant working with other Alts. None of them would be happy about training an Alt-killer.

"How did you get control?" he asked.

Hannah rubbed her arms, her face scrunched in that adorable way she had when she was in deep thought. "Bloodsurfing? I'm not sure. Once you recognize the trigger, it's pretty easy. At least for me."

"What trigger?"

She bit her lip. Scott gripped the back of his chair to keep himself planted instead of tossing her back onto the bed. He'd never felt so out of control with a woman before.

"It's almost a physical click in my head right before I enter your body. I have to make the decision to bloodsurf, but it's not a passive decision or a casual one, like turning off your alarm in the morning or making a right turn in your car. I have to think to myself: I want to bloodsurf. Then I have to be in a position to do it: I need to touch skin. I can't surf through clothing. Then I think about how I need to do this right now or else bad things will happen, and poof! I'm inside."

"Want versus need," he repeated. "It's not enough to want to use your power, you have to need to use it. There has to be urgency."

"No, not always urgency. It's more like desire, powerful desire to use your power."

If she repeated the word *desire* again he would haul her back into bed. Oblivious to what she was doing to him, Hannah looked around his room before pointing to a comb on his dresser. "Try translocating the comb."

He shook his head. "No way. I'm in enough trouble as it is."

"C'mon. We've already broken the rules, this can't make it worse. Try it once and let's see if you can do it. If you can't, we'll let it go."

His curiosity overrode his good sense. Catherine didn't make rules to be broken. The consequences were too high. He'd shot his own brother as a result of breaking the rules. Still, they were talking about a comb, not a gun. He stared at the comb and tried to call it into his hand. Nothing happened.

"This isn't going to work."

"Do you always give up this easily?" She taunted, recrossing her arms. "How did you ever graduate from the police academy?"

Ouch. He'd worked his ass off at the academy. He stared at the comb, small, flat, and light. Still nothing.

"How badly do you want it?" she asked.

"I don't want it at all. I already used the comb, so I don't need it."

She pushed off the wall and walked over to him. In a second, she'd attacked his head. He could smell the fresh scent of soap through her blouse and closed his eyes. Soap and skin and the uniqueness of Hannah. Star Haven had never seemed farther away. "Ow. You don't

201

have to pull my hair out by the roots. I get what you're trying to do."

"Don't be such a wuss." She mussed his hair one last time. "Now you need a comb."

He started to reach to pat his hair back into place, but she slapped his hand away. "No cheating. Call the comb to you."

He didn't have to. To his complete shock, the comb appeared in his left hand.

"Wow. You catch on quick." She took the comb from him and put it on the dresser again. "Try it again."

He stared at it for a long minute. Nothing happened.

"What were you thinking of before it worked?"

Her scent, but he'd be damned if he'd tell her that. It also wasn't true. He'd been thinking about her right up to the point where she'd chastised him for cheating. Something had changed in that brief moment. What, though? He closed his eyes to concentrate. What had he been thinking of before the Left Fist lighter appeared in his hand? He'd run through several scenarios on how he could use it as a weapon to gain advantage over the Left Fist sitting in the car. And the peanuts? He'd been thinking about how hungry he was and how satisfying even a small bag of peanuts would be. His phone? He'd wanted to call his precinct. He had to let everyone know that he was okay and that they didn't have to add him to the list of hostages. Scott opened his eyes, spied the comb, and thought about combing his hair.

A subtle, quiet click and the comb disappeared from the dresser and appeared in his left hand.

Hannah let out a whoop and jumped up and down, but Scott couldn't help thinking of the guys back in Star Haven — Juan, his partner, and Pearson, his lieutenant.

He'd worked hard to earn their respect, worked even harder after he'd shot the Alt, to prove it hadn't been a lucky shot. He knew how disappointed, even angry, they would be when the found out he'd become an Alt. Had always been an Alt.

"Let's try it again." There weren't many other objects in the room he could pull. Hannah surprised him by placing her hand on his forearm where he kept one of his knives.

"Take this off."

Not only did Hannah have confidence, she was getting downright bossy. He did as she asked, though, and pulled off his jacket again to remove the sheath with the knife still locked in place. She grabbed both and placed them where the comb used to be.

"Try to pull the knife, but not the cover," she said.

Again he tried to think only about holding the knife, but it remained on the dresser. If he thought about using the knife, he'd default to a combat posture. Before the thought went further, a dull ache wrapped around his body. He was tired of fighting. Instead, he refocused the image. When else would he use a knife? His stomach rumbled. Dinner. He hadn't eaten since the night before. He imagined himself at a restaurant, someplace classy, with Hannah sitting across from him wearing a dress, black and sexy. A thick, juicy steak covered in sauce sizzled on his plate. He imagined using his knife to slice it.

The knife disappeared and reappeared in his left hand. The sheath remained behind.

Hannah clapped. He had the key, though he didn't believe for a moment Catherine would let him off the hook for training. At least he wouldn't have to start at square one.

He watched Hannah prowl around the room searching for another object for him to use as a target, but he was done. He needed a decent meal and some sleep. He wanted time to think.

The wall intercom buzzed. Scott reached up to answer it. "Yeah."

"It's Thomas. I just received a call. The police want you back. They have a few more questions."

He still had Nik's phone, which is why he had given the cops Thomas's number. "Can we stall them for a couple of hours. I need sleep."

"I'll see what I can do."

Hannah's face slipped from joy to worry. "I'll leave you alone."

She headed for the door, but before she got there, he reached for her arm. "It'll be okay. They couldn't get me to give you up before. They won't get anything out of me now."

Her smile, a mere shadow of the one she'd worn when the knife appeared in his hand, touched his heart and a few other places.

"I know," she said. "I'll see you before you leave."

She tugged her arm out of his grip and he let her go. It would have been comforting to sleep with her in his arms. That pesky word *desire* floated through his consciousness as she shut the door behind her. How easy it would have been to translocate her back into the room.

Ice cold fear crept over the rising heat he stoked. Want versus need. He wanted Hannah, like he'd wanted nothing else in his life, but need? To the point where he'd risk her life translocating her back into his room just to hold her one more time?

Scott looked at the sheath still lying on his dresser and pulled. The sheath disappeared and reappeared in his left hand. The energy behind his desire dissipated leaving only fear in its wake. He jammed the knife back into the sheath and rose from his chair.

The more he used his power, the more he enjoyed it. Old thoughts of working for T-CASS rose and stretched, like a sleepy bear waking from hibernation. This time the dream had a shiny, new element: Hannah, by his side, wearing some crazy-colored uniform, hands on her hips, her wavy, red hair dancing in the wind.

Like he'd told Hannah, he knew nothing of what it took to work for T-CASS because it had never been an option for him. He hadn't just let his dream die, he'd kicked it into a locked box and slammed the door shut never believing he'd open it again. It hurt to remember those early days, when he was just a kid and everyone thought he'd make a fine new addition to the Alt community, whatever his power turned out to be. Even his grandfather had treated him like one of the family.

He'd done a lot of remembering these past few days. Memories of being left behind — in school, after school, on the playground — surfaced and begged him to lock up his dream again. He remembered how happy he'd been in Star Haven — new friends he'd never see again, a job he loved but couldn't return to.

Flopping back into bed, Scott wrapped his arms around himself. Want versus need. He had to decide between what he wanted and what he needed, but how could he choose?

CHAPTER SIXTEEN

For the second time, Scott found himself alone under the harsh lights of the Thunder City police interrogation room. He'd left all his weapons at the house. No point in wasting time stripping down only to have to put everything back on again when they released him. If they released him. As good as Thomas's lawyers were, there was no guarantee they could argue for his release again. This time, the Thunder City cops had a smug look about them and insisted he didn't need a lawyer.

Five minutes passed, then ten. Had the police called in the T-CASS telepaths? The presence of telepaths during routine interrogations had been a huge bone of contention when Catherine first signed the agreement with the City as to where and how the telepaths would use their ability. It was the presence of telepaths that had driven many Norms over to Star Haven.

Fifteen minutes later, the door opened.

"Mayor Dane." Scott stood up more out of surprise than courtesy.

"Officer Grey. I wish we could have met again under better circumstances." She signaled for him to sit.

"Yes, ma'am." Scott remained standing until Dane seated herself across from him. After hearing Hannah's accusations, he tried to see Dane in a new light. She'd always projected herself as a classy, professional woman and today was no different. Her beige suit, notched at the neckline, and her layered brown hair gave her the neat, clean look of a spokeswoman in a television commercial, instead of the harried, distressed appearance of a parent upset over a missing child. It was almost as if by perfecting her look, she could hide the monster underneath. If the monster existed. Scott needed to be sure.

"Before we get started, I want you to know this conversation remains between you and me. No recordings, no Thunder City police, no lawyers, and no telepaths." Dane set her briefcase on the floor and pulled out her tablet.

"I understand." He could understand the lack of telepaths, since no one could prove Hannah's life was in immediate danger, but to bring him to an interrogation room and then turn the interrogation over to the mayor of Star Haven? It made no sense.

"You are aware of my continued attempts to find my daughter?"

"Yes ma'am. My entire precinct spent a lot of time looking for her."

Dane smiled, perhaps to put him at ease, but if so she failed. Instead her smile had a predatory look, and his suspicions flared. Had her smile always looked like that, but he'd been too blind to see it? Had he bought into her anti-Alt message so deeply he'd ignored all of the defenses he'd built to protect himself while he lived in Thunder City?

Of course he had. He'd left Thunder City, he'd left Thomas, because of Miranda Dane's promise to build an Alt-free zone. He'd lived in Star Haven, where his hatred of Alts had been fed and nurtured. In his quest for independence, he'd become a slave to someone else's ideology. He'd wanted to believe in Mayor Dane so much that he'd ignored all the evidence that had been shoved in his face for the past three days. Dane's message had hurt people he should have been protecting. Why hadn't he seen it before now?

Hannah. You have feelings for an Alt. You can run from your family, but you can't run from yourself. Hannah has changed everything for you.

"I appreciate your devotion to your duty regarding my daughter. However, I've come across some evidence that you found her." Dane tapped the screen of her tablet.

"Evidence, ma'am?"

Dane spun the tablet around so he could see the screen. "A witness saw you carry my daughter into the emergency room of Star Haven Memorial."

She showed him a grainy security camera shot of him carrying Hannah into the emergency room of Star Haven Memorial. The angle of the camera was bad, so only the top of his head could be seen and Hannah's face was tucked into his shoulder. He could argue against the definitive nature of the shot, except Dane had said she had a witness.

"Your witness is correct." No point in denying it, but he'd stick to the story he'd given Juan. Scott reached over to enlarge the picture, which Dane allowed without flinching. Either she trusted him enough to get so close, knowing he wouldn't try to attack her, or she trusted the cops standing outside to

208

protect her should Scott become violent. "I did locate your daughter on the roof of the hospital."

Dane turned off the image and set the tablet aside. "Officer Grey. You knew I was looking for her. Why didn't you contact me immediately?"

At least here he could tell the truth. "Given the circumstances, it wasn't the right thing to do."

"What circumstances would lead you to think that telling me you'd found my daughter was not a priority for you? You've seen the missing child posters all over the city."

"Yes, ma'am," Scott agreed. "However, your daughter is no longer a child. She turned eighteen last Monday. I remembered her birth date after the ER nurse dismissed me. If Hannah doesn't want you to find her, it's not my place to tell you her location."

Dane's nostrils flared. She didn't seem to care much about Hannah's age or her legal status.

"Tell me more about your interaction with my daughter, Officer Grey. What happened on the roof?"

If Dane really was behind his ransacked apartment, then Scar would have told her about pushing him out of the helicopter.

"Well. After the Left Fists shoved me out of the copter, I figure an illegal Alt must have caught me in mid-air, then knocked me out so I couldn't identify them. When I woke up, your daughter was at my feet, and unconscious. I figured the Alt must have found her hiding place and knocked her out too, so I brought her to the emergency department."

"And you left her there? Unguarded?"

She didn't even blink when he told her about falling from a helicopter. She knew what had happened to him. She already knew, and had hired professional

209

thugs to go after him. Hannah had been right all along. He should have trusted her. "Well, yes, ma'am. I did."

Dane's red fingernails tapped the table top. "Why? Why did you not stay with her?"

Scott shrugged. "The nurse ordered me to leave. The entire ER was in turmoil. I figured it would be best to let the nurse do her job and not get in the way."

The staccato tapping increased in speed. "Where did you go after you left my daughter?"

"To the men's room and then to the cafeteria."

"Did you make any phone calls during this time?"

"Yes, ma'am. I called my precinct."

"You called your partner, actually." Dane pecked at the tablet again. "You had a two minute conversation with him."

His phone had been compromised? Before Nik had destroyed it? No, Thomas's counter-measures would have prevented any information from falling into Dane's hands. She must have ordered Juan's phone records pulled. She might have even had his partner's phone bugged by now, had him followed. Shit, he'd have to find a way to warn Juan, but how? Would his partner believe him after all this? "Yes, ma'am. For the record, I did plan to call Commissioner Becksom, because I wanted him to know he could call off the search, in case he hadn't noticed her birth date."

Dane heaved an irritated sigh. "When did you notice your ear had grown back?"

"My ear, ma'am?"

"Don't play stupid. Your right ear. You didn't have one at the commendation ceremony."

Scott reached to touch the regrown lobe. "I'm not sure. My best guess is that the illegal Alt who caught me somehow fixed it."

210

"While you were on the roof?"

"Yes, ma'am."

Dane's eyes narrowed. "I see."

She sat there and stared at him for a full minute. "I don't know about you, Grey. Your story is reasonable. Maybe you know the truth about Hannah and maybe you don't. If you don't, then I'm sorry, but this situation is untenable. I must find Hannah."

"The truth, ma'am?"

"My daughter is the Alt who fixed your ear, Grey. I've tried to hide her condition all these years, much to my regret. She used to be a sweet, obedient child, and if she had remained so I would have sent her away as soon as she graduated. Instead, she learned how to use her Alt power in the most cunning and manipulative ways."

"You mean she grew up." What appeared as cunning and manipulative to one parent was perfectly reasonable behavior to another. His brothers were proof.

"Yes, she did. Something you must have noticed."

Miranda hit his code red defense mechanism. He leaned forward to protest, but Miranda raised her hand for silence. "She likes you as only a young girl can like an older man."

"Not that much older..."

Miranda talked over his protest. "You have all the qualities of a classic handsome hero who would rescue her from the mother who only wanted what was best for her. She took advantage of you."

"No, she didn't," Scott said. "When I pulled her off the roof, she was unconscious. All she asked for was assistance leaving Star Haven. I gave her safe passage, nothing more."

211

"I don't think you quite understand the situation, Grey. My daughter has the power to heal. She fixed your body, regrew your ear, and manipulated your hormones so you would fall in love with her and do her bidding."

Cold shock shut down his protests. Manipulate his hormones? Make him feel things he didn't want to? Could Hannah really do that? Had she done that?

White hot anger melted his shock into a puddle. He'd done it again, trusted someone and got his back stabbed. Just like he trusted his brothers, trusted Catherine. They'd all betrayed him. He knew how desperate Hannah had been to leave Thunder City; he'd never considered that she could — would — use her power that way. He never should have touched her. Had she planned this all along? Had she healed him so he'd owe her?

If she had, why does she still want you to stay with her? She doesn't need you now. She has the rest of the Blackwood family to protect her. When you touched her this morning, she didn't need you, but she wanted you anyway.

Scott grabbed hold of that tenuous logic and held on tight. "She wouldn't do that."

"She would and she has."

"Where? To whom?" His grasp slipped and doubts crept back into his thoughts. He was a cop. Maybe Hannah manipulated him, and maybe she hadn't. He needed to keep Miranda talking, find a flaw in her story. Any flaw, if there was one.

"Hannah had an affair with my husband, Roger. She manipulated him, used him for her own selfish reasons."

Not possible. Hannah might have extensive knowledge of the human body, but he had enough

212

experience to know she was still a virgin. Why bloodsurf if you were ready to have sex with someone you cared about? She bloodsurfed because she wasn't ready and had enough sense to not continue. Scott slowly inhaled to cover for the slight relaxation of his shoulders. He'd found the crack in Dane's story, the one he needed to see her as Hannah did.

Dane sat back and crossed her arms over her chest. "I've had to live with the consequences of her actions. When she killed Roger, I decided enough was enough. It's time I brought my daughter to justice."

So Dane planned to accuse Hannah of murder to force the Thunder City police to find her? "Forgive me, Mayor Dane, but I read the report about your husband's death. Roger Dane died because of a heart attack he had while behind the wheel of his car. It plunged into the Bay."

"Who do you think induced his heart attack?" Dane leaned across the table, viciousness pulling back her upper lip and baring her teeth, the monster set free. "Roger was as healthy as a man his age could be. He had access to the best physicians available. Nothing in his records indicated he was a candidate for a heart attack."

A single fingernail jabbed the top of the table. "Before you ask — no, I can't prove it yet. What I can prove is Hannah's direct violation of the Alt ban. She remained in Star Haven for six months after the ban went into effect. Our laws are clear: she's to be arrested and prosecuted."

Scott closed his eyes, his gut curled into a tight ball of pain. He knew the law as well as any other Star Haven cop. Dane was right.

"I'm afraid I don't have any more time to play games, Grey. Tell me where my daughter is."

"I don't know." He opened his eyes, keeping his gaze as steady as he could on Dane.

"We've had your family's home under surveillance and we've confirmed the house is empty. Did you bring her to your parents? Are they hiding her?"

Dane had to be talking about the decoy house Thomas kept in Fargrounds.

"No," he lied.

"You don't realize how much danger they're in. Every moment your parents are exposed to my daughter is another moment she has to get them under her control. The way she controls you."

"I don't know where Hannah is right now."

"Well, then, you leave me no choice."

Dane stepped out of the room and two men stepped inside. They wore Star Haven badges, but Scott didn't recognize them. "Officer Grey, you are under arrest for aiding and harboring a fugitive."

Aiding and harboring a fugitive. He'd do time if convicted. Time in a jail filled with Left Fists. No wonder the Thunder City cops looked so smug. They might have a case against him for shooting Electrocyte, but Dane had a stronger case against him for helping Hannah. Thunder City would see him in jail even if it meant sending him back to Star Haven.

The detectives cuffed his hands behind his back. "Let's go."

He shouldn't have wished so hard to return home.

***

214

Hannah ate her dinner at the formal dining table this time, but tasted nothing of the roasted chicken and vegetables. All her thoughts were of Scott. She didn't blame him for not appreciating her first attempt at seduction. For him it was just another one-night stand — sort of — or stress relief after reliving the horror his brother had put him through, only to have his brother offer a heart-felt apology.

If there was one emotion she was well acquainted with, it was turmoil — to have your entire world shaken, your entire belief system collapse on itself. He needed time to pick at the situation like a scab and seek validation for the job that you really can love and hate someone at the same time. Like how she loved and hated her mother, the woman who had raised her, educated her, used her, and would now kill to control her.

Carraro had assured her he had Scott's situation monitored and would let her know if anything happened. Evan attempted small talk, but neither of the twins could coax her into a conversation. No matter how hard she tried, her voice sounded distant, forced, not like her own. Nik had clicked off the television after the twelfth news report about Scott's recall by the police for continued questioning. She cleaned her plate out of respect for those days when she'd had nothing to eat, but she didn't accept seconds when offered.

A wall monitor beeped behind her. Alek shoved back his chair to answer it.

"Yeah."

"It's Thomas. Is Hannah with you?"

"We're having dinner."

"When she's done, would you ask her to join me in my office?"

Alek looked over at Hannah. She waved her palm over her empty plate to indicate she was done.

"She's finished."

"Good. Thank you."

Hannah pushed her own chair back. "Where's his office?"

"I'll take you." Nik stood, looking strong and powerful. He'd slept most of the day and swore he had no lingering effects from the gunshot. Hannah had offered to bloodsurf once more to make sure she hadn't missed anything, but Nik insisted it wasn't necessary.

"You mean though the walls?"

He held out an open hand. "It's safer than flying. I promise."

She glanced at Evan who winked at her.

"If you say so."

Without further warning Nik tugged her into a loose embrace and... *Yikes*. She surfed, but not through blood. Instead, the rough innards of woods and metals raced past. She closed her eyes when it looked as if they would crash into a wall, but her sense of touch remained and the cement foundation scraped past without a scratch.

Did Nik lose his sense of time when he traveled like this? Could he lose himself inside and never come out again? Hannah held fast until a shove and a pop pushed her face up through a floor. Under her backside, the plush carpet squished.

From above, Carraro leaned over a huge oak desk, amused.

"You can breathe now." Nik's voice reverberated through the room.

Hannah gasped. "Thank you."

The walls around the office shimmered. "Any time."

He disappeared.

Carraro walked around the desk. "How was your first trans-mansion journey?"

Hannah checked to make sure her clothes hadn't disappeared in transit. Green cotton shirt, jean capris, and gold sandals — still intact. "Incredible. It's like bloodsurfing, but without the blood."

He grinned as he grasped her sleeve to pull her to her feet. "Except for the occasional fight, usually reserved for football season, we're generally a blood-free home."

Carraro indicated she should sit in the swivel chair next to his executive one. On his desk sat a computer with multiple screens similar to the one in Scott's apartment. One screen displayed a spreadsheet, another a chart, and a third one showed a blueprint.

"I sent the files I didn't download from your stepfather's records to an engineer friend of mine. I asked him to review the imported materials and give me his best guess as to what they would create if they were put together."

Hannah watched the scroll of data on the spreadsheet. "What did he say?"

"We're not one hundred percent sure, which is why I wanted your input. After he eliminated the materials common to most buildings — cement, drywall, and the like — we came up with four distinct possibilities."

Carraro highlighted a section of the spreadsheet. "The first group seemed innocuous - a gymnasium or arena. This one, though, would be much larger with no stadium seating as you would expect at a sporting event.

The materials to make up the floor, however, were provided by the same company contracted to build the Thunder City Arena, which tipped us to its possible use."

Hannah shook her head. "Miranda has no use for sports, though she often puts in appearances at Sabers games to keep her supporters happy. Why smuggle this sort of material, though? It must be readily available and it's not illegal."

"Good question." Carraro highlighted a second list on the screen. "This group lists medical equipment for a clinic or doctor's office, and a third group lists a half dozen walk-in freezers."

"Freezers?" A few ideas came to mind. "Maybe to be used by the concession stands at the arena? Along with an infirmary?"

Carraro nodded. "Could be."

So it made sense, but she still didn't understand why someone would feel the need to *smuggle* freezers into Star Haven. Lots of places must use them — grocery stores, laboratories, florists.

"Here's where I became concerned." Carraro brought up a fourth list — much longer than the first three. "Put together this last list and you have yourself a prison. Not a large one, but secure enough for most hoodlums."

An idea brushed Hannah's thoughts before it lost itself in the cloud of her confusion.

"Were you able to figure out who changed the records?" she asked. "I mean maybe you missed something two years ago, or the hacker has taken on other jobs and left a pattern you could trace?"

Carraro shook his head. "No. Whoever they are, they've managed to stay under my radar. Which could mean he or she is either a one-time opportunist or they're being paid to not take other jobs. If they had taken them, I'd know."

This bothered her more than the list of materials. Despite his shady reputation, Hack-Man had worked enough legitimate jobs in cyber-forensics to earn his reputation in the open, otherwise Roger would never have hired him. You would think Thomas Carraro would have his fingers on the pulse of any other hacker who could pull this off before they could disappear so thoroughly.

Carraro turned away from the screens to face her. "I know we've mentioned keeping an eye on your mother since she ran for Mayor on an anti-Alt platform, but you know her better than any of us. What do you think this is about?"

It was the oddest feeling, having a well-respected adult ask her for an opinion — as if she too were an expert. When it came to her mother, she guessed she was an expert. The only one left alive willing to warn people about her.

"We don't even know for sure if Miranda is behind this," she said, more to remind herself of her lack of evidence. Isn't that what Scott had demanded of her? Evidence? She still had none to offer.

"True enough," Carraro agreed. "Go on."

"Miranda wasn't anti-Alt at first." *Careful. You can still be arrested, just like Scott.* "Once she realized what I could do, she encouraged me. Trained me, in her own way. While most kids were reading Dr. Seuss, Miranda gave me health books, or biology books, most of them way over my grade level. She'd have me practice on her: smooth this wrinkle, remove this pimple, eliminate this fat pocket. It was easy and I wanted to please her."

"It's natural to want to please a parent," Carraro said. "So she never had strong anti-Alt policies until she ran for Mayor?"

"She needed the votes." Hannah shrugged, at a loss to explain her mother's change of heart. "Star Haven already had a reputation for harassing Alts. Most two-shoes worked as vigilantes and they had to wear masks or they'd never be left alone. Miranda tapped into the Norms' fear of losing their jobs to Alts, or telepaths manipulating them, or any of the other dozen or so conspiracy theories Norms use as an excuse to hate Alts."

"Fear of the Other." Carraro leaned back in his chair and laced his fingers across his stomach. "Let's theorize for a moment. If your mother is behind the change in records and these materials are meant to build what we think they're supposed to, what is she trying to accomplish?"

That pesky thought hit the back of her brain again, but Hannah shied away from it. "How big a prison would the materials make?"

"Not big." Carraro twisted the monitor with the blueprint toward her. "A dozen cells at most. Double occupancy and you have twenty-four prisoners."

"A prison with an arena? Like those awful movies where men fight each other to the death for an audience?"

Carraro gave rueful laugh. "It does have horror story overtones, doesn't it? Does it sound like something your mother would involve herself in?"

He sounded doubtful.

"She could use it to raise money for her re-election campaign." Lame, so lame.

"There are easier, safer ways to raise money, even through illegal means."

He was right, of course.

"It also doesn't explain the freezers," he added.

The thought Hannah had avoided punched into her forebrain.

"A prison for Alts. Oh, God." Hannah covered her mouth. This really was a horror story. "She's using the freezers as time-out rooms."

Carraro frowned. "Thunder City has a prison built specifically for Chaos Alts. We even have an agreement to house Chaos Alts from Star Haven dating from long before the Alt-ban."

Hannah shook her head. It all made sense. *Oh, God, what have I done?* "No. Not a prison for Chaos Alts. A prison for Alts — any Alts."

Carraro straightened as he followed her thoughts. "What are you saying, Hannah? Tell me what you think."

What did she think? Her mother had used her to heal not just her henchmen, but Chaos Alts, or so she said. No prisoner could have gotten the types of injuries she was healing unless they were being deliberately hurt. She knew it, but she hadn't known it. She'd bought into her mother's excuses. They'd tried to escape, they were caught fighting, it's too expensive to keep bringing them to the hospital. But Chaos Alts weren't kept in the Star Haven jail. What she was doing was so wrong, so sick, but she couldn't face it.

She had to come clean, tell the truth. "It's a prison to keep Alts. Those names, the list of names of the missing Alts Catherine showed me yesterday. I saw their names on a list my mother kept. They're all missing, because my mother — because Miranda — has

221

them. They're in a prison built for Alts. They'd lived on the fringes of society. No one was supposed to look for them. *And I helped heal them!*"

"What do you mean, Hannah?" Carraro reached over to take her hands, but this time Hannah yanked her hands back. "Why would Miranda want to keep a prison full of innocent Alts?"

"To control them." The sobs overtook her, choking her words. "I should have told you about the things Miranda made me do. I'm sorry. I'm so sorry."

"All right. All right. Relax. Take a deep breath. Let's think about this for a moment." He handed her a tissue, which she snatched to wipe her eyes. "Miranda had you healing Alts, possibly snatched off the streets and incarcerated. What was she doing with them? Experimenting?"

Stop crying. Think! Focus. Get yourself under control. It was Miranda's voice yelling at her, strong enough to stop the tears. Miranda's voice, not her mother's, not her mother anymore. "Maybe she wants more Alts to control? Maybe create an army of them? All under her command. What better way to start than with prisoners who have no choice?"

Her whole body shook. This must be what Roger had tried to warn her about. He had discovered Miranda's plan, which might have included Hannah, and he'd told her to meet him at the marina. Miranda had killed him before he could get there. Hannah had heard the gunshot over the phone. She had known at once that he was dead and that she had to escape on her own.

Whatever Carraro thought of her speculation was cut off by his phone.

222

"Yes," he answered, then paused. "What are the charges?"

Hannah bit the back of her hand. Scott. The phone call had to be about Scott. "Keep him in sight. Let me know where they bring him. It'll probably be the airport."

He shut the line. "Son of a bitch."

"It's Scott, isn't it?" she asked, her voice thick with unshed tears.

"Yes, it's Scott." He pressed the phone to his lips.

She had to know the truth. "Tell me what happened."

"Your mother's here in Thunder City."

She gagged on the vomit before she forced it back down. Carraro reached for a bottle of water but Hannah waved him to stop. "How do you know? What has she done?"

"She just arrested my son for aiding and harboring a fugitive: you."

It was all starting to come together. "Thunder City allowed this?" she asked, while she put together pieces of Miranda's puzzle.

Carraro dialed another number. "Thunder City Norms love their Alts, even the Newcomers. Scott's killed two. They're out for blood."

"We have to get him back."

"We will."

"No, you don't understand." She flung her hand at his computer screens. "This? This isn't about Scott. She doesn't want him. She wants me."

"We're not going to give you up that easily."

Carraro said no more because Catherine picked up the line. She already knew about Scott's arrest; it was all over the news. The polished wood bookshelves lining the walls vibrated. The Blackwood family was on the move.

Her mother must have known that the Thunder City Alts would protect her. She would have planned for such a reaction. The blueprint of the prison glowed on the computer screen. Someone would be killed if the Blackwoods went after Scott.

She'd give herself up first and no one, not even Catherine Blackwood, Captain Spectacular, could stop her.

Chapter Seventeen

Hannah watched the Blackwoods suit up from the doorway leading into the parlor, their movements controlled, efficient, well-practiced. Carraro had offered her a drink, this time scotch or brandy, something dark and potent to calm her hysteria. Her body no longer shook, the trails of her tears were dry against her skin. Inside, she was screaming. Every possible conclusion to this scenario ended in blood, Scott's blood. Her ability had never felt so useless.

Carraro — Hack-Man — stood behind her in the hallway, his ear pressed to his phone.

"What are you going to do?" she asked no one in particular.

"We don't know yet," Catherine said, paused, and in a blur changed into her uniform. When Catherine was in uniform, Hannah would always think of her as Captain Spectacular. "Legally, we can't do anything."

"What can you do illegally?" There had to be flexibility when someone's life was in danger, especially someone the Blackwoods cared about. "You can't let Miranda transport Scott to Star Haven. We'll never see him again."

Alek hooked a mic over his ear and curled it around to his mouth. "We don't have a lot of choices.

If we yank him out of police custody now, it could cost us our agreement with Thunder City. We can't have the Norms thinking the Blackwoods are breaking the law to protect an Alt-killer, much less an Alt-killer from across the Bay — who, oh by the way, we're related to."

Alek's sarcasm made her want to punch him. Scott's antipathy had been aimed at Evan, and Evan had apologized, but apparently Alek hadn't read the memo yet. Would Alek really help rescue Scott? Or would he hold back? She'd have to keep an eye on him.

"This isn't an arrest," she said, channeling her aggression into words. "Miranda won't turn Scott over to the Star Haven police, or if she does, she'll make sure the officers involved are loyal to her."

"We'll keep a line open to the Star Haven police," Carraro said. Hannah looked over her shoulder as he pulled his chin away from the phone. "If Scott isn't processed within an hour, we'll start raising alarms. Thunder City wants their chance to prosecute him as well. We can use that to our advantage to make sure he doesn't suffer from any accidents."

"In the meantime, we need a plan." The Captain adjusted her ear bud. "First, we need to establish where she's going to take him. Even if she does take him to jail, there's more than one in Star Haven."

Over the Captain's shoulder, Hannah could see the muted television. The camera shot showed Scott, still handcuffed, being marched toward a helicopter at the Thunder City airport. A group of heavily armed police officers surrounded him.

The next shot showed a group of protesters waving signs demanding Scott remain in Thunder City custody for prosecution. A third set of protesters demanded the right of Star Haven Alts to return home and testify against him. Two Alts raced between the groups, keeping them behind the police barriers. So much support for the Alts. It was everything Hannah could have wanted from Thunder City, but twisted into a sick joke. Scott would pay the price for Thunder City's loyalty.

"Mach Ten and Stampede have things under control at the airport. Flame is on her way," Evan commented.

The camera shot swung back to the helicopter. The doors to the cabin closed. The rotors spun faster and faster. She couldn't watch, but at the same time she couldn't turn away. White hot anger turned to vertigo. Never had she hated Miranda more than she did at this moment.

"She's going to faint," Evan said, reaching for her. "Stay with us, hon."

Carraro's hand landed on her shoulder. Stars appeared at the edge of her vision. It was either breathe or scream.

"I'm fine." Liar. "I just want Scott back. I want him to be safe." True enough.

On the screen, the helicopter lifted off. Scott was officially out of reach.

Carraro's phone buzzed yet again. He listened for a moment, then said, "No, I understand. You do what you are comfortable with." He disconnected the line. "We have another problem. Pathia is pregnant. She'll help from home, but she won't go into the field."

"Can't blame her," Captain Spec said, though she didn't sound happy about it.

"Who's Pathia?" Hannah asked.

"T-CASS telepath," Carraro answered. "Very powerful. She'll keep a connection between Scott and herself for as long as she can."

"What do you mean 'as long as she can'?" *Watch your tone of voice, young lady.* Miranda again. Would she never get that woman out of her head? But Hannah heeded the warning. Her nerves had turned her request into a demand. She'd better watch it. She couldn't afford to alienate anyone, especially the Blackwoods.

Carraro didn't appear offended, at least. "Even the most powerful telepaths have limitations."

"But if she's a telepath, can't she read Miranda's mind? If she can tell us what Miranda has planned..." Everyone in the room shook their head. "Why not?"

"It's one thing for Pathia to establish a link with Scott," Nik said, already changed and seated on the sofa. "They were classmates once and she could argue she only wanted to send him a telepathic message in the context of friendship."

"It's something else entirely to go into a Norm's mind, someone you don't have a personal connection with, and dig for information," Alek continued, as he zipped up his uniform, ready for action. "It's a class A felony. She'd get jail time if anyone found out."

"Now you're worried about committing a felony?" She whirled on Carraro, her tone of voice be damned. How could they be so fucking casual about their own flesh and blood? "You were a Neut, you still are when it suits you. You downloaded Roger's records without permission. Isn't that considered theft?"

"Sure it is," Carraro said. "And if someone can prove I did it, I'll go to jail. Given how Roger hired me to look at the records in the first place, who's to say he didn't also give me permission to download them?

228

However, committing a felony yourself and asking someone else to do it places the burden of responsibility on the person you're asking. Pathia has always been a two-shoe. Asking her to commit a crime even in this situation makes her position untenable: she either has to refuse my request, and risk alienating someone she trusts and relies on for operational support, or acquiesce to my request, which makes her a criminal. I prefer not to place her in either situation, so I'm choosing not to ask."

His answer stoked the fire burning her last nerve, but she had enough control now to keep her mouth shut.

"Everyone ready?" Captain Spec asked.

"Ready for what?" she asked, trying not to sound bitter.

The Blackwoods looked at each other then back to her.

"What?" she snapped. With all of her worry about Scott, she hadn't paid attention to what was going on around her except for a brief thought to how cool the Blackwoods looked in their uniforms. Except for Carraro. He wore the red polo and black slacks she'd seen him in when he first pulled her onto his boat. Maybe this was his uniform?

"We might as well bring her along. She's already a two-shoe and she'll eventually join T-CASS," said Nik.

"I'll take her," Evan offered.

"Take me where?" She'd had enough surprises to last her for a century.

"Headquarters." Evan joined her in the doorway, motioning her to move so he could exit the parlor. "Underneath the Thunder City Arena."

"Where the Tornadoes play?"

229

"Yeah," Alek said. "Thunder City owns the land and it's central to where everyone lives. Underneath the building is where we meet, schedule, deploy, monitor, and host the occasional party."

"And you're going to fly me there?"

Evan grinned. "Thomas could drive you, but flying is much faster."

"And safer," said Alek, coming up from behind Evan.

"Let me take her," Nik said as he emerged from the wall ahead of them. "She's already traveled with me."

"No way." Evan put his arm around shoulder. "You had your chance. It's my turn."

"No fighting over the girl," Captain Spec said. "Hannah, pick your poison, but we have to leave now."

No brainer. "I'll fly with Evan."

"Fine."

There was no ceremony, no rallying cry. Nik merged with the nearest wall and disappeared. The rest of them walked out the front door, Evan pausing to hold the door open for Hannah. In the sunlight, Captain Spec wrapped her arms around her husband and flew away. Alek followed her, a gust of air vortexing in his wake.

"Ready?" Evan placed a hand on her back.

"No, but I want to be there for Scott."

"I've never dropped anyone," he said.

A gentle breeze tickled her ankles.

"As the cushion grows, lean into it. We'll fly head first, just like Mom."

A soft pillow, invisible except for the ripple in her clothes, pressed against her knees, then her hips, and finally her shoulders.

"Go ahead. Lean into it."

At first she only stretched her calves as far as they would let her.

"A little more," he encouraged.

Afraid to fall, even with Evan standing so close, she bent her knees instead.

"Okay. Here we go."

A stronger swoosh of air yanked her feet out from under her. She yipped, but the air pillow turned dense and captured her weight. Beside her, Evan mirrored her prone position. They gained height while he guided her in a slow, smooth circle around the mansion.

"Keep your eyes open."

She hadn't even realized she'd closed them. Reality blew away her imagination. She pushed her hair off her face so she could see the fountain and rose-covered trellis in the backyard. Another quarter swing and Mystic Bay sparkled in the sunlight dotted with colorful boat sails. More height and another quarter swing and she could see the backyards of nearby neighbors. A group of kids played in a sandbox. A man floated on a doughnut in his pool. Further ahead, two-story homes turned into small office buildings until they reached an oblong cluster of mirrored skyscrapers in downtown Thunder City. The Arena punctuated the south end of the cluster, its spires surrounding the main building.

"We're going to straighten out now and go a little faster."

Yes. The joy of flying gave way to thoughts of Scott's flight over the Bay into whatever nightmare Miranda had planned for him. Determination to track him down and get him back added fire to her anger.

"Not a little faster," she said. "A lot faster."

Evan pulled her closer. "Are you sure?"

"I can take it."

He laughed. "I don't doubt it. Hang on."

She did, as tight as she could. Below her, the world blurred and the wind carried her forward.

***

The euphoria of flying came to an undramatic end when Evan lowered her onto the roof of the Arena. This roof was much higher and a hell of a lot less cluttered than the one at of Star Haven Memorial. She had a ringside view of the banners fluttering on the individual spires, each representing a different sports team. She and Roger had rooted against all of them at one time or another.

"This way." Evan motioned her ahead of him through a metal door. Despite her request to go faster, she suspected they were the last ones to arrive.

Once inside, he directed her to an elevator. She expected him to hit the button to whatever floor they needed to get to, except there wasn't one — only a flat pad with a screen, but no buttons.

"Identify," demanded a female voice too perfectly modulated to be real.

"Rumble. Evangelos Blackwood. Three-Eight-Two-Seven."

A panel slipped open like a disc player. Evan placed his hand on top. It flashed colored lights under his palm.

"Identity confirmed. Identify."

Hannah knew the voice was asking for her information, but she didn't have a moniker or a number.

"Hannah Quinn," she said so the software wouldn't set off alarms if she failed to say anything. Nothing happened. Evan motioned her to put her hand on the panel. It felt warm. The lights flashed far longer for her than they had with Evan.

"Restricted access granted."

She let out the breath she'd been holding as the elevator doors opened. "Did you have my name buried in a database somewhere?"

"Thomas must have added your name after you arrived, when it became obvious you were one of us."

One of them, she thought, as the elevator descended. Evan made it sound so easy. Would the Thunder City Alts still think of her as one of them after they rescued Scott? After they figured out she and Scott had...had what? A fling? An affair? A one-day stand? Would standing by Scott ruin her chances of staying in Thunder City?

She needed to find Scott first and bring him back home. Once he was safe, then she'd worry about how to classify her relationship with him. If you could even call it a relationship. They'd made no promises, and he still wanted her to break his power. If the other Alts rejected her, she'd do what she'd always planned on doing. She'd run.

The elevator bumped to a halt. The doors slid open. Hannah stepped out with Evan's hand pressing gently on her lower back. Swarms of people dressed in black slacks and yellow polos stood scattered about a huge, low-lit conference room. Four screens the size of swimming pools lined the lower edge of a domed ceiling. Data streamed across two of them, while the other two silently displayed the current news broadcasts with closed captioning, one channel for Thunder City, the other for Star Haven. Underneath the larger screens, dozens of computer stations ringed the room. In the center a large, round table sat on a platform about two feet above the floor.

She spotted Captain Spec seated on the far side of the table from where she and Evan had entered. Nik and Alek flanked their mother, but Carraro was nowhere she could see. Evan brought her around to an empty seat next to Alek.

"Stay behind my chair," Evan whispered, as he levitated her up the platform. "I don't know how all this is going to play out. You might be asked to speak."

She did what Evan said. At least her late entrance hadn't interrupted the meeting.

"Thank you all for coming on such short notice," the Captain said, speaking into a microphone so her voice could be heard around the room, even over the background noise of the computer equipment. "A situation has arisen, and I need feedback from all of you before I proceed. First, I want to introduce all of you to Hannah Quinn."

Hannah didn't need a mirror to know that her face had turned the same color as her hair when the Captain pointed to her with an open palm, but she didn't look down either. One by one, she met each pair of eyes at the table. Some of the Alts smiled at her, others stared, but none of them appeared hostile or angry. Yet. She recognized a few of them — Hopper, from her kinky, bouncy hair, and Spritz from her bright blue and white uniform, and a few others from the news articles she had collected over the years. She hoped it was custom for Alts to use their moniker instead of their real names while inside the Arena.

"Hannah is a Newcomer and one of the most powerful Alts I've ever met. Her mother, however, is Miranda Dane, the Mayor of Star Haven."

The Captain paused a beat for the information to process. Variations of "are you kidding" and "did she say daughter" and "how powerful is powerful" were whispered among the closer Alts, who took a second, more careful look at her. Hannah pressed closer to Evan's chair. He reached a hand back to clasp hers in a quick, supportive squeeze. She guessed by this point rule-breaking was also a Blackwood family trait, so she squeezed his hand back.

After waiting out the initial shock, the Captain continued. "This is the situation I wish to discuss with you."

For the next ten minutes, Hannah listened as the Captain relayed the events of the past three days to her fellow Alts.

"I understand most of you won't have any sympathy for Scott Grey, given his history," the Captain said. "However, if what I suspect is true and Officer Grey is an Alt whose power only recently manifested itself, then he deserves a chance to prove himself to us. Let us find him and bring him back here to train. If he finishes his training and commits himself to the protection of Thunder City, then we will have gained two new Alts to add to our roster of city defenders."

No mention of Scott Grey's real identity. Did no one know Catherine had a fourth son?

A black man in fatigues with huge shoulders and a high-and-tight haircut leaned forward to speak. "Captain. I think I speak for all of us when I say I have a few concerns."

As he spoke, his fingers formed small cubes at their tips. Blockhead. He was even more impressive close up than he was on television.

"Only a few?" the Captain asked, but before Blockhead could continue she interrupted. "I wish we had the luxury of time to address everyone's concerns about Grey. Unfortunately, we don't. It is my belief, and the belief of Ms. Quinn, that Miranda Dane may try to harm Grey in hopes of luring Ms. Quinn back to Star Haven. Our only concern right now is his rescue."

"Wouldn't bringing her Alt-daughter back to Star Haven violate the very ban Dane pushed through the City Council?" A very pale Alt wearing thick glasses with white lenses over his eyes asked the question.

"It would," the Captain confirmed.

Blockhead leaned forward again. "It would appear, to me at least, that Miranda Dane herself has violated her own law by returning Scott Grey to Star Haven. Could Thunder City not bypass the Mayor's office and deal directly with the Star Haven Attorney General? Most of Thunder City wants Grey returned so we can prosecute him ourselves."

The Captain nodded. "I agree we will pursue all legal options available once we confirm Grey has been delivered to the Star Haven police. At this time, however, Dane does not know of Grey's Alt status. I would like to keep his ability out of the media. It could endanger his life if Dane discovers what he can do. The Police Commissioner agrees."

"Do you think Grey will not be processed?" Blockhead continued.

"We believe there is a strong possibility Dane will bring Grey to an undisclosed location to lure her daughter back."

Another Alt, dressed in bright yellow with a matching feather pinning back her thick black hair, motioned for a chance to speak. The Captain nodded in her direction.

"You said Ms. Quinn is one of the most powerful Alts you've met, but you haven't actually said what her ability is. Could you please tell us what she can do?"

The Captain signaled Evan to let Hannah sit in his chair. Evan rose, pulled the chair out for her, and pushed the chair back in as she sat down. The chair automatically adjusted its height so she could speak into the microphone. In front of her, the flat screen monitor embedded in the table shut down. Restricted access, she supposed.

"Ms. Quinn calls herself a bloodsurfer," the Captain said. "I've seen her use her power. She transfers herself into the bloodstream of others in order to heal them."

Another long silence, then Yellow Feather asked, "Heal how? Explain, please, because even with the extraordinary power sitting around this table, this isn't an ability we've ever seen before."

The Captain turned to Hannah. "Would you please elaborate on what happens when you bloodsurf?"

Miranda used to badger her to explain what she actually did when she bloodsurfed. And yet, every time she tried to explain, her words felt inadequate. "Well, if you break a bone, I stitch it together. If you're sick, I can destroy the bacteria or virus causing your illness. If you've been shot, I can repair the damage and remove the bullet if necessary. It's something I would have to show you if you have more questions."

Three seats to her right, on the other side of the Captain, Nik stood up. Without prompting, he unzipped his uniform and slipped the material off his upper body. Underneath he wore a black t-shirt, which he yanked up to expose his chest and torso.

"You all watched the news last night. You saw what happened at the harbor. My...Scott Grey shot Electrocyte and the bullet passed through him and hit me square in the chest." Nik ran his hand over his muscled body. "Do you see the wound? Do you see any scars? Some of you have known me since I was a kid. How many fights have I gotten into? How many accidents have I had while chasing down Chaos Alts? You don't walk away from those situations unscathed. Look at me. There's nothing there. Half of my past has been erased because Hannah didn't just save my life by healing the gaping hole in my chest. She erased every scar I've ever had. The only reason why I'm sitting here now is because of her. If that doesn't make her the most powerful Alt in this room, I don't know what would."

Nik tugged down his shirt and zipped up his uniform.

"A potent demonstration to be sure," Yellow Feather said, before she leaned back. The group turned their eyes back to Hannah. She could see their concern as they calculated the risk of rescuing Scott against keeping her in Thunder City. Regardless of what they thought of Scott, they must know the danger of Hannah returning to Star Haven.

"What exactly do you want us to do, Captain?" Blockhead asked. "We can't cross the border to rescue Grey. To do so would bring Star Haven's law against us and put Thunder City in the middle of a messy legal battle. We can't do that to the Norms who have stayed by our side and helped us build this city."

The Captain tapped her tablet a few times. A blueprint of the prison Carraro had shown Hannah earlier appeared as a holograph in the middle of the table.

"I discovered through an informant that Dane's late husband's import business was used to smuggle construction materials into Star Haven. After reviewing the list and consulting an expert, we believe this is what the smuggler is trying to build."

Blockhead squinted at the blueprints. "What is it? It looks almost like the Arena on top of us, but what are those open spaces on the side?"

"Cells," the Captain said. "We think it's a prison. One designed to hold Alts. The current theory is — and please remember it's just a theory at this point — that Miranda Dane is using this prison to hold the missing Alts on the list I distributed to you yesterday. In fact, she may have more Alts than what I had listed."

Blockhead looked down at his station's computer screen. "If we can prove there's a connection between the missing Alts and this theoretical structure, maybe we could get permission to send some Norms over to Star Haven to investigate further."

"We don't have time for investigations." Oh, shit. Did she just speak out loud? She must have because everyone was looking at her again. "We need to figure out where this structure is located immediately. Miranda — my mother — has probably taken Scott there. I intend to get him out, with your help or without it."

Evan's hand landed on her shoulder, but not with a lot of pressure. Miranda would have used the gesture to shut her up. Evan used it to give her the strength to keep talking.

"You need to understand this: Scott saved my life and gave up everything he ever wanted in order to do it. He knew that once he crossed the Bay he could never return. He gave up his home, his friends, his job — all of it destroyed because he dared follow his duty to the extreme limit: to keep me safe at all costs, even from my own mother. I owe him my life, so the least I can do is give up mine for his. I will cross the Bay to Star Haven if it means I can bring Scott back here alive. If you won't help me, then I'll go it alone."

The gauntlet thrown, she leaned away from the mic. She'd backed T-CASS into a corner, but she didn't care. Either they would help or they wouldn't. There was no more time to waste.

Out of the corner of her eye the Captain glanced down her screen. A frown creased her brow and she closed her eyes for a long moment. Too long, in fact. Nik leaned close to her.

"Mom, are you okay? What's wrong?"

With a subtle touch she scrolled the screen down before looking back up to address the table.

"Pathia has contacted Hack-Man. She's lost her telepathic link with Grey. He's either beyond her range, unconscious, or dead."

As one, Alek and Nik pushed back their chairs. Evan released her shoulder. Hannah spun and saw he had already floated off the platform. From the shadows, Carraro appeared, headed for the elevators.

"Stop!" The Captain's voice echoed across the room. "We are not crossing the border into Star Haven. Not yet. As much as I want to go after Cor — after Scott Grey myself, we do not have enough information to find him. Until we do, we stay here. Understand."

No response. Even Carraro stayed in place.

240

"Please, don't make me force you to stay," the Captain said.

Nik and Alek reseated themselves, and Hannah gave her seat back to Evan, his face ashen, hard, filled with pain. He would bolt at the first opportunity. When he did, she would join him.

The Captain addressed everyone. "For now, I need all of you to take this blueprint and show it to the Newcomers you're training. Ask them where a structure this big might be built. It could be underground, it could be anywhere. Ask them if they've seen anything unusual and send your reports directly to me. By first light tomorrow, I want to know where Dane is imprisoning Alts. Dismissed."

CHAPTER EIGHTEEN

"That's it?" Hannah winced as her question echoed around the room. All of the Alts could hear her, but she ignored them. Scott wasn't dead. Miranda wouldn't kill him until she had Hannah secured. She had to believe that. "We're going to do nothing except hope one of the Star Haven Alts knows about a clandestine construction site?"

"No," Evan said, his voice low. He motioned her out of the chair, away from the mic. "We're going to do a lot of things while the others interview the Newcomers. Hang in there, Hannah. This is going to be a long night."

He lowered her back to the floor. Off to the side, she saw Carraro intercept his wife with a hug, Alek beside her. A group of Alts gathered around Nik. Yellow Feather poked him in the chest. Nik laughed, grabbed her hand and kissed the tips of her fingers. How could they act so casual with Scott's life on the line?

She had to believe he was only unconscious. Maybe that's what all of T-CASS believed. Unconscious didn't mean healthy, though. Miranda could have had one of her men knock him out, or she could have drugged him.

"C'mon." Evan tugged at her sleeve. "There's a smaller conference room in the back. We need to..."

"Hey, Hannah Quinn."

The Alt with the all-white glasses broke away from Nik and double-stepped in her direction. Up close, he looked about her age. His skin and long hair were almost as white as his lenses. His burnt-orange uniform — this one with a large padded pocket over his heart — loaned him some color.

"I'm Asher," he said, though he didn't hold out his hand for a shake.

It seemed silly to give her name since he already knew it. "Uh, hi. Nice to meet you." She started to walk past him to follow Evan, who had headed over to his brother, now standing among the cluster of Alts surrounding Nik.

"You probably haven't heard of me yet, but I'm called Seeker. I just graduated and this is my first official T-CASS mission."

Oh, great, an inexperienced Alt. How many other T-CASS Alts had just graduated? How useful would they be in finding Scott?

"I can see through anything," Asher said, determined to have a conversation with her. How could she shut him up so she could find Evan? Evan had to know what Captain Spec and Carraro were up to. This Asher guy couldn't possibly know anything.

Asher raised his glasses. Instead of the usual complement of cornea, iris, pupil, and sclera, his eyes were all black. The sharp contrast between his pale skin and hair and the pitch black of his eyes gave him a demonic appearance.

"Wow." Curiosity quashed her antagonism. No, Asher's eyes weren't just the sclera turned black to blend in with the pupil. Black ichor had replaced his eyeballs, like pools of dark blood. "What exactly do you see?"

"Whatever's below the surface. It's all I see. I can't see walls or skin, just what's underneath."

Like through the walls of a prison cell? "What do the glasses do?"

"Creates a barrier so I can see you as you are and not just your skull."

Creepy, but at least he didn't leer and talk about how he could see through her clothes, which he probably could. Too bad the glasses weren't a substitute mask. If they were, she wouldn't be the only Alt who had to wear one if she joined T-CASS. Still, even the practical nature of the glasses made her feel less like an outsider. "I'd love to bloodsurf through your eyes and see how they work."

He grinned. "Good. I'd like to work with you too. When I'm not training with the police, the Captain has me triage disaster victims for an ambulance service. I can tell more quickly who needs immediate medical attention. I think we'd make a great team."

Team? Work together? She wasn't even a member yet. Another Alt walked over before she could sputter a response. This one wore a fire red uniform, skintight and all attitude. "I'm Klara, Flame. You can heal anything?"

"Yes." Her response was automatic. More Alts headed in her direction, surrounding her instead of Nik.

Klara gave a single nod. "We'll talk after you're trained."

The other Alts tossed questions at her, making Klara's curtness less abrupt. Panic bubbled up her veins; she started to shake. She'd never been the center of attention without Miranda nearby.

"Will you start training immediately?"

"Have you picked out your uniform yet?"

"Where are you staying? Do you need a roommate?"

A sharp whistle cut short the questions. Evan returned to her side. Nik and Yellow Feather stood behind the group.

"Who's the woman in yellow?" she whispered to Asher.

"Highlight. T-CASS trainer," he whispered back.

"What's the first rule of the Arena?" Highlight shouted.

"What happens in the Arena, stays in the Arena." Everyone except Evan, Nik, Alek and Hannah responded.

"So there's no gossip," Nik said, arms akimbo. "Hannah is staying with the Blackwoods. The threat against her by Miranda Dane is real. No one is to discuss her whereabouts, even upstairs during practice."

"If you have a regular job, you can return," Highlight continued at full volume. "If you're not working and feel ready for some drills, I'll be upstairs. Otherwise, all of you are on call until further notice."

Most of the crowd followed Highlight, except for Asher.

"I know you're staying with the Blackwoods," he said, "so you don't need anything, but if you just want to talk or go somewhere to hang out after all this blows over..."

Evan and Nik loomed over both of them, arms across chests.

Asher backed away, slowly at first. "...uh, they have my number."

He ran the rest of the way toward the elevators.

"You didn't have to frighten him," Hannah said. The two tree trunks didn't budge.

"It's been a while since I've had to scare a Goob," Evan said.

"Goob?" she asked.

"Newbies. Recent graduates." Nik lowered his arms as the last elevator doors closed behind Asher. He directed her toward a side exit. "The ones who join T-CASS right out of high school because they've trained for most of their lives."

Evan followed. "But they don't have enough experience in the field for trainees of their own."

"And they have just enough confidence to get themselves, and you, into trouble." Nik pressed his hand to another pad beside the door. The door opened and Nik motioned her through first.

"Highlight will drill with them," Evan said. "If the Captain does call for a raid, they'll be ready."

No amount of drills would prepare them for Miranda. Her mother would have planned for Alts to try and come after her. A raid would only get Scott killed. The Captain had better have a different tactic in mind.

The smaller conference room had a set-up identical to that of the main room, minus the large television screens. Carraro sat at the head of an oval table, multiple devices in front of him and a set of headphones covering his ears. He slipped the headphones off as she approached.

"He's not dead," she said.

He gave her a wan smile. God, to have a parent who loved her as much as Carraro loved Scott...Roger had come close, but she'd never seen her stepfather this distraught. Not until it was too late. "I know, but he's not conscious either."

"You said he could be outside of Pathia's range."

Carraro motioned for her to take the empty seat next him. "To get so far outside her range so quickly, Miranda would have to have transferred him to a supersonic craft. She doesn't have access to one. We'd know it if she did."

"Or she has an Alt who could fly." Her hopes were getting ahead of her. "We don't know what she's doing to the Alts on the list."

"If she even has them."

"Right, but if she does and one of them flies, maybe all she's done is bribe them to work for her."

"It's a possibility," Carraro agreed.

He didn't believe her any more than she believed herself. Scott wasn't dead, but he wasn't out of range either. At least they had a range to work with, which gave her some small comfort.

She glanced around at the bustling activity. The smaller conference room was brighter and louder than the Arena, with computer stations in each corner and technicians in blue polo shirts running information across multiple screens. The Blackwoods sat themselves at the table with her and Carraro, Evan choosing the seat to her left. This time the screen embedded in front of her lit up and information scrolled. Hannah recognized the names of the missing Alts. The noise from the computer stations dimmed as one by one, the techs joined them at the table — two men and two women.

247

"What reports do we have from Star Haven? Carlos?" Carraro asked.

The tech sat on the other side of Evan. She guessed that the blue shirts indicated some sort of advanced team. She could hope, anyway. "There have been no public reports of Scott Grey's arrest. None of the police precincts are showing signs of increased activity or preparation for his arrival."

Carraro nodded. "Sylvia?"

"No flight plan was filed for the helicopter. It could be going anywhere. We tried to track it, but once it reached the Lazy Eight Islands, we lost it."

"Could it have landed there?" Alek asked, across from her.

The other female tech chimed in. "I called the University and they put me in touch with their Island Conservation program director. She's going to contact a small team of faculty and students out on the islands to see if they saw the copter. She promised a call back within the hour."

Which meant more waiting.

"Shinzo?" Carraro asked the tech at the opposite end of the table.

"I found a possible discrepancy in the warrant for Grey's arrest. The judge who supposedly signed it has been in the hospital for the past two days with pneumonia. Whatever paperwork Dane showed the TC police, it could have been forged."

"The Thunder City police were so eager to see him in jail, they didn't bother to check." Hannah's bitterness didn't help, but it was all she had to contribute.

"Thunder City has had collegial relations with Star Haven regarding the extradition of Norms who've committed crimes in one city and fled to the other," the

248

Captain said, from her seat to the left of Shinzo. "With the mayor of Star Haven standing there, I'm sure our commissioner had no reason to think the paperwork was faked."

How could the Captain sound so calm? Had Scott been right? Did the Captain...Catherine...really care more about Thunder City than she did her own son?

Carraro cleared his throat to bring attention back to him. "As soon as you get confirmation of a forged document, contact our legal representatives. We can use this as leverage to get permission to cross the Bay and search for Grey."

"I think it's safe to say at this point that Grey isn't under arrest, but he is a hostage," the Captain continued. "He's unconscious, so none of our telepaths can track him, and Dane may keep him under until she needs him or decides to...dispose of him."

Was that a small break in the Captain's perfect decorum? It wasn't enough. It would never be enough.

Carraro continued. "We need a plan to locate this prison. Yes, Shinzo?"

"I'm checking for bids on construction contracts. See who's working without one. No contract might indicate under the table payments."

"Good thought. What else? Hansa?"

"If Dane has a project this big anywhere in Star Haven, even if it's underground, it could require or cause a change in traffic patterns. I can compare patterns over the past five years across the major expressway exits and roadways and see if there are spikes. Perhaps even roadblocks to prevent civilians from seeing something they shouldn't."

"Get it done. What else?"

Hannah didn't want to hear *what else*. "What are you doing?" The room hushed. Everyone stared at her. "Traffic patterns? Construction bids? Miranda would have thought of all of this. Just like she thought of how to get the material into Star Haven in the first place. Why do you think she bothered to marry Roger Dane? She didn't love him. He had an import business she needed. Not even Hack-Man could figure out who altered the records. This isn't how we're going to find Scott."

Evan leaned back so she could see every face around the table, including the Captain's. "If you want to find Scott before Miranda becomes desperate enough to hurt him, then you have to set up an exchange. Him for me."

The Captain was already shaking her head before Hannah finished the sentence. "We can't give you to her. Even if I thought she would let Scott go, which is doubtful, what would she do to you in retaliation?"

"Nothing she hasn't done before," Hannah insisted.

"You think so? I don't." The Captain stood. Oh, fuck, now Hannah understood why they called her The Captain. With all of her intimidation aimed at Hannah, Hannah wanted to crawl under the table and beg forgiveness. "You can't heal your own body. You said so yourself. You don't know how many bones she'll break to compel your compliance with her scheme — which, by the way, is still theoretical. If you return to her custody, I can't guarantee we can get you out alive."

Hannah dug deep to find her courage, a small pocket nurtured by Roger, untouched my Miranda. Somehow she kept her voice from quivering. "I found my way out once, with no help from the Thunder City Alts. I can do it again."

"You don't know if you can."

"You don't know that I can't." Her anger ran past her courage, hot as hell. "We both know Miranda will kill Scott if I don't offer to replace him. She won't let him go, because whatever she's up to, she's trying to hide it from you, and right now he's a magnet for Alts who want him back in Thunder City."

Out of the blue, it all made sense. The whole scheme laid out in plain sight. "Her plan, whatever the end result is, has to remain hidden from Alts. Why else would she champion a ban that rids Star Haven of all Alts, but keep her daughter behind? She can't have Alts, any Alt, figuring out what she's up to. How could she accomplish this with telepaths reading her mind? Or aerialists flying over her construction site? There's no one left in Star Haven to interfere. The Star Haven Norms are so damn happy we're gone, they'll never question anything Miranda does, including flying off to Thunder City in a police helicopter with a fake warrant."

She rode the crest of her argument to stare down Captain Spectacular, her hero. "Give me a phone. Let me make the deal. Have Pathia track me as far as she can — she has my permission. It can't be illegal if she has permission, right?"

She looked at Carraro, who nodded. He glanced at his wife. It had to be hell, having to choose a side, knowing both the Captain and Hannah were right. No matter what they decided, Scott could die.

She had more to say. "If I can, I'll try to get a message to you from wherever Miranda takes me. If she lets Scott go, you can pick him up and leave. Don't interfere, and when I escape again, you're the ones I'll run to."

No one spoke or tried to make eye contact with her.

"You'll need back-up," Captain Spectacular said, after a long minute. She scrubbed her face, her weariness finally showing. "I can't send an untrained Alt into a situation like this without it."

Did the Captain just concede? Had she won? Beaten back the Captain's objections? "I'll give you an hour to figure out how to make this work. After that, I'm making the call."

She might have won, but it would be a pyrrhic victory if Miranda killed Scott anyway. Stars danced before her eyes. Evan grabbed her arm and tried to guide her to sit again.

"No." She pulled her arm away and dashed for the door. "I need to be alone."

***

Scott woke to a splitting headache and fluorescent lights. He tried to reach up to rub the back of his skull, but his right arm jerked to a stop with a handcuff tight around his wrist. The same type of cuff locked around his left arm. *Shit.* He'd been coldcocked by one of Dane's mercs not two minutes after the helicopter lifted off. At least he hoped they were mercs and not cops. He hadn't recognized them from his own precinct, but he'd hate to think any Star Haven cop would do something like this to a fellow officer. Juan sure as hell wouldn't.

A quick glance around showed him what looked like a hospital room, not so different from the one

Hannah had been in yesterday, but much smaller. The gurney Dane had him chained to took up much of the space. No, not a hospital gurney. There were no sheets or a pillow. She had him chained to a table. A small sink and cabinet occupied the corner opposite the door.

He lay his head back down and thought of Hannah. Evan had sworn on his life he'd let no one harm her. Scott closed his eyes and made a vow. He'd forgive Evan if his brother kept his promise. He'd even forgive Catherine, too if he ever got the chance. For Thomas, he'd make the effort to reconcile with his family, if only they could keep Hannah from harm.

He raised his head again to look around. Dane must have figured she'd throw the telepaths off his scent if she knocked him out. It wouldn't stop T-CASS from tracking her, but she had no doubt counted on T-CASS obeying the law, the Neuts Thomas employed not getting paid in time, and any Chaos Alts on T-CASS's radar not willing to cooperate for any price.

She'd risked everything to get him out of Thunder City, so the stakes had to be high enough to make the danger worth it. What the hell could Dane be up to? How did it involve Hannah? And where the fuck was he?

He tilted his head back, grimaced at the throbbing pain, and saw the camera in the corner of the room. Even if he could translocate a paperclip or something to pick the lock, whoever watched him would notify Dane before he could free himself. Which left him flat on his back unless...

He jiggled the left handcuff. Would his Alt ability work on cuffs already locked around his wrist? He was right handed, but when he'd called the lighter it had wound up in his left hand. Everything except the gun had landed in his left hand. How would it work if he tried to remove the cuff from his left hand? Would it land in his right hand, which would make the translocation obvious to whoever watched him? Or would it remain in his left hand and much less obvious? How long would it take to remove both?

No wonder his mother was such a stickler for training. A T-CASS Alt would know exactly what they could do with their ability in a situation like this. There would be no questions, no hesitation, just action.

The door's locks — there must have been at least six of them — clicked open one by one, and Dane entered. She stood over him, arms crossed, her lips puckered.

"I'm disappointed, Officer Grey."

If his head hadn't hurt so much, he'd have thought of a much wittier comeback than, "I'm sorry."

His apology failed to appease her. "Your Alt friends were supposed to at least try to rescue you."

Had Dane's mystery hacker cracked Thomas's cover? "I don't have any Alt friends."

"Then tell me where my daughter is." She slammed her hand next to his head, making his ears ring. "You didn't just drop her off on a street corner somewhere. If your parents are still protecting her, I will find them."

At least she didn't know his real identity. "I'm not trying to be difficult, Mayor Dane. Really, I'm not, but your daughter is an adult. She has the right not to return to Star Haven. And honestly, I don't know where she is. She's not with my parents. They're on vacation."

"Where?"

"You think I'm going to tell you? Chained like an animal? Am I even under arrest? For real?"

Dane paced. Just like Catherine would have. He doubted either of them would appreciate his observation.

"Even if your parents don't have her, you wouldn't have just left the girl on a street corner somewhere."

"Of course I wouldn't." He'd stick to the big, dumb Boy Scout routine. "I gave her specific instructions on how to find a shelter. There are at least a dozen of them all over the city. She was supposed to call one of them. I don't know which one."

"A homeless shelter."

"Yes."

"You told my daughter to call a homeless shelter."

Her outrage was almost funny. "Where else was she supposed to go? Any of the shelters would take care of her. She'd get the help she needs. Food, clothes, maybe even some counseling. She might come back to you, ma'am, if you give her some time and space."

She leaned over him, her face twisted, ugly. "I do not have time to wait for that brat to return."

Scott pushed his head as far away as he could, which was not as far as he'd like.

"She wouldn't have wasted time on a homeless shelter," Dane said. "She would have run to the first Alt she could find. The Alts have her."

"Okay," he agreed, because what else could he do?

"And I have you."

"Which means, what?" he asked.

"It means you had better hope the T-CASS telepaths are paying attention. You had also better hope my daughter is very grateful for your assistance, because I'm going to hurt you until she crawls out of whatever hole you dug her into and gets her ass back to Star

Haven. And you'd better pray that happens before dawn."

She yanked open the door and stepped outside. "Deal with him."

Scott recognized the scar-faced thug from the Left Fists who replaced Dane in the doorway. His shit-eating grin told Scott just how badly this was going to hurt.

CHAPTER NINETEEN

Hannah opened the conference room door, her hands cold and her knees like jelly. She'd spent her hour on the roof of the Arena where she could be alone with her thoughts, her fears.

Three days ago, she'd never thought she would ever get out of Star Haven. Then Scott Grey dropped out of the sky and rocked her world. Not only did he get her out of Star Haven, he gave her a family, his family. She cared about the Blackwoods, and damn it, she cared about Scott despite his history. So much so she'd chuck the Blackwood family and all of the security they offered, in order to return to the devil's trap of Star Haven and get him back.

Damn Miranda. Damn her to hell.

The techs had returned to their stations, their computer screens flashing information faster than she could follow. Carraro stood away from the table talking on his phone. Captain Spec and her sons huddled around a holographic map of Star Haven hovering over one of the table's imbedded tablets. There was no sign that they'd developed a plan beyond finding the prison. She'd given them an hour and they still had five more minutes before she made the call. A lot could change in five minutes.

Evan motioned her over to his side. On the map, a red block shaped like the prison maneuvered into position.

"No luck." Alek pushed his chair back. "They would have had to knock down half the Swamp to get it to fit. Plus it's too close to the Bay. They'd risk flooding."

"It was a long shot. Try again. One district over," the Captain said.

Alek used his finger to maneuver the prison to another portion of map and enlarge it. Hannah sat down and watched the red block shift locations. Alek rotated the prison on its axis, attempting a different angle, trying to find an area where it would fit and still be out of sight of the population.

"Thank you, Gavin. We'll give it a shot. It's the best news I've heard in several days." Carraro closed his phone. "We have a lead. One of Gavin's — Blockhead's — trainees used to work as an operator at the water treatment plant west of the city. He mentioned a detour set up almost three years ago across the only road leading to the facility. It services the Northern Star and Havenside districts."

Without being asked, Alek shut down the red prison image and readjusted the map. A few clicks later, the water treatment plant came into view.

"When they increased the treatment plant's capacity, the project paid for a secondary road to detour away from the main road. This secondary road swerved far to the north before doubling back. The roadblocks on the main road have remained up even though the project has been completed," Carraro said, moving around the table to get a better view.

A satellite image of the roadblock — cement barriers wrapped with barbed wire — came into view.

"What else is out there?" Nik asked.

"I don't know," Carraro said. "You tell me."

Alek scrolled the image back from the barriers. One of the techs — Shinzo — wandered away from his station to look over his boss's shoulder.

"The road leads to an abandoned resort in the foothills about an hour from the water plant." Alek pulled up an image of the resort's remnants. "That far from the city, no one would notice any construction. I suppose the guest lodge could serve as a bunker for security guards, with a kitchen and showers already in place."

"How old is the resort image?"

Alek checked. "Last December, but the resort went bankrupt five years ago."

"It's too flimsy," Carraro said. "They would have had to carve into the surrounding geography to install the prison. Keep looking in this general area."

Roar panned down from the lodge.

"Wait. I saw something. Southwest of the lodge," Nik said.

Alek adjusted the image again. "Looks like a crop circle."

"It's a quarry," Evan said.

"I had forgotten about the quarry." Captain Spec leaned forward. "Nothing has come out of there in three decades."

"It's a huge area." Alek sharpened the view. "Far enough from the city. No one would notice any construction unless they stood right on top of it."

"There isn't even a paved road anymore," Nik said. "Just a dirt trail, which intersects with..."

"The main road," Alek interrupted. "Right where the barriers stand."

"Zoom in on the dirt road." Captain Spec hovered over her son.

Alek did as she asked.

"Those grooves in the trail are track links, not tires."

Alek pulled up the red block of the prison. He overlaid the image onto the quarry. "It would work. All they would have had to do besides the construction is run a water line out there. With enough generators, they could have themselves a hidden prison within the quarry."

Carraro's phone buzzed again. Hannah circled around to take his place along with everyone else in the room. A quarry so far outside of Star Haven sounded perfect for a hidden prison. Had they finally gotten a break?

"Pull out!" Carraro violently twisted around, almost knocking over Shinzo. "Break your connection. You're done. Don't do anything more. We'll find him."

Something had happened to Scott.

"Pathia," Carraro said, as he sank back into a chair, his face tight with anguish. "She re-established a link with Scott. He's awake, but..." He stopped and closed his eyes.

Captain Spec approached her husband and put her arms around him as she knelt by his side. "Miranda's hurting him?" she asked.

Carraro nodded, but didn't, or couldn't, speak. He pressed his forehead to his wife's cheek. They held each other close.

Hannah had no one to share her pain with, so she turned to Evan. "Get me a phone. Any phone. Let me make the call."

Evan shook his head. "Hannah, you can't."

"I can. It's my decision to make. Miranda will smack me around, nothing more. She needs me alive and mostly unharmed. I can handle it. I'll find another way out."

She kept her eye-lock on Evan firm. She had to make him believe her, believe she could handle Miranda. A cold assurance coated her fear, covering her uncertainty. *Believe me, Evan, I need you to believe in me.*

The soft sound of Shinzo clearing his throat caught her off guard. "She doesn't have to go alone."

Nik rolled down the sleeves of his uniform, getting ready for...something. A fight? To spy? No. Captain Spec stayed next to her husband, her arms still around him. Nik wouldn't dare cross the Bay without permission. Of all the Blackwoods, Nik seemed the least likely to break the rules or the laws. "We appreciate your offer, Shinzo, but even sending Norms would be too high risk."

The tech shook his head with a small, embarrassed smile. "I'm not offering, not that I wouldn't if I were an Alt. What I mean is the quarry, if it does turn out to be Dane's secret prison, is deep in unincorporated territory. It's not covered under the Alt-ban. I've read the text of the law and it's quite specific. It only bans Alts from occupying territory within the city limits. The quarry hasn't been incorporated since it shut down. It's in no man's land. Either Dane knows this and selected the site to cover her own ass if she was discovered hiding Alts out there, or..."

"Or she fucked up the ban," Nik said.

Shinzo nodded. "Yeah. She fucked up the ban, or rather the City Council did, by not using language to expand the law's reach beyond the edge of Star Haven proper."

A vicious hint of pleasure spiked through Hannah. So, Miranda wasn't perfect after all. One slight imperfection could crack Miranda's plans wide open. They just needed to get Hannah inside. She'd find a way to break Miranda's stranglehold over Star Haven. She had to, for Scott's sake.

Carraro pulled out of the Captain's arms. "There's no guarantee Miranda is holding Scott at the quarry."

"There's no guarantee the quarry is anything other than what it appears to be — an abandoned pile of rocks," Shinzo countered. "At least now you can find out. Legally."

Carraro looked at his wife.

"I'll take a look," she said.

"No." Hannah stood, the rush of emotion giving her raw power, courage she never thought she'd possess. "Not until after I make the call. Regardless of where Scott is, Miranda is torturing him. I want it stopped. I make the call and negotiate from there. If we can make an exchange and get Scott back, then Miranda will bring me to the quarry or wherever she's hiding the other Alts. You can track me and stop her once and for all."

Everyone looked to the Captain. With obvious reluctance, she nodded. Hannah had to believe the Captain loved her son, and wanted the torture stopped more than she wanted to protect Thunder City, more than she wanted to protect Hannah. Another crack appeared in another seemingly impenetrable wall.

Evan handed Hannah his phone. "Dane can't trace it."

It didn't matter to Hannah one way or the other. She turned her back so she couldn't see everyone in the room staring at her. No one tried to stop her. She dialed the familiar number.

"Where are you?"

Miranda's voice speared her soul like an ice pick. Hannah almost lost what courage she'd gained, but she thought of Scott and found her voice. "Doesn't matter. Stop hurting Officer Grey."

"So they are monitoring me with their telepaths. That's a gross violation of every Alt law here and in Thunder City. I'll have the telepath extradited for this. Whichever one it is will be buried alive in Star Haven."

Miranda didn't deny that she had a hand in Scott's torture, but she didn't admit it either. "The telepath is monitoring Officer Grey. Not you. She only knows what you're doing to him. You have to stop."

Her mother snickered. "You tell whoever is protecting you that I won't release Grey from custody until you are back where you belong."

She'd release him, but not stop torturing him, and still no admission of guilt. "I'll do whatever you want, but you have to stop hurting Officer Grey right now and you have to release him."

"You're in no position to dictate to me, you little bitch. Tell me where you are."

Hannah bit her tongue against lashing out. "I'll meet you at the marina. Bring Scott, alive. I'll want time to heal him. If you agree to this, I'll do whatever you want. I won't fight you. I won't try to escape. I won't cause you any trouble."

"And if I don't agree?"

Despite her terror, Hannah held fast. "I'll cause you more trouble than you can afford, Miranda. You need me or you wouldn't be so desperate to get me back. You need me alive and unharmed and willing to cooperate. Betray me in this exchange and I'll find a way to destroy you. You know I will."

Seven seconds of silence never felt so long. "Five minutes. I'll give you Grey and you'll have exactly five minutes to heal him. Not a second more."

An admission of sorts, but at this point it didn't matter. "Fine. Five minutes. I'll be at the marina in two hours. If I find out you're still hurting him..."

The line went dead.

"You have two hours to get me to the Star Haven marina. Miranda will bring Scott, alive. I'll have five minutes to heal him, then I leave with her peacefully," Hannah said to Catherine.

"We'll be waiting for you at the quarry," the Captain said.

Where Miranda would be ready for them.

***

"Couldn't sleep?" Carraro asked Hannah as she joined him.

He'd suggested she try to rest, but after a half an hour of tossing and turning in the *Elusive Lady's* guest room, she'd grabbed a bottle of water and headed back up to the deck. She shook her head as she twisted off the cap and took a swig.

"Neither could I," he said.

They remained quiet together. Roger had never been this quiet unless Miranda was around. If he'd been here, he would have peppered her with all sort of interesting stories about Mystic Bay and his childhood spent boating along the coast with his own father and grandfather. For the first time, Hannah could think of him without overwhelming grief.

"He'll be okay," Carraro said, though she wasn't sure if he spoke to her or to himself. "So long as Miranda doesn't kill him, he'll get through this. My son has the heart of a lion."

Hannah took another sip of water. "I hardly know him. He didn't have to bring me out of Star Haven. He could have turned me over to Miranda, looked the other way, and pretended I was just another runaway. She would have rewarded him, given him another medal, maybe even recruited him into her scheme." That thought gave her a shiver. "He took good care of me. In his apartment, he kept asking me over and over, 'What do you need, tell what you need, Hannah'."

Carraro smiled. "Loyalty and dedication are two strong Blackwood traits. A Blackwood will stay by your side through thick and thin."

"Unless they feel betrayed." Did she really want to poke around Scott's past? "Evan betrayed Scott and so did Catherine. I know Evan's apologized, but it took quite some time to get there."

"Betraying a Blackwood is almost as bad as killing one." Carraro faced her. "It's harder to forgive a family member than it is an outsider. Perhaps because blood is thicker than water, it hurts more when a Blackwood bleeds from wounds inflicted by one of their own. I've hurt both my wife and my son at various times, but they forgave me a lot faster than they could forgive each other."

"But you're one of them," she said. "Scott loves you as if you were blood."

Carraro closed his eyes. "Some days I wonder why. I never intended to become a father. I didn't have the interest or the temperament. I took Scott into my home with the intention of using him to attract his mother. Who would have thought her son would win me over all on his own. In doing so, he made me a better man, one worthy of Catherine."

"I'm so glad Scott found you," she said.

"No, no, I found him." Carraro wagged a finger, a small smile cracking his frown. "Don't let him try to tell you otherwise. It wasn't long after I agreed to mentor him that he decided he was good enough to be my son. The adoption was incidental to the bond we'd already formed."

She wanted to weep for Carraro and Scott, but she'd already shed too many tears. "You're a good man, Mr. Carraro."

"Thomas." He corrected her. "And you're an extraordinary woman, Hannah. I'm so glad my son found you."

"I don't know. I'm not feeling extraordinary at the moment."

"How do you feel?" he asked. He sounded concerned, and honest, and so much like Roger her heart broke all over again.

"Angry," she said after a moment. "And scared, but mostly I'm angry. How did it get this far? I always knew Miranda was ambitious, but how did she get to the point where she'd torture someone to get what she wants? Maybe I didn't pay close enough attention. Once I hit middle school, I did everything I could to stay out of her way, while still doing whatever she asked of me. Do this, not that. Stay here, not there. Play with this friend, not that one. Stop listening to that awful music. No, you can't go to the movies, no, you can't go the dance, no, you can't have a computer, no, you can't date, interrupt me again and I'll show you what pain is all about." The dam broke and she spilled her heartache in uncontrolled gasps. "It never stopped. She never stopped."

She took a deep breath to get herself back under control. If she poured all of her agony out now, would it leave her alone once Miranda had her? "Her husband's weren't much better. When she married Roger, he was a godsend. I never realized just how abnormal Miranda was until he paid attention to me. Me as a daughter, not a competitor for Miranda's attention...just me and him on the couch, rooting for the Sabers, or sailing around the Bay, or just eating dinner together."

Thomas offered her handkerchief to wipe her eyes. Miranda didn't need to see her tears.

A shadow blocked the sun.

"Fifteen minutes," Blockhead said, before he left them alone again.

Her stomach contracted as she wiped her eyes one last time. She and Thomas and Blockhead had discussed various scenarios and how to handle them if Miranda attempted to renege on her promise to let Hannah heal Scott. Doctor Rao also waited below deck in case things went wrong.

The marina appeared on the horizon.

"You can still change your mind. If you don't want to go through with this, no one would blame you," Thomas said.

How kind of him to say so. "No. I started this, I'll finish it."

He opened his arms and she stepped into his hug. "I'll be right beside you."

She nodded, taking the comfort he offered, then pulled back. "I'm ready."

Time sped up as the marina came into view. Blockhead returned to their side of the boat with binoculars. "It looks like she cleared out the entire place. There's police tape across the security gate on both the north and south ends. All the berths are empty."

"Do you see Scott?" she asked.

"No...wait...yeah. I see him."

He sounded resigned, not hopeful.

"What? What's wrong?" Hannah demanded.

Blockhead lowered the binoculars. "He's on the ground. It doesn't look good."

"I can fix him." For her, five minutes was a lifetime.

Thomas put his arm around her shoulders. Blockhead retreated below the deck to keep himself hidden as the pilot guided the yacht into the nearest berth. Thomas kept his arm around her after the plank extended, and they walked off the boat together.

At the far end of the marina, five of Miranda's thugs waited for them, dressed as cops and armed with semi-automatic weapons they didn't even try to conceal. At their feet lay Scott, bare-chested and still. Even from this distance, she could see the blood covering his face, his chest.

"They probably broke bones," she said to Thomas, choking on her words. "Get your belt between his teeth. If he's conscious, this is going to hurt. Three chest compressions at the four minute thirty second mark, so I'll know when to get out."

As soon as they reached the group, one of the thugs snarled, "Five minutes. Not a second more. Starting now."

Hannah dropped to her knees and slapped her hand over Scott's heart. Inside. First, his ribs. Most of them had fractures that needed repair, but she only stitched the actual breaks. If she had time later, she'd come back and take care of the rest.

Next, his left kneecap had shattered and needed a complete overhaul. His right ankle was also swollen. Scott's body jerked as she moved the bones into place, which only made her work faster. Done and done.

She surfed up to his face. His broken jaw and nose took priority over his blackened eyes. A few loose teeth took precious time away from other repairs, but she handled those as fast as she could.

She managed to reconnect the retina, clean up the hemorrhage, and seal the blood vessels of his right eye, before three waves knocked her off course. No, not yet. She muttered every curse she'd ever learned as she took a look at the other eye. Swollen, but not as bad the first. She sealed as many vessels as she dared before she returned to her own body.

"I took care of the worst of it," she said, panting. Thomas's hands cradled Scott's head. "He'll be okay."

Even as she made her report, Scott moaned and twisted on the ground. "Hannah?"

He reached for her, but before she could grab his hand, one of the thugs yanked her off the ground.

"Hannah?" Scott coughed, his voice too hoarse. She'd seen his vocal cords, red and raw. "Where are you? I can't see you?"

Thomas bent over his son to whisper in his ear.

The thugs shoved her toward the exit gate. She didn't fight, as she'd promised. Miranda didn't need more ammunition to use against her.

"Nooooooo!"

Thomas must have told Scott what she'd done. She heard nothing more before she climbed into the back of a van. Scott would live. Even if she accomplished nothing else, he would live.

CHAPTER TWENTY

"Where is she?" Scott reached for Hannah, but only grasped air.

"She's not here. Can you stand?"

Thomas. Thomas was here. Strong hands held his head in place. He couldn't remember anything but pain.

"I heard her. Hannah was here." His throat stung. He tried to open his eyes, but one refused to open, and the other couldn't see past the sunlight. "You have to get her out of here, Thomas. Get her out."

"I promise you, we'll get her out, but we cannot stay here, Scott. Can you stand?"

Yes, damn it, he could stand. He rolled onto his stomach and pushed himself to his knees. A pair of hands slipped under his arms, steadying him. "Where am I?"

"The marina," Thomas said.

How did he get to the marina? He remembered fists pummeling him, his shirt ripped right off. His knee, the same one he leaned on, broken so Dane's men could hear him scream. They must have brought him here after he passed out.

"I've got you. Just a little bit further."

Scott pushed himself to stand. Thomas held him close, pulled Scott's left arm over firm shoulders. They took a couple of steps together, uncoordinated, until Scott found his own rhythm and Thomas matched him. His leg didn't hurt as much as it should have.

Hannah. She had healed him. Who else could do it as fast as she could? "Where is she?"

"Keep walking, Scott. I promise, I'll answer your questions, just keep moving."

Scott listened to Thomas. Thomas had never led him wrong. Thomas pushed him up the plank to the *Elusive Lady*. Even half blind, he'd know Thomas's second home anywhere. A shadow rose in front of them. Instinct overshot logic and Scott took a wild swing.

"Scott, no." His father held him back, arms wrapped around his chest. "It's okay. It's Blockhead. He's not going to hurt you. He's with me."

Out of his one good eye, Scott saw Blockhead back off, hands — blocks — raised.

"I'm going to let you go, Scott, but you have to promise me you won't try to hit anyone."

Scott looked around. Blockhead moved farther away. Near the door leading below the deck, Doctor Rao stood watching. Why was the doctor here? Was Hannah hurt?

"Promise me, Scott. I'll let you go, if you promise not to hit anyone."

Two more of Thomas's crew stepped into view, tense, ready to pounce to protect their employer, but out of range for the moment. What were they waiting for? Oh, the plank. The *Lady* had to leave the marina. Blockhead was an Alt. He'd get arrested in Star Haven. Nothing about this made sense.

"Thomas?"

"Yes, son."

"Where am I?"

"You're at the marina."

"I know, but how did I get here?"

"Miranda Dane's men brought you here so I could take you home."

Miranda Dane. Hannah's mother. "Where's Hannah?"

"She's not here."

"Where is she?"

"You need help, son. You've been badly beaten. Doctor Rao here needs to examine you."

"Hannah healed me. I heard her."

"Yes, she partially healed you, but there's still a lot of damage we need to fix."

"I want Hannah."

"I understand. You'll see her again, Scott. Please come with me."

Scott moved slowly, like an old man. His head spun, and the dizziness made it hard to think. "Why isn't Hannah here?"

"She had to go away for a little while, but she'll come back soon. C'mon, son. Stay with me."

He trusted Thomas, so he followed him toward Doctor Rao.

"Hello, Scott."

"Doctor."

They went downstairs and through the galley and the salon to the guest bedroom. Thomas kept his arms secured around Scott.

"Lie down right here and let's get you fixed up right."

He did as Thomas asked. He could smell the faint scent of Hannah. Something cold and wet touched his arm. "What are you doing?"

"Shhhhh. It's okay. Just relax." Thomas pushed him back onto the pillow.

A needle pricked his skin. "No!"

Thomas pressed him to the bed. "You promised me, no fighting."

Already his one good eye was closing against his will. "Where's Hann..." He couldn't finish the sentence before he lost his voice. The world turned black.

***

Hannah woke to pitch black and perfect silence. The last thing she remembered was the van's engine, loud inside the hood the thugs had jammed over her head. What else? Oh, yeah, the sharp sting of a needle in her shoulder. They'd knocked her out with drugs. She couldn't feel the scratchy fabric of the hood anymore, so they must have removed it. It was so cold, she almost wished she had the hood back to keep warm.

She'd been right. The freezers smuggled in through Roger's business were used to keep Alts under control. Just trying to remember how she got here took far more effort than it should.

Damn her promise to Miranda. When her mother let her out of here, and eventually she would have to, Hannah would keep her promise to not cause trouble — until she figured a way out. After that, all bets were off.

Since she couldn't see anything anyway, she tucked her head down to her knees to keep her nose warm. It worked until the door opened. The sudden burst of light blinded her.

"Get up."

Miranda. Hannah rolled onto her knees.

"I said, get the hell up." Miranda grabbed her by the hair and pulled. She was tired of being manhandled like a rag doll. Miranda pushed her toward the door. "Six goddamned months of my life you've wasted. I don't have any more time to spare for you. Move it."

Hannah tried to walk toward the open door, but missed by about two inches and hit the doorframe. Miranda yanked her back and pushed her through the opening. One of the four large guards dressed in black caught her in his gloved hands before she fell. The other three had their guns ready.

Miranda didn't wait for her to get her bearings.

"Turn her around."

The guard did as she asked, forcing Hannah to face Miranda. The freezer was warmer than Miranda at that moment. With her reflexes so slow, Hannah couldn't avoid the back of Miranda's fist when it slammed into her cheek. She would have fallen back to the floor except the guard dug his fingers into her arms to keep her upright. The second Hannah turned to face forward again, Miranda slugged her other cheek even harder.

Blood dribbled down her chin. Lesson learned. There was more where that came from.

Miranda turned and walked away. The guard shoved Hannah to follow. The forced movement and warmer air made her toes and fingers tingle. The guards stayed on her heels, pushing her along when she slowed.

Hannah tried to keep up with the stream of curses and threats Miranda spewed, but it became repetitive. Six months ago such a tirade would have had her knees knocking together while she cowered in a corner until it stopped. Now it just goaded her inner rebel. She'd stop Miranda, no matter the cost to herself.

The walls of the complex didn't change as Miranda turned a corner into another corridor. The same dull gray sheet metal reached about ten feet from floor to ceiling and the florescent lights shone through metal cages. She hoped the Blackwoods had been right and Miranda had set up her operation in the quarry.

Miranda was still bitching her out a mile a minute even as she turned another corner and stopped in her tracks. Hannah almost collided with her. A palm pad similar to the one she'd used at the Arena extended. The door clicked with Miranda's identification and swung open.

Miranda pushed Hannah through. Inside, three tables stood side by side. Each one had a person lying on the table, hooked to an IV. Even from the doorway Hannah could see the shackles.

"You know what to do. Get to work."

"I'll need water." The words stuttered so badly through frozen lips she wasn't sure Miranda had heard her.

"What?"

Hannah paused to breathe deep to clear the stars from her eyes. "I need water. I get sick after I heal because I'm dehydrated. We thought it was exhaustion, but it's not. It's dehydration. Keep me hydrated, I'll be able to heal more people faster."

Miranda's silence was almost as frightening as her rages. She turned to one of the guards. "Get her a box of water from storage."

"Yes, ma'am."

The guard left. Miranda slammed the door closed behind them and set the locks. The other guard pointed

276

his gun at her, but Hannah ignored him. She approached the nearest patient.

She recognized the man who lay there, one of the Alts her mother had made her heal before. He was also one of the names on the Captain's list. His gray hair was mussed, with a stain of blood running from his left nostril to the corner of his open mouth.

He wheezed with each breath he took. His loose-skinned arms overhung the sides of the table. His eyes were open, but they didn't track her as she gently pulled down the thin blanket.

She expected to find mottled bruises in various shades of blue and purple, but instead she saw only one large bruise covering most of his chest. She replaced the blanket and pulled up the end that covered his feet. The right foot was encased in a surgical boot.

For all of her knowledge of human anatomy, she wasn't a doctor, much less a diagnostician. She didn't need to know what was wrong with a patient before she healed him or her. In this case, she guessed this man hadn't been given the same treatment as Scott, but that didn't make his pain any less significant. No one had repeatedly hit him; instead, he had received one massive blow to the chest, which might have sent him tripping backwards and caused him to break his foot.

She had a hand in this, his anguish. Miranda had made her heal him more than once, then had sent him right back into a nightmare of endless pain. Beatings, experimentation, and it never ended. Not for these prisoners. She had to put a stop it. She had to make up for her role, but how? If she refused, what would Miranda do? Torture them more until Hannah caved? And she would cave. She'd returned to Miranda because she couldn't stand the thought of what her mother was doing to Scott.

She covered her distress by checking the IV. The label meant nothing to her, but she hoped it contained a painkiller or sedative. If not, this was going to get messy. Her heart heavy, she placed her hand on the man's chest and surfed.

He needed a lot of work, most of it associated with the natural aging process, but Hannah stuck to just his chest wound and his foot. She wanted to finish the other two patients before Miranda returned. Before she emerged, though, she decided to make a quick trip through his brain. The microscopic thread that fed his powers lay across the midline.

She couldn't have been inside more than a minute or two, but when she emerged she found the second guard had returned with the box of water in hand.

"May I?" Hannah pointed to the box.

The guard dropped it on the floor and left. The guard who remained backed up to the door. The gun he'd slung around his back shifted forward in his arms. He cradled it like a baby as she approached the box. He watched her, tense, unblinking. She wondered if they had participated in Scott's torture.

"You've never seen an Alt use their powers up close before, have you?" she asked, while she twisted off a bottle cap.

His fingers tightened around the gun's grip and butt. "Seen your kind plenty of times."

"Incapacitated, like them?" She indicated the injured Alts with the bottle. "Or functional, like me?"

"They functioned just fine until..."

"Until what? Give me a clue. What's going on here?"

"I don't get paid to talk."

She'd pushed too hard too fast. "I'm not getting paid at all. At least give me something to work with so I know what to look for when I bloodsurf through those other two."

He gave her a blank look.

"My Alt ability — bloodsurfing."

His eyes narrowed. "I've heard rumors you can heal anything."

"True enough." She sipped the water, the cold soothing her split lip.

"Diseases?"

"Yes."

"Old age?"

"Of course."

"Why don't you heal yourself?"

Already her face felt twice its normal size. She took another sip of water, tainted with her own blood from the inside of her mouth. She considered a half dozen lies and half-truths. Confess the truth to the enemy? Like hell she would. He didn't need to know she couldn't heal herself. "Why would I? Miranda will just beat me again. She likes to see evidence of her power. I've stopped the pain for now. It's enough to keep me going."

"You must think you're some sort of god."

There was the sneer she'd expected. "What I think is that I'm an eighteen-year-old who thought she'd graduate from high school, get a job, fall in love, get married, and have a couple of kids. Instead, I'm a prisoner to my mother's ambitions." One long, last swig of water before she got back to work.

He stared at her and said nothing further, so she turned to the second patient. This Alt was a woman, one she hadn't healed before. She was younger than the first patient, with thinning brown hair. Her injuries looked similar to those of the first: a broken arm, a concussion, and fractured ribs.

When she had finished bloodsurfing, she drank another bottle of water. The guard still hadn't lowered his gun and she didn't want to antagonize him, so she said nothing. The third patient only had superficial wounds: a dozen or so bruises along his upper body. She was in and out in under a minute.

The guard moved even farther away when she reached for another bottle of water. "What are you so scared of? What could I possibly do to you besides clear your sinuses?"

He almost laughed this time, which was progress. It wouldn't hurt to have a sympathetic guard on her side. Maybe he wouldn't shoot her in the back if she made a run for it? Stupid thought. He worked for Miranda. Of course he'd shoot her.

At least she had no headache. In fact, she felt better than she ever had after healing someone. Her body had also warmed up enough that the tingling sensation in her toes and fingers had disappeared.

Thunder slammed through the room. The water in her mouth sloshed down her chin and windpipe. The lights flickered and snapped off. For a moment Hannah thought to make a run for it, but the lights snapped back on and the guard still blocked the door.

"What the hell was that?" she choked over the water. A split second later, a second boom shook the room and made the door squeak. The guard moved toward her and away from the door.

"Well?" she demanded. "Are we under attack?" Had Thomas gotten Scott back to Thunder City by now? Had Captain Spec ordered an attack? She had no idea how much time had passed.

The guard stood still, only a few feet from her, tense and waiting. A third boom followed. Then a fourth.

Between the booms of thunder, a soft wheeze rose from her first patient. Hannah walked over to his table. He wheezed again, trying to speak. She couldn't understand his words, though she knew there was nothing wrong with his vocal cords. It must be the drugs from the IV keeping him half sedated. A thought, devious enough to impress Miranda, came to her. Hannah sat on the edge of the table, blocking the guard's view of the patient's arm.

"Joe," he wheezed.

"Who's Joe?" she asked, while she placed her hand over the tape keeping the IV in place. With her thumb, she rolled the edge of the tape back to expose the embedded needle.

"Friend."

"Joe is your friend? Is he here?" She slipped the needle out of the vein.

"Changed."

"Changed how?" Keeping the needle on top of the vein, Hannah covered it with the tape.

"Monster."

Hannah rose from the table, trying to appear nonchalant as she tucked the man's arm under the thin sheet. "What does he mean," she asked the guard. "They changed Joe into a monster?"

Before the guard could answer, the locks to the door clicked open. Miranda entered with the second guard. "Are you done yet?"

"Yes." *No.* She wanted more time to do the same trick with the other two patients. All she could do was hope that she had made the right decision. Give this guy a chance to escape. *If* the IV was drugging him, *if* he had an Alt ability he could use to defend himself and the other patients.

"Come with me."

The first guard stepped aside, but followed close behind. Miranda kept silent this time. In the corridor, more guards rushed past them. A double boom knocked everyone into a wall and the lights flickered again.

An elevator ride brought her up one floor. Hannah waited until Miranda stepped out before following.

In front of her was a long bank of computer stations. The bank faced a thick window that stretched the length of a hockey field with a skybox view of an arena. The arena floor was black with a grid pattern of yellow stripes, and ran the length of the glass and twice the distance perpendicular to the computer stations.

Miranda demanded a status update. Ignored for the moment, Hannah stepped up behind one of the techs sitting at a station.

Another boom, closer, louder, and more powerful, shook the entire skybox. Hannah fell to her knees. The tech fell out of his chair as his ear jack went flying off his head. Hannah grabbed the jack as she stood. The arena appeared empty, so what had caused the quake?

From the bottom edge of the glass, a head rose. Huge hazel eyes that had to be bigger than a truck's tire, appeared along with shaggy brown hair falling like ropes around ears she could get lost in. Blood ran in rivulets from its forehead along the creases of its face.

The head backed up, ducked, and slammed into the wall below the glass. The whole room shook and she fell back again.

"What the hell?" she asked of no one in particular.

"I need my ear piece." The tech motioned her closer. She handed it to him. She noticed all the techs dressed the same — jeans with white dress shirts. "You can hang onto my chair," he said.

She did. "What is it?"

"An experiment run amuck."

"Experiment?"

"You're new here?"

The creature made another charge at the wall, but this time Hannah hung on.

"Uh, yeah. I'm Miranda Dane's daughter."

If he wondered about her bruises, he didn't say. "And she hasn't told you about this?" he asked, instead.

Another hit. The tech's computer screen flickered.

"We don't communicate very well."

The monster backed up again. This time Hannah noticed he was naked. He eyed the entire length of the control room before retreating to the far corner of the arena.

"Thank God," the tech said, running a hand through his dark, shaggy hair. "Getting thrown to the ground every three seconds by a mutated Alt wasn't in the job description."

Mutated Alt. The guy in the arena must be Joe. There had been a Joseph Austin on the list of missing Alts. What the hell had Miranda done to him?

Miranda returned from the other end of the room. "Pay attention. Do you see the Alt in there?"

"He's kind of hard to miss."

Her sarcasm went over Miranda's head. "His original Alt ability included enhanced strength, but not as powerful as Catherine Blackwood's. We still don't know how Alts get their powers, but we tried to increase his strength to double hers."

If Miranda had telepaths involved in this project, she could find out from Hannah where Alts got their powers. Miranda's fifth husband had once said he'd rather die than have a telepath read his mind. Hannah had scoffed because at the time she didn't believe there were any secrets worth killing yourself over. Suicide didn't seem so silly now.

"We've studied Blackwood over the years, so we know her limits. Six months ago, we introduced a mutated gene into Subject B's body. It enhanced his strength times three. Two weeks ago, we added another mutated gene, one designed to increase his strength times six."

"It has a side effect."

From her expression, Miranda didn't think much of her pointing out the obvious. "Clearly. His brain swelled along with his body. The damage destroyed his control. He's more animal now than Alt."

As if Joe could hear her, he leapt to his feet and charged the wall. Prepared this time, Hannah and Miranda grabbed the tech's chair as Joe launched off the floor to smash his head into the glass. A small crack spider-webbed the glass, but it held, and Joe slid back down to the floor. Hannah swore she heard a sob, but she couldn't tell if came from Joe or from herself.

"You need to return him to his original state. Undo the genetic mutation." Miranda tugged down her blazer where the hem had folded.

As if this day couldn't have gotten more insane. "Back to his original state? Are you kidding? I wouldn't know where to begin."

"You have four hours, so I suggest you think quickly. His heightened metabolism breaks down drugs faster than we anticipated. We can't knock him out, but we can slow him." Miranda signaled a guard. "Bring her to the entrance, but don't let her inside until we get Subject B under control."

"Wait."

Miranda stopped, her patience at an end.

Nothing Hannah could say would make this right. Nothing she could say would make it easier either. If Thomas had managed to track her, if T-CASS was on its way to rescue her, they would need to be warned about Joe. If the mutant Alt managed to escape the confines of the arena before T-CASS arrived, he could put all of Star Haven at risk. "I'll need more water."

Miranda huffed. "Get her more water."

Then her mother stormed away, snapping out orders as she returned to the elevator.

"Can you really make him normal again?" the tech asked, looking at her with open skepticism. "I mean, back to his regular Alt form?"

Hannah looked at the creature who now huddled himself in the far corner of the arena. "I have no idea."

Even as she lied, the bare bones of a plan came together. Hannah hardened her heart against her own disgust. It was a plan that would guarantee her exclusion from T-CASS. No one would trust her after this. Scott would wish he'd never rescued her, had never touched her. She'd lose him forever for not telling him the truth about her power. For not telling him what she was capable of.

285

At the end of the day, when push came to shove, she was truly her mother's daughter. And she hated herself for it.

CHAPTER TWENTY-ONE

"What time is it?" Scott forced open his one good eye. Sticky tape stretched across his skin. He could feel the low rumble of an idling engine. He was still aboard the *Elusive Lady.*

"Nearly eight."

Thomas sat next to the bed, dark circles under his eyes. When was the last time his father had actually gotten any sleep? He'd been working in the background non-stop since Scott's deployment to the Swamp. Before Scott had his life turned upside down by Hannah.

"She has her, doesn't she?" The bristles of his beard scraped against his palm as he scrubbed his face, reawakening all his sore spots, which were everywhere. "Miranda has Hannah."

"Yes, she does."

How like Thomas to sound so agreeable in a crisis. "Did you try to stop her?"

"What would you have me say?" Rumpled clothes rubbed against the fine leather upholstery. Thomas must have spent most of the day at his bedside. "I tossed a young woman to the sharks to save my son. She volunteered. I told her if she changed her mind, I would support her decision. She didn't change her mind."

Would Hannah have changed her mind even if Thomas had forbidden her to go? Knowing firsthand what Miranda was capable of, he understood just how big a sacrifice Hannah had made for him. Any doubts he might have had about her intentions shriveled to dust. She had never used her ability to manipulate him into caring about her. If she had, she would still be safe, hidden away in Thunder City. "Where's Catherine? The others?"

"We believe Miranda has built a prison of sorts in an abandoned quarry southeast of Star Haven. T-CASS has gathered near there to scout the territory. Catherine will decide what to do when we have more information."

"A quarry? The one near the resort? Why?"

He listened as Thomas told him what they suspected about Miranda's secret prison.

"If nothing else, T-CASS will have set up surveillance by now." Thomas leaned forward to grab a mug off the nightstand.

Scott knew where he needed to be. "Take me out there."

"No," Thomas answered, before Scott finished his demand.

"You have to."

"No, I don't."

"Miranda has Hannah."

"Hannah gave herself up to keep you safe. Don't undermine her efforts."

"I can get her out."

"How do you propose to...oh, no, no, no." Thomas slammed the mug back onto the nightstand, coffee sloshing over the side.

"Why not?"

"It's not safe." Thomas knelt next to the bed. Scott had never seen his father look so frantic.

"Neither is leaving her with Miranda," he argued.

"You have no training."

"Neither does Hannah." Scott pushed his elbows to sit up.

"Hannah at least has the benefit of having been an Alt since she was born." For a moment, he thought Thomas would grab his shoulders to force him to remain in bed.

Scott flinched in anticipation, his muscles remembering the restraints Scar had used. Thomas saw his reaction and shifted so he only leaned on the mattress. "She knows what she's capable of. You've only had your Alt powers for three days. You don't know what will happen to her if you try to translocate her out of the quarry. What happens if you leave a piece of her behind, like her heart or her intestines?"

"I could be her last chance." *Her only chance.*

"Or you could put her in more danger. What if it doesn't work? What if she gets stuck inside a rock? What if she bounces back to where she started? What will happen then? You'll have killed her and exposed T-CASS to Miranda."

"I won't kill her," Scott said, but doubts started to creep into his logic. "They'll fight it out. It's not as if T-CASS has never handled a raid before. All the Chaos Alts sitting in Rocklin Prison are there because T-CASS put them there."

Thomas grabbed his mug again and sat back in his chair. "Don't be so quick to volunteer others to fight for you."

"Fine. If you won't take me there, I'll go myself." The building adrenalin rush gave him the strength to swing his legs over the edge of the bed. He stopped, closed his eyes. Images of Scar and his buddies working him over yanked back his bravado. Their laughter pinched every nerve he had. They'd taken their time, made him guess at which bone they'd break next.

"She didn't have time to heal everything," Thomas said.

No kidding. On top of the muscle pain, Doctor Rao had wrapped his ribs so tight he couldn't take a full breath. It didn't matter. He was going to find Hannah. T-CASS and Thomas would have to get over it.

"I'll get you some painkillers." Thomas stomped out of the bedroom.

"The blue bottle, not the red," Scott called, in case Thomas had forgotten which ones he preferred. He looked down to examine the bruises he could see while he waited for Thomas to return.

"You're determined to do this, aren't you?" Thomas handed him a blue bottle and a glass of water.

Scott shook four pills into his palm and swallowed them. "I owe her. She needs me."

Thomas sighed while he sat back down. "We're at the Lazy Eight Islands. It'll take us at least forty-five minutes to reach the mouth of the Bay. From there, I'll contact an Alt to fly us to the quarry. We won't trespass into Star Haven's airspace. Don't be surprised if your mother refuses."

Nothing Catherine did would surprise him. "If she does, if all of T-CASS refuses, I'll find another way. Even if it means hiring a Neut."

Thomas slumped back. "When did you get to be so damn stubborn?"

Scott remembered exactly when. "When I first met you. You praised me for not giving up in the face of adversity."

Thomas snorted. "Not the day you insisted I adopt you?"

Scott shook his head. "A mere formality. You were already my father."

"Really?" Thomas asked. "You were never a child who needed a parent."

Why would Thomas think that? "Yes, I did. I didn't know it at the time, but I needed a father and a mentor and a friend. You gave me all three wrapped in one arrogant, sophisticated package. I couldn't have asked for better."

"Then you've forgiven me for marrying your mother?"

He'd forgive Thomas for everything and anything, but marrying Catherine was different. Scott had never forgiven his biological family for anything. Every slight became a personal attack, an open wound, with no hope of healing. No wonder Thomas had doubts about Scott forgiving him. He had to make Thomas understand. "I forgave you a long time ago. I should have said something. I figured since we still met every week after I moved to Star Haven, you understood. We should have talked about it. I guess..."

"...you were too stubborn," Thomas said.

Scott wasn't sure if Thomas truly understood what Scott meant. They needed more time, but there was no time left. Miranda had Hannah. He thought of what Scar would do to Hannah if Miranda snapped her fingers. Scott squeezed the edge of the mattress. When all of this was over, when Hannah was safe and Miranda behind bars, he and Thomas would have a long talk.

Thomas clicked the intercom on the wall. "Lie down. Let the painkillers go to work. I'll set us a new course."

He did as Thomas asked, but with a promise to make it right.

***

Three hours later, Scott sat on the low edge of a half-crumbled brick wall that ringed the old resort. Highlight had transported him and Thomas from the mouth of the Bay to the staging ground at the bottom of the foothills. The Alt, now clad in black instead of her usual yellow, had said nothing while Thomas gave him a boost onto her light slide. Once they arrived, the other Alts kept their distance, including Evan and Alek. Just as well. He had nothing to say to any of them. He'd apologize to Nik for not giving him back his phone, which would have prevented all of this, but justifying his actions to the others? Not a chance.

T-CASS hunkered down around him, in groups of four or five. They were all waiting for Nik to report. Having so many Alts around made him edgy, tempted by his instinct to call his precinct and have them all arrested. Except he was an Alt too, at least for now. He only recognized some of the old guard, relying on half-remembered faces since they all wore black. A handful of Goobs formed around the more experienced Alts, reviewing battle strategies should the Captain call for a raid.

The cool breeze cleared his head of the fog created by pain and painkillers. Next to him, a group of techs worked on tablets, with Thomas sitting on the ground close by, offering his suggestions and advice as needed.

Everyone had something to do except him. He'd already checked all his weapons before he left the boat. Though he'd promised Thomas not to use his Alt power, his father had said nothing about Scott using conventional weapons. Out of respect, he'd keep the guns hidden unless he needed to use them. He didn't have the stamina to endure a protracted argument with T-CASS.

The sound of dirt tumbling down the small slope caught his attention. Ten feet away, Nik phased up from the ground.

"We have a problem," he announced, just loud enough to get everyone's attention.

The groups broke up and surrounded his brother.

"The entire quarry is a minefield. I damn near tripped one buried about a hundred yards from the northeast edge. Aside from the mines, there are larger, more powerful bombs attached to the quarry itself."

A female voice rose over the murmur of the crowd. Scott didn't recognize the speaker, a woman with hair a shade darker than Hannah's. "At least we know the prison is here."

From the sky, Catherine dropped right next to Nik.

"I saw a string of autocannons circled around the edge of the pit. Motion activated."

More murmuring.

"What's the point?" another Goob called out, too loud and his buddies shushed him. "Dane has to know we can take out all of the mines and the guns."

Scott agreed, as did the Catherine. "This isn't about stopping us. You don't set up an operation all the way out here to draw attention to yourself. They've relied on stealth and so far it's worked. The weapons are about stalling us. Dane knows we're risk-averse. There are only a handful of T-CASS members who can withstand a barrage of bullets or outrun an explosion. The rest of you will have to wait until we can secure a clear field into the prison."

"Every minute they stall us is time they have to erase their computer systems and escape," Thomas continued, stepping next to his wife. "Once they know we're here, they'll know they've lost control of the facility. They'll want to destroy evidence, prevent us from following them, protect their secrets. We can't let them get away with it." He looked at his wife. "Right?"

Catherine smiled at her husband. "Right."

"Aren't there any sentries? Human sentries, I mean?" Blockhead asked.

"No. I checked halfway up the mountain. It seems they've focused their manpower inside the prison," Catherine said.

"Do you have a plan?" Highlight asked.

"Of course." The Captain looked over the crowd. "Seeker, where are you?"

A pale young man stepped forward.

"You and I are going to fly over the minefield. I need you to map out exactly where each mine is located."

Seekers jaw dropped. "I'm going to fly? With you?"

294

"You're not afraid of heights, are you?" Catherine asked.

"No, of course not."

Scott chuckled at the way Seeker puffed out his chest.

"Good. Where's the map he's going to work off of?"

One of the techs stepped forward to hand Seeker a tablet. "When you see a mine, tap the location on the screen. It'll automatically transmit the coordinates to us and we'll send an Alt to clear it."

Seeker nodded.

"That's only part one," Catherine said. "Part two is if I can find a safe spot closer to the quarry, or if we can clear a path fast enough, I'm going to create a foxhole for you. I want you to watch the activity inside the prison and report back to us."

Scott guessed Seeker would have grown paler if it were possible.

"Ready?" Catherine stepped behind the Alt and slipped her hands around his waist.

Poor Seeker startled at the contact.

"Don't tell me you're ticklish," the Captain stage whispered.

"No, ma'am."

"Okay. Here we go." Off she flew with Seeker secure in her arms.

"Guess that leaves me to deactivate the mines." Blockhead stepped forward. Scott wasn't surprised. He'd met the former marine a few times when he was a kid. Back then Blockhead had no use for Norms, just like Catherine's father, Scott's grandfather. He and Blockhead had formed a mutual dislike of each other long before Scott ran away.

"I'll help." Another Alt — Mach Ten — stepped forward. Another original T-CASS member, but Scott had never met him.

"Me too," Nik said, breaking away from the group.

Since when did his brother have the skills to disarm mines? He'd have to ask, should ask, but did he have time? What if one of the mines blew up and his brother didn't phase fast enough? Maybe waiting to ask wasn't such a good idea.

The crowd broke up and returned to their previous groups. Scott took a step toward Nik, but Thomas intercepted him.

"Clearing those mines could take all night." He kept his voice low, though several Alts had ways to overhear him if they wanted to. "You can still return to the boat if you want to."

His body said *yes*, but he shook his head. Even if he wanted to return, there was no way he was going to ask Highlight to chauffeur him back and forth again. "I want to be here for Hannah. There has to be a faster way to get her out of the prison."

"This is the safest way to get to her. If we activate any of the mines, Dane will know we're here, which will put Hannah in more jeopardy. We need to keep the mines silent for as long as possible. Remember, Dane needs Hannah."

Dane needs Hannah, Scott repeated to himself as he wandered back to his original seat. He needed Hannah, too...no, stop thinking about it. He couldn't afford to accidentally activate his Alt power and pull her out now. What if Thomas was right and he left pieces of her behind? If he could focus on something else for a while, something other than his aching body, she'd remain secure inside the prison until he knew where she was. He wouldn't translocate her unless he had no choice.

If he didn't have a choice though, it would be easier if he could confirm her location first, wouldn't it? He walked over to Nik, who stood with Highlight's group.

"I need to talk to you."

Nik touched Highlight's shoulder and signaled he would be nearby. Highlight's gaze flicked to Scott, unreadable, but she said nothing. Once Scott had Nik far enough away he said, "I want to join Seeker in the foxhole."

Nik squinted. Scott knew his brother would guess why, and would calculate all of the possible scenarios. The same scenarios Thomas had already thought of. "You can't do it, Cory. Don't try to translocate her out of there."

"I'm not going to. I promise. I already promised Thomas I wouldn't. I just need to know if she's okay."

Nik ran his fingers through his hair. "What if she isn't okay? What will you do then? You'll be stuck in a hole with a Goob. If the quarry's guns start firing, or if a mine explodes...we already thought we had to bury you once this week. Don't make us do it for real."

"You won't. Please, Ghost...Nik. I need to be there. I need to be closer to her."

Nik looked to the stars with a heavy sigh. "Are you armed?"

"Yes. Is that a deal-breaker?" He didn't know much about T-CASS operations, but he did remember one rule: No guns. It had been a concession to the Thunder City police, to show respect for police training. But Scott was a police officer himself, and he wasn't a member of T-CASS. The rule didn't apply to him and his brother knew it.

One of the techs approached Nik and handed him a tablet. "We have three coordinates," he said.

Nik gave the screen a cursory once over before he tucked it into his uniform. "No, it's not a deal-breaker. It's justification if the Captain asks why I even considered bringing a half-blind, untrained Alt so close to the action. The Goob's alone, and if Dane's guards attack before we clear the minefield, you can at least fire back."

Scott released the breath he'd been holding. "Thanks, Nik."

His brother grimaced. "Don't thank me yet. I still might blow myself up before morning."

Scott started to ask where his brother got the training to disarm mines, but Nik phased into the ground before he could.

***

Two hours later, Nik sought out Scott, who'd stretched out on top of the brick wall, giving his body time to rest until he needed to move.

"Ready?" Nik asked.

"You're finished?"

"We only need a path to the front door and there's a reason why they call Jack Mach Ten and not Mach Two and a Half."

Before Scott could respond, Catherine landed nearby. "Ghost, Rumble, Blockhead, Roar, Hopper, Mach-Ten, Highlight..." She didn't name her husband, but Thomas joined her too. She wanted a conference with the old guard, the Alts with the most experience in the field. Nik half-smiled an apology and Scott found himself once again on the outside looking in. He didn't like it any more now than he had as a kid.

A few minutes later the group broke up and each of the experienced Alts started organizing the Goobs. Nik returned as he had promised.

"If you want me to take you to Seeker, we have to do it now."

"What's happening?"

"The Captain's calling it. We're going to raid the prison." Nik took Scott by the elbow and led him away from the brick wall, behind a scraggly bush where they wouldn't be seen.

"What's changed?"

"Seeker saw something. We don't know what it is. It's big, it's loose in the prison, and shots have been fired."

Shots fired. Scott's hand automatically checked his guns. "What about Hannah. Did he see her?"

"She was alive as of five minutes ago."

Hundreds of lives could be lost in five minutes. "What aren't you telling me?"

"Nothing, Cory. We don't know the details yet. I'm taking a huge chance bringing you to Seeker. Please don't harass the poor kid with questions he doesn't have answers to."

Scott nodded, though his mind raced with worry. "Okay, okay. I'm sorry. I'm ready whenever you are."

Nik held Scott by both forearms and sank them both into the ground. A moment later, Scott coughed and sputtered as Nik pushed him up through the gravel into a foxhole carved out of the ground. Seeker jumped at the unexpected visitor. Then he slipped his glasses over his eyes. "You're Scott Grey. I recognize you from the news reports."

Nik hadn't surfaced with Scott, so Scott was on his own with the Goob. The last thing he needed was the kid giving him a hard time about the shooting. "Yeah. Can you see Hannah Quinn from here?"

Seeker didn't press the issue. Instead, he took off the glasses and stared at the gravel wall in front of him. "I've been trying to track Ms. Quinn, but there's so much activity. I can't keep up with it all and the thing in the arena. It's huge. The guards keep shooting it, but it won't go down. How can anyone stop whatever it is?"

Seeker was panicking, so Scott laid a hand on the kid's shoulder. He'd been a rookie once. He understood the power of excitement mixed with fear, praying you didn't screw up. The way he'd prayed before he shot the first Alt. "Focus on one thing at a time. The creature — is it an immediate threat to us? Do we need to evacuate this foxhole?"

"No." Seeker took a slow breath. "We don't need to evac yet."

"Good. Do you see Hannah Quinn? Is she in immediate danger? Do we need to evac her?"

Seeker had no eyeballs, so Scott couldn't tell if the Goob was looking around. After a moment, the Alt replied. "No. She's on the second level of the arena. Where you would expect skyboxes to be if this were a sporting event. I think it's a control room of sorts."

"Is Miranda Dane with her?"

"No."

"Do you see Miranda Dane?"

Long pause. "Miranda is on the lower level — in an infirmary, I think. There's three people lying on tables with IVs attached to them."

Why would Miranda visit an infirmary? Why would she need one? He had no immediate answer when Seeker jumped again.

"One of the patients just attacked Miranda," Seeker said.

"Is he winning?" If Miranda died, the guards could shut the place down. Maybe let Hannah go? He knew it was wishful thinking on his part, but it was better than thinking of Hannah held hostage by a group of mercs who had just lost their paycheck.

Seeker shook his head. "I don't know. He's doing something to her. She's pinned to the floor. No, now she's pinned to the wall...now she's pinned to the ceiling. Hang on. A guard just came in. He's shooting the patient. I think I should call this into the Captain."

"Not just yet. Keep an eye on Dane if you can. Is Hannah still in the control room?"

Before Seeker could answer, a loud *clank* echoed across the quarry followed by the hiss of hydraulics. The ground shook. Bits of rock and dirt fell from the walls of the foxhole.

"What's happening?" Scott asked.

"It a door. Huge. Right in front of us."

A square section of camouflaged rock cracked open not twenty yards in front of them.

"Oh, my God." Seeker backed up to the far edge of the hole, as far as he could go without climbing out. "It's coming right at us."

CHAPTER TWENTY-TWO

Six guards surrounded Hannah as they stood outside the arena. She jumped up and down to pump up her circulation, keep herself moving, banish her fear. Of course, Miranda had made herself scarce while her daughter prepared to walk into the mutant's den. If she didn't know better, she'd call Miranda a coward, but in reality, she did know her mother. Miranda didn't care what happened to Hannah so long as her daughter got the job done.

Well, she would finish the job. In the past twenty minutes the prison population had developed a frantic edge. Everyone ran around, shouting orders, distributing more weapons. She heard the word "Alt" more than once, but didn't know if it referred to Joe, or to the other patients in the infirmary, or to someone else. Deep down she hoped Captain Spec had found the prison. If not, her escape plan could end with her still in Miranda's custody.

One benefit to all the activity was that in the confusion she'd managed to take a count of the guards. She didn't think more than fifty worked inside the complex. If there were more, they had to be outside. Fifty guards, plus the dozen techs in the control room, plus Miranda. Not quite the fortress Hannah had expected.

"The three of us will go in first to subdue Subject B," the guard she'd met in the infirmary said. "We'll need to get at least a dozen tranquilizer shots into him before he'll even start to feel it. Once he's down, you'll come inside with those three. Be careful, he might thrash around. We'll have to keep firing at him to keep him down."

"Wait, how can I communicate with you? I mean, with all the noise?" Hannah asked.

"Why would you need to?"

He asked the question without sarcasm, as if he'd listen to her if she gave him a good reason. Maybe talking to him earlier had produced a positive effect? He saw her as a person and not just an Alt? "Because I don't know what's going to happen while I heal him. He may shrink back to his normal height and weight. If he does, and you keep firing tranquilizers, you could kill him before I can break down the tranquilizer. It also makes my job harder if I have to keep sewing up the holes you're making. Miranda wants this done quickly, so why waste time by forcing me to fix more holes?"

She hoped the guard didn't sniff out the bullshit in her story. She couldn't communicate once she surfed, but it would help to have a com unit on hand.

"Here's my spare." He handed her the small square unit. "Clip it to your waist."

She did. Now, for the hard part.

"I'll need you and your men to take off your gloves, too."

She heard one of the guards behind her scoff.

"Because?"

This time his voice wasn't quite sarcastic, but he was losing patience.

"If you get hurt, I can't heal you if I can't touch your skin."

A snicker rose from behind her, along with a muttered comment. "No damn Alt is touching me."

The guard signaled his team to hush.

"Listen to me," she said, tempted to grab his sleeve, but she resisted. "I'm a healer. Aside from that, I'm Miranda Dane's daughter. If I try to pull a stunt, and I can't even begin to think of what I could possibly do, you know she's going to hurt me bad. What happened to the cop your men beat up is nothing compared to what she'll do to me if I try to escape."

He knew about Scott. The way he flinched, he must have seen Scott either during or after his beating.

Another boom right on the other side of the door interrupted her. She didn't need all of them to listen to her, just the one guard. The others might follow.

"Do you really think all of your men are going to walk out of there unscathed? Why take the chance? You've seen what I can do. You know I'm good, I'm quick. I can have you healed and walking out of here pretty as you please."

Another boom dented the metal door. The guard lowered his gun and yanked off his gloves. "I'm not ordering any of you to remove your gloves, but if you're going to do it, now's the time."

Four others followed their commander's lead. He raised his gun again and the door slid open. Three of the guards entered. Once they crossed the threshold the door slid closed again.

Nothing happened as Hannah counted the seconds. She made it to four before the first shots were fired, followed by an inhuman howl.

Joe was in pain because Miranda had mutilated his body, but if Hannah returned him to his pre-mutated state, Miranda would only subject him to more experiments. Mutate them and heal them in an endless cycle of experimentation. Her guilt hardened her determination to make it right. She would put a stop to this madness once and for all.

"Ready?" one of the guards from the second set asked.

"Yeah," she replied.

The door slid open. She let two of the guards go first, before she followed. Joe lay on the ground, heaving.

"Move, move, move!"

The guard behind her pushed. Inside, the arena looked bigger than it had from the control room. "Whatever you're going to do, do it now."

The guards had Joe surrounded on all sides, his naked body sprawled on the ground. She needed privacy, so she headed toward Joe's upper body before she crouched down and crawled under his armpit. The stench repulsed her, but she slapped her hand to his upper arm and surfed.

Such damage. The poor guy didn't stand a chance in this condition. She did what she could to ease the swelling in his skull, but didn't have time to fix everything. It took a strong sense of self-preservation to pull herself out of Joe's body.

She pulled the comm off her belt. "I'm dehydrated. I need water. Can someone get me a bottle?"

"You've only been in there twenty minutes."

"Hey, his brain is the size of a small moon. Give me a break."

A moment later one of the guards, not the one she knew, crawled in after her.

"Stinks like a pile of shit at high noon," he muttered handing her the bottle.

"No kidding. And I'm sorry."

She grabbed his hand and surfed. After spending all of those years emotionally forging an obedient daughter, Miranda had forgotten the first lesson of parenthood: children learn by example. Miranda, the nurse, had taught Hannah to use her power to heal because that was what she needed. Miranda had used her daughter as a weapon of cruelty, making her heal abused Alts only to see them returned to prison where they were abused again, or making Hannah heal her hired thugs to keep them operational. Miranda never once asked if Hannah had any other abilities, and Hannah learned through example to lie by omission.

Hannah had never told Miranda that whatever she could heal, she could also harm.

Two, four, six. With precision, Hannah dislocated the joints in the guard's shoulders, elbows and knees, then followed up by cutting his vocal cords. He couldn't move or call for help by the time she emerged. Luck stayed with her as Joe twitched.

"You okay in there?"

She heard the voice over the guard's radio. She snatched up her com.

"Hey, we need help. Your guy got scrunched by Joe's arm. Can you pull him out? I'll heal him when I'm done."

She drank from the water bottle as two more guards ducked into her shelter.

"Let me help you," she said, while positioning herself between the two guards. She grabbed one hand. Two, four, six, slash.

"What the hell?"

Before the other guard figured out what she'd done, she grabbed his hand, too, and repeated her attack.

Three down, three to go. Time to push Joe into giving her a hand. She surfed inside. His system had already metabolized most of the tranquilizers, but even as she surfed, she could hear the guns firing outside, injecting more into his system. She helped speed up the destruction of the drug and stimulated his production of adrenaline. She waited as long as she dared, then surfed back out and ran out from under his arm.

"He's getting up," her guard yelled. "Fire, fire, fire."

Hannah retreated against the wall to where the three guards she had disabled lay. One of them still had his dart gun next to him.

Two of the guards left in the room dodged and rolled out of Joe's way, while her guard called for backup. She picked up the dart gun and positioned herself near the door with her back to a wall. The door slid open and two guards ran right past her.

At such close range, she couldn't miss. She nailed both of them in their backsides where they didn't have any armor to deflect the darts. They fell with a flop. To make sure they stayed down, she dislocated their joints and ripped their vocal cords as well. She also grabbed a regular pistol from one of them, careful to keep it pointed away from her.

An empty corridor greeted her, though the flashing red lights signaled an emergency situation. She ran over to the elevator and pressed her hand to the control pad. Nothing happened. A moment later a whole squad arrived.

"He's killed three men," she shouted at the guards, careful to keep the pistol behind her back. "You have to stop him. I need to find my mother. Send me up to the control room."

One of the guards slapped the floor number for her, then disappeared. Alone in the elevator, Hannah leaned back. Sweat dripped down her face.

The door slid open. All of the techs stood over their stations, watching the massacre below. She approached the one nearest the door, the same one whose chair she'd held onto earlier, and pointed the gun at his head.

"How did they get Joe into the arena?"

The tech froze. "Whoa."

"Keep your hands where I can see them."

He pulled his hands back from his station.

"Don't make me have to ask again. How did they get Joe down there? The door I came through is too small for him to fit."

The tech glanced down at his colleagues, but they paid him no attention.

"Who's Joe?"

"Subject B, asshole." She pressed the gun harder against his chin. "The poor slob your guards are torturing down there. The one they mutated into a monster."

"Oh. We brought him in through the loading dock at the back of the arena. It's how we brought in all of the equipment to construct this place."

A loading dock would lead outside. "Open it."

"I'm sorry?"

308

"I said, open it."

The tech smirked. "Or what?"

"I'm not playing games," she answered.

"Yes, you are," the tech said. "The loaded chamber indicator tells me the gun is empty. Not to mention, your hands are shaking so bad, even if you took a shot, you'd miss."

True, her hands had been shaking the whole time, but the shaking got worse the longer she held the heavy weapon. "You know what? You're right."

With her left hand, she grabbed the tech's wrist as he tried to hit an alarm. He screamed when she smacked his elbow joint out of place. Back in her body, she grabbed the gun from where it had fallen on the computer console.

"Open the damn door or I'll dislocate the three hundred other bones in your miserable body." She turned to the rest of the room. "The rest of you get the hell out of here."

No one moved, so she fired the gun over their heads. Something sizzled as a light went out. The crew scrambled for the exit on the opposite side of the room. She ignored them, and turned back to her tech.

"You lied to me about the gun," she said, pointing it at his head again. "Open. The. Damn. Door. Now."

He lowered his good hand to the computer and tapped a few keys. A rumble rolled through the arena. Behind the chaos below, a large door opened in the back.

She stepped away from the tech so he couldn't grab her, and glanced out the window at the area. "What's outside the door? I don't see anything."

"It's a tunnel. Short. A hundred meters at most."

"Is it lit?"

"Emergency lighting."

Would it be enough for the Thunder City Alts to see? She couldn't hang around to find out. "Let's go."

"Down there?"

Joe still raged, but he was slowing again as more of the guards used tranquilizers on him.

"Yeah," she said. "You better hope Joe likes me more than he does the guards. Now take your shirt off."

"I can't even move my arm." He wagged it up and down.

"Not my problem."

He tried to stall, but when she grabbed his upper arm he ripped the shirt off faster.

"Walk."

She backtracked down to the arena, using the tech's handprint to activate the elevator. By the time they reached the entrance, the arena was empty. Joe had found his way into the tunnel — she could hear his footfalls echoing. The guards who hadn't fallen under Joe's wild swings followed him. The only person missing was Miranda. Where the hell had her mother gone?

She pushed the tech through into the arena and kicked the door closed behind her. "Lock it."

The tech used his good hand to manipulate the pad next to the door. She didn't trust him for a minute, though, so she kept one eye on the trail behind her as she forced him to navigate around the bodies of the unconscious or dead guards.

They'd almost made it to the tunnel when the whole arena shook violently.

"What the hell's happening?" The vibrations stopped for a second, then started again.

"External security," the tech said. "The autocannons on the roof have motion detectors in case the Alts find us."

"How many?"

"About fifteen, maybe twenty. I'm not in acquisitions so I'm not sure."

"Not sure? It's your job to be sure." She borrowed some Miranda-style sarcasm. "Keep walking."

"Could you at least fix my arm?"

"So you can slug me? Not a chance, pal. Move." She pushed him into the tunnel. The emergency lighting did little more than show her the smooth dirt floor. Joe's bellow echoed off the rock walls.

"Do you really want to go out there?" the tech asked, after twenty feet.

"Do you know you talk too much?" She didn't know if she wanted to go out there. At any moment, a guard could discover them, or Joe could double back into the tunnel, or she could walk right into a bullet.

"Look out." She pulled the tech toward the wall as two guards did exactly as she feared. With one hand on the tech, she leveled her gun as the guards ran close.

They passed her without even stopping.

"That can't be good," the tech said.

"Keep walking." She marched him to the beat of her heart, which pounded as fast as the guns fired. Almost there.

"What happens when we get outside?"

"I haven't figured that part out yet."

More guards raced toward them and Hannah pressed against the wall. Again the guards didn't slow down.

"Hey!" she shouted.

One of the guards stopped. A woman. It was dark enough so maybe she didn't recognize Hannah or realize she had a hostage.

"What's going on outside?"

"Alts. Gotta be at least thirty of 'em. It's a raid. Between Subject B, the Alts, and the guns on the roof, we're all retreating inside. It's more secure."

The guard turned and ran.

"Go." Hannah pushed the tech back toward the arena. "It's safer in there."

"What about you?"

As if he cared. "Believe it or not, I'm safer out there."

He seemed okay with that, the jerk. "Would you..." He held out his arm.

"This is going to hurt," she warned. She surfed inside and pushed the joint back into the place. He hollered.

By the time she emerged and reoriented herself in the dark, he was already backing down the tunnel. Even in the poor light, she could tell he wasn't looking at her, but over her head. He turned and ran.

Hannah had pivoted only halfway before Joe's huge hand wrapped around her waist and lifted her off the ground.

***

"What's coming?" Scott asked.

"The thing. The creature. There's a corridor and it's heading right for us," Seeker said.

Shit. "Now you can call the Captain for an evac."

Seeker stuttered as he called in his report. The foxhole was too deep, so Scott couldn't see over the

312

edge. The ground shook harder with every step the creature took.

"Ghost's on his way," the Captain's voice broadcast from Seeker's tiny comm unit. "Do not try to run. We'll get you out."

Cannon fire rocketed overhead. Seeker put his glasses back on so he couldn't see through the gravel wall. "I can't do it anymore. I can't look at it."

"You did fine, Seeker. You did just..."

An angry roar, followed by earth shaking steps coming closer, and closer. Rocks rained into the foxhole.

Nik popped up from underneath. Scott shoved Seeker into his brother's arms. "Get him out. I'm staying."

"No way. Do you hear that thing? How can you help Hannah if you're dead? It'll rip you to shreds if it finds you."

"Then I'll make sure it doesn't find me. Get me up there," he pointed over the edge of the foxhole.

"The autocannons..."

"Are pointed at the Captain, not me. Please, Ghost. I have to find her."

Nik set Seeker aside and grabbed Scott's arms. A second later, Scott lay at the far edge of the hole. He could see what frightened Seeker. Holy fuck! The kid hadn't exaggerated.

Nik lay beside his brother. "Now do you understand? Let me get you to safety."

"No. Take Seeker and get out of here."

"Damn you!" Nik disappeared. Scott looked into the foxhole. Nik grabbed Seeker and, with one last withering look at his brother, sank into the earth.

The creature roared and spun around, its ugly ass in Scott's face. From between its legs, he could see a squad of Miranda's guards fire at it. Scott considered joining them, but what good could his Ruger do against eight tons of ugly? Not to mention, he only had one good eye to aim with. The creature lashed out to pound a fist into the mouth of the tunnel. As debris hit the guards, half of them fled back into the tunnel, abandoning their unconscious comrades. The creature stepped forward to follow them, squishing one unfortunate soul.

Scott prayed Hannah had found a safe place inside the prison, someplace small and tight, where the creature, or Miranda, couldn't reach. If he could get inside, he could find her. He wouldn't stop looking until he did.

The cannons lit up the night sky. Scott couldn't see Captain Spec zoom in to smash the first gun into tiny pieces, but he heard the screech of twisted metal just fine. She'd probably flown Blockhead up there with her so they could take out double the cannons in half the time. Behind him, a mine exploded. He hoped it was because Evan or Alek had hit the device with lightning and not because some Goob had stepped on one.

Staying low to the ground, Scott scurried toward the tunnel. He couldn't get too close because the creature had stopped just inside the entrance.

Scott pulled his Ruger just in case. If he could get close enough, maybe he could hit a vital organ, or an artery, or something to bring down the creature once and for all. The thing pounded its fist into the ceiling before it swung its arm down. It looked as if it had grabbed a guard.

Scott aimed for the thing's head and fired.

***

"No. No. NO. Joe stop. Please." He squeezed Hannah so tight, her own ribs cracked under the pressure. She had no chance to pull herself out of his grip as he lifted her toward the top of the tunnel. At the last second she bent as far as she could to get under his thumb, so his knuckle hit the ceiling instead of her head.

She knew what would come next. She'd watched his wild swings in the arena. He would slam her body into the ground. With a final breath, she surfed.

No time. She had no time to heal him. No time to fix what was wrong. She had no time, because even as she swam up his arm she could feel it swing down. How could she stop him? How could she make this right? She had no time.

Without pause or true thought, she aimed for his spinal cord, smashed his brain stem, then plowed through his brain to the interthalamic adhesion. Clipping the thread wouldn't stop his swing, so she increased the pressure, sucking in air and water, pushing the organ beyond its tolerance until it exploded.

Joe didn't make a sound until his body flopped onto the ground.

Hannah emerged, still trapped in his hand. Outside, the cannons continued to fire. She tried to pull herself out his grip, but the huge hand held her firm. His thumb, slick with blood, wouldn't budge.

She still had the comm unit the security guard had given her, but would any of them respond? Could she contact T-CASS with it? She dug her hand between her

315

chest and Joe's fingers, but she couldn't find room to get to the unit clipped to her jeans.

"I always knew you were a mistake."

Miranda. Her mother's hair fell about her face in a tangle, her fine blazer ripped along a seam. She had never looked so disheveled.

"Help me," Hannah said.

"No."

Her mother's refusal didn't stop Hannah from trying to wiggle her way out. "Why? What did I ever do to you?"

Her mother pursed her lips. "Nothing. You were a means to an end, nothing more."

Hannah wished she could recall the numbness from the freezer. You couldn't hurt so much if you were numb. "After everything I did for you? All those Alts I healed so you could torture them? All those thugs I helped so you could send them back out to hurt more people?"

Miranda stumbled over the huge rocks scattered on the ground. She only wore one shoe. "And yet when I needed you the most, you ran."

Hannah tried to tug her way out one more time, but failed. What little strength she had was gone. "A little kindness might have kept me by your side."

"I doubt that." Miranda bent over to pick up the pistol Hannah had dropped. "Roger had too much sway over you."

"He paid attention to me. You were always too busy."

"Everything was always so simple for you." Miranda shook her head, raining dirt from her hair. "You have the power to control people."

"If I truly had that kind of power, don't you think I would have made you love me a long time ago?"

"Why didn't you?" Miranda actually sounded curious.

"Because it wouldn't have been real and it wouldn't have lasted."

Her mother sat on one of the larger stones, her fingers brushing dirt off the gun's barrel. "They'll kill me, you know. Subject B was supposed to be our big breakthrough. If you'd been here I would have had time to perfect the gene mutation. They would have given me anything I asked for."

Hannah dropped her chin onto her hands, exhausted. "Who are they?"

Miranda waved the gun. "It doesn't matter now. They'll kill me for losing Subject B. Since I'm a dead woman anyway, I might as well take my revenge now and destroy Subject A."

She leveled the gun at Hannah's head.

"How can you do this?" Hannah asked. "How can you shoot your own child?"

"Simple. You're not my daughter. Your mother is dead. I know, because I killed her."

Hannah screamed as Miranda fired.

***

What the hell happened? There was no way Scott's puny Ruger had caused the creature's head to explode.

Careful not to trip over any debris, or slide on splattered brain matter, Scott crept forward. He paused at the mouth of the tunnel, not yet ready to commit to getting too close. Nearby, he could hear a sob and a voice. Whoever the creature had grabbed was still alive.

317

A scatter of gravel fell from the ceiling as another mine exploded. He ducked back and waited. When no more rocks fell, he crept forward again, circling around to the creature's elbow. He cursed his impaired sight, but once in the tunnel, the emergency lights had enough illumination for him to see the situation.

Hannah, covered in blood, was caught in the thing's death grip and Miranda sat nearby with a gun.

Scott couldn't hear what Miranda said to Hannah, but when she raised her gun there was no mistaking her intent.

He knew he should pull Miranda's gun, but his thoughts were only of Hannah. A fierce sense of protection overrode his police training and triggered his Alt ability. Hannah disappeared as Miranda fired, and reappeared at his feet, screaming. Miranda turned, saw her daughter at his feet, and fired again. Her shot was wild, uncontrolled.

Anger sharpened Scott's senses. He had all the control in the world, so he locked his will onto the bullet in the chamber. No matter how poor his aim, how badly his arm shook, he fired. The slug disappeared, then reappeared right before it slammed into Miranda's forehead. Her body jerked once before she joined her creation face down in the dirt.

Hannah's screams reached hysterical levels. Just as he had done on the roof of the hospital, he knelt next to her. Before he could check her for injuries, she threw her arms around his neck. His ribs ached, but he pulled her closer and rocked her back and forth.

Time stalled. The mines stopped exploding. Hannah's hysteria calmed to gasping hiccups. He had no idea how long he'd been sitting with her in his arms when Catherine appeared at his side.

"She's injured," Catherine said.

"It's not her blood," he replied.

Catherine nodded. "I'm going to get both of you out of here. Hang on."

The Captain...Catherine...his mother lifted both Scott and Hannah into her arms and launched. She kept her flight close to the ground. In his arms, Hannah started to shake.

"Hurry," he said.

Catherine picked up speed, but not too much. She flew them all the way back to the *Elusive Lady*. A hint of sun rising over the Bay lit the deck as Doctor Rao met them.

Scott wouldn't surrender Hannah just yet, so he carried her below to the guest bedroom.

Catherine stood in the doorway as Scott laid Hannah on the bed. "Do you want me to stay?"

Scott looked up at his mother, then back down at Hannah, still shaking. Doctor Rao began his exam.

"There's nothing you can do. They need you back at the quarry."

She came forward, pulled him into a hug. "If you need me, or if her condition changes, call me. I'll come back."

He returned the hug, a small trickle of love widening the hole already created in his defenses. He believed her.

"Scc...Sc...Scott?"

Hannah tried to sit up, but Scott knelt next to the bed, his hand on top of her head, wiping away the blood. "Shhhh. Don't talk. Let Doctor Rao finish."

The tears were starting again. "She said she wasn't my mother. She killed my real mother."

Scott ran his thumb along her hairline, soothing her as best he could. "Miranda's a liar. She said it to hurt you."

"What if she wasn't lying? She killed Roger. She killed her other husbands. Can you find out?" Her eyes, bloodshot and puffy, fluttered closed as Doctor Rao injected her with the same sedative he'd given Scott.

"Yes. We'll investigate Miranda all the way down to her dirty underwear. Now sleep. I'll be right beside you when you wake up."

CHAPTER TWENTY-THREE

Scott had kept his promise. Hannah awakened to find him sitting next to the bed, all bruised and bandaged. She reached out to bloodsurf again, swearing she'd fix him up right this time, but he blocked her hand before she could touch him.

"Don't even think about it," he said.

She flinched at the sharp retort. "I'm sorry."

Scott shook his head. "Don't be sorry. Don't ever be sorry for trying to heal someone. Now is not the time. You need to heal yourself first."

Only then did she notice her wrapped ribs and the IV line. While she was asleep, someone — Doctor Rao she hoped — had washed her free of blood, including her hair, which hung damp and limp. At least she wasn't dehydrated from bloodsurfing so much.

"Do you want to tell me about it?" Scott asked. His one good eye, soft as a cloud now, stared into hers as he knelt next to the bed. "Tell me what Dane said to you? Did to you?"

She started to speak, but both sides of her face sent waves of pain through her head and neck. She ached a hundred times more than she had when Miranda first punched her.

"Hurts," she said instead. "My body hurts too much," she clarified.

Scott unwrapped a prefilled syringe. "Doctor Rao is helping T-CASS over at the quarry. He said to give you one injection if you felt you need it."

The medicine worked quickly. Hannah could feel her muscles relax and the pain ease. Scott had asked her a question, though. "No, I don't want to talk about it. Not yet." Her emotions were far too raw to put into words. After a deep breath she managed to croak, "Can I have a few minutes alone?"

Scott must have understood her slurred speech because he nodded. "I'll be up on deck. You can use the intercom to call me if you need me. Don't say a word, just hit the button."

She waited until he disappeared into the salon to let the dam burst one more time. It took longer than a few minutes, but eventually her well of tears ran dry. The emotional pain fed her physical pain. If she could have lain in bed all day she would have, but a muffled boom told her that the *Elusive Lady* was docked somewhere near the quarry, and that T-CASS was still destroying mines. She removed the IV and change into a pair of sweatpants and a t-shirt — Catherine's she suspected — that someone had left on one of the chairs.

She hobbled as far as the stairs leading up to the deck, but couldn't quite get her legs to lift high enough to climb.

"Scott! Help!" she tried to call, but he didn't hear. Another intercom box sat embedded by the door. She hit the button.

He appeared, and though he looked as bad as she felt, they leaned on each other as he helped her to the deck. Not all of T-CASS was participating in the cleanup. Catherine, Thomas, Nik, Evan, and Alek had also gathered while Thomas placed a call to one of his techs on speakerphone. The sun had passed its zenith, heading down to meet Mystic Bay, but it was still warm enough to unfreeze her bones. In the distance, another boom barreled across the land. Smoke rose from where T-CASS worked to collect evidence against Miranda, but Hannah turned her head away from the horror she had left behind.

Scott helped ease her onto a deck chair and adjusted the back so she could sit mostly upright. Then he pulled his own deck chair over to sit next to her.

"If you need anything, you just tell me," he said, his voice low. "Food, sunscreen, whatever."

The numbness of the painkillers kept her comfortable. She didn't need anything for the moment. Hannah listened carefully to Thomas's phone call to catch up on what she had missed.

"Go ahead, Shinzo. What did you find?" Thomas asked.

"I sent you a file. You need to read this."

Thomas scrolled a finger across the screen. "Okay. What am I looking at?"

"Text messages sent by one of the guards at the prison," Shinzo said.

Thomas scrolled through the notes. Hannah wished she could read it, but settled for the commentary. "How did you get this?"

"There were breaches in security. Some of the guards had clandestine tech hidden around their quarters. This guard figured no one would notice an older model cell phone."

"How did you think to look for this?" Thomas asked.

"Pure frustration," Shinzo said. "Dane's hacker — I'm assuming it was the hacker you've been chasing — started a low-level format before we ever got inside. We probably won't find anything useful. I thought maybe one of the guards might have snuck in some outlawed equipment and I was right. Most of the rooms had gaming consoles and e-readers, but this guard had a girlfriend on the outside he texted regularly."

Catherine looked over her husband's shoulder as he continued to scroll through the entries. "What the hell is the Court of Blood?"

"I don't know, Captain," Shinzo said. "I ran a general search, but came up with nothing."

"Tag it," Thomas said. "If the guard happens to be one of the unfortunate souls who tangled with Hannah, he might know more. Run a background check on the girlfriend too. If she's just his girlfriend, we'll leave her alone. If not..."

"On it."

"Thanks, Shinzo."

Thomas closed the line. Everyone now looked at Hannah, except Scott, who reached over to hold her hand while he glared at his family. Still the rule-breaker, his hand was both soft and strong. He gave his support if nothing else.

"I don't know anything either," she said before Scott could pick a fight with his brothers. "Miranda never told me anything. I've never heard of the Court of Blood. If I had to guess, they're the ones who ordered her to..." her throat closed up, so she waved in the general direction of the quarry. Eventually, she'd tell them more, about Miranda murdering her real mother and kidnapping her.

"I'll work with Shinzo," Nik said. "I have a few contacts who can help."

"What about the guards Hannah disabled? They must know something," Alek said. "We'll have to interrogate them."

Hannah winced at the word *disabled*. The guards, if they weren't dead, would have been hospitalized. She wondered if Doctor Rao had examined them first, maybe with Seeker's help. Seeker would have seen the dislocated joints and cut vocal cords. It wouldn't take a genius to figure out who could inflict that type of damage to so many in so little time. Eventually all of T-CASS would know about the dark side to her power.

"If we can get them extradited to Thunder City, we'll question them," Catherine said. "Right now, Star Haven is leaderless. Commissioner Becksom has disappeared and so has half the city council. The Star Haven police have taken the guards into custody anyway. Like it or not, Star Haven will investigate what happened at the quarry as well as the death of Miranda Dane. They're going to want to investigate us, as well. How much they're willing to work with Thunder City to find the truth remains to be seen."

"What about the Governor? Has anyone contacted the Capitol?" Evan asked.

Catherine shook her head. "The Governor refuses to send in the military reserve. He said it sounded like we had it under control so why should the State interfere?"

"Spineless jackass," Alek muttered.

"It's just as well," Thomas said. "Other cities consider themselves Alt friendly, but only Thunder City has legislated equality. The entire country is watching us. We don't want to attract too much outside interference."

Everyone fell quiet. Both Thunder City and Star Haven would investigate the quarry prison. Guess who would be at the center of it all?

You can still run.

Could she? Would she? A dozen different scenarios played out in a matter of seconds. She could do it. Easily. She'd eluded Miranda for six months. Leaving Thunder City would be even easier. All she had to do was evade T-CASS, including their telepaths. Sure, no problem.

Hannah looked down at Scott's hand wrapped around hers.

"What about you, Scott?" Thomas asked.

Scott kept her hand in his. "What about me?"

He sounded defensive already. She squeezed his hand, but she had no strength to make him feel it.

"If you're going to return to Star Haven, now's the time to do it," Thomas said. "We can concoct any story we want about the shooting — an undercover Newcomer translocated the gun, but sent it to you by accident. Thunder City won't investigate too deeply because you're not in their custody. You helped Hannah cross the Bay because she was eighteen and you didn't know she was an Alt. Star Haven will understand how a sneaky Alt, aided by her Alt-loving mother, tricked you. The Attorney General will drop the charges and you'll be free to live in a city where you're still a hero."

Hannah's hope rose and fell in the same moment. It would work. She could see Star Haven believing such a story. No matter what the Star Haven investigation into the quarry turned up, Mayor Dane had betrayed the city by hiding her Alt daughter for eighteen years. No one would miss her or Miranda. The sooner both of them were buried, literally and figuratively, the better. Scott could have his old life back.

Scott looked at her hand, still tucked into his. He had the oddest look on his face, though, as if he hadn't realized he'd taken her hand in the first place. He looked at her for a long moment, but didn't let go.

"One of the many reasons Norms dislike Alts is because they view you — us — as irresponsible," he said. "Vigilante Alts create so much damage, personal and property, and they never take responsibility for their actions. Your car gets trashed while an Alt chases down a bank robber. Tough luck. Call your insurance company and hope they don't blame you. You break a bone while an Alt pulls you from a burning building, same thing. The Alt should have been more careful, now you're out of work and stuck with the bills..."

"It's not like that in Thunder City," Alek protested. "We fix what we break, even if we're not responsible. We pay for everything even when we shouldn't. We apologize even when it's not our fault. We give a hell of a lot more than what we get back."

"I know," Scott snapped back. "I'm talking about perception, not reality. Even in Star Haven, things aren't as bad as they're perceived to be. The damage inflicted by the Left Fists can't be blamed on the Alts, because there are no more Alts in Star Haven. No matter what the hard-core anti-Alt advocates say, they can't pin all of the destruction in the Swamp on Alts."

"They'll try," Alek said.

"Yes," Scott replied. "They will. The only way to change the perception though is for Star Haven Alts to

327

take responsibility for everything. Like they do in Thunder City."

Scott stopped, closed his eyes for a moment before he continued. "On the other hand, I'm also an Alt-killer."

Thomas leaned forward this time, to protest, as did Catherine.

"Let me finish," Scott said, before his parents could speak. "I've killed two Alts in three years. Even for a Star Haven cop, that's unheard of. I can justify both, but in Star Haven I don't have to, and in Thunder City I haven't been given the chance. I need to show the Alts of Thunder City I can also take responsibility for my actions as a police officer — a Norm police officer. Let them listen to my testimony and decide if I made the right decision."

"Some might be willing to listen," Nik said, but then he glanced at Alek. "Others might not want to hear what you have to say."

"I'll never be completely accepted in either city," Scott said. "But the fact is, I'm an Alt and a cop. I have to reconcile both and maybe do some good while I'm at it."

Hannah sniffed. Her pride in Scott spilled over. He was staying in Thunder City. Staying with her, or at least near her. He wasn't asking her to break his Alt power.

In the background, another mine exploded.

"You three better get back to the quarry," Catherine said to her oldest sons. "I'll join you later."

Hannah tensed. Scott had chosen to take responsibility, but what about her? She'd flirted with running away, and from the look on Catherine's face, Hannah's fate was next on the list of topics to be discussed.

Alek and Evan took to the sky, with Evan carrying Nik. Hannah guessed Nik couldn't phase through the Bay.

Scott scooted closer to Hannah.

"I guess you want to know what happened inside the quarry," she said.

Catherine nodded. "Pathia monitored you as best she could once you regained consciousness, but telepathy isn't as accurate as the media would have you believe. We'd like you to fill in the blanks."

Had she spent all her courage facing down Miranda? Why didn't she feel powerful anymore? T-CASS knew she'd used her ability as a weapon. She hadn't just disable the guards — she'd blown up Joe's brain. Even she hadn't known she could do that until she had to. She'd killed. Would anyone trust her to heal again?

She looked at Scott. He could have run back to Star Haven, back to his old life, but he wasn't. He was staying. Taking responsibility. If he could do it, she could too. She should. How would Alts ever achieve equality with Norms if they hid?

"Do you have a recorder on that thing?" she asked Thomas, pointing to his tablet. He nodded. "Please turn it on. I really don't think I can repeat all of this again. This is what happened."

The most difficult thing she'd ever had to do was talk about what happened inside the prison. She left nothing out, from her hatred of Miranda, to Miranda's confession about murdering her mother and kidnapping her. She didn't worry about whether or not Catherine, or Thomas, or even Scott, believed her. It didn't matter anymore. She could only control her testimony, not their reactions. If they couldn't accept

329

what she'd done, then she'd move on. Not running, but moving forward in a direction she'd choose on her own.

They listened. Scott never dropped her hand. When she finished, she said, "You know what I know. There's nothing else I can add."

Thomas clicked his tablet off. "Thank you, Hannah. Others will have to hear this, and we'll continue our investigation. If anyone in Star Haven tries to hold you responsible for what happened to the guards, or to Joe, we'll have your testimony to fight them."

He tugged Catherine to stand and they both headed below deck leaving her alone with Scott.

"Now what?" She looked him in his one good eye. "I mean between us."

He shook his head. "We don't have to talk about this. It can wait."

"No, it can't." Hannah tried to sit up straighter, but her muscles spasmed. She slumped back in the chair. "I need to know where I stand with you. There's too much uncertainty in my life right now. Don't make me have to wait find out if you care, even a little bit."

He let go of her hand. Well, she'd asked for it, but at least she knew he didn't want her.

"I don't know," he said. "If you're asking if I'm in love with you, I...I don't know."

I don't know was better than just plain *no*. Her hope climbed, but not too far.

"I mean," he continued, "we don't really know each other. Do we have anything in common besides really fucked up families?"

She tried to smile, but suspected it looked more like a grimace. "Yeah. You rescued me, though."

"And you rescued me," he pointed out.

She had, hadn't she? "Riding off into the sunset together isn't as easy as it looks."

"Not with our injuries at any rate." He picked up her hand again.

"So where do we go from here?" she asked. "I don't mean the investigation. We can't control that."

Scott leaned back in his chair. The sky was in full twilight, but with clouds billowing from the quarry. Gray, just like Scott's eyes. "Catherine will still insist on training both of us. We can't get out of it if we're going to live in Thunder City. T-CASS won't be happy to see me, but they won't fight Catherine. Especially if the old guard lets it leak that I'm really Cory Blackwood, Catherine's forgotten son."

"Will you change your name back to Cory Blackwood?"

Shrug. "Maybe. I became Scott Grey when Thomas adopted me. As much as I respected Thomas, I wanted my own identity, wanted to have the power to name myself. We'll see how many people actually remember me. Keep in mind, even as Cory, I'm legally Thomas's son, not Catherine's. Maybe I'll compromise: Cory Carraro."

She laid her head back and they both remained quiet for a long time. Stars appeared in the sky before she could speak again. "What am I going to do? Who am I? Miranda's first husband's name was Quinn, but she always said my father was some guy she picked up in a bar and she never got his name. I don't even know if Hannah is my first name."

"We'll find out." Scott let go of her hand to massage her temple with his thumb. "I can check your birth records."

"She said she killed my mother." Dammit, the tears were starting again. Would they ever stop?

Scott shook his head. "We'll search the hospital records too."

"At Star Haven Memorial? Good luck finding them." Her bitterness burned.

"Hey, don't give up on me yet." He stroked his forefinger along her jawline, careful to avoid her puffy cheeks. If her ribs didn't hurt so much, she'd return the affection. "I might be a cop, but I've got some mad skills in the detective department too. Plus, I'm connected. Nikolaos Blackwood is a damn fine private investigator. He'll give me a hand. Maybe even give me a family discount."

Hannah shrugged, though she wanted to smile. "There won't be anything to find. Miranda didn't pick me out at random. She called me Subject A. She was going to kill me so the Court of Blood couldn't have me."

Scott leaned over and gave her a friendly kiss on the nose, so not playing fair. "See, we already have information to start our search. Please, Hannah, trust me. I'm not going to give up on you. You'll have answers before you're all healed."

"This could take a month or more." She ran her hands down the bandage wrapped around her chest. "I wish I could heal myself as fast as I can heal you."

He pulled away. "I told you before: No bloodsurfing."

"I know, I know, until I'm trained." She tried not to pout.

He nodded, slowly. "Yeah."

"How can I keep that kind of promise, though? I've turned my back on too many people who were sick or injured. I killed Joe. I injured the guards protecting me from Joe. Not bloodsurfing makes me no better than Miranda."

"You're nothing like Miranda." The way his good eye clouded over, so dark and passionate and focused on her...she believed him. He said he didn't know if he was in love with her, but since he planned to stay in Thunder City she'd have a chance to change his mind. "Even after you're trained, even if you have permission to heal people, you can't possibly heal everyone. We need to establish protocols, boundaries..."

"Rules," she said.

He smirked. "More like guidelines."

"Where do we go from here?" she asked again.

"I can't stay at the estate," he said. "Too many bad memories I'd rather avoid. I'll move into the penthouse downtown until I can find my own place. I'd like to try to reconnect with Catherine. She's been trying in her own unique way. The least I can do is give her a chance."

"What about your brothers? Evan and Alek?" His expression darkened even further. Had she pushed too far, too fast?

"We'll see."

Not a commitment or a promise, but not a resounding rejection either.

"What about you?" he asked. "What would you like your future to look like?"

Damned if she knew, but Scott had shared his plans, the least she could do is dream a little. "I guess I'll stay at the estate for now. It's not like I can afford an apartment. If I train fast enough, maybe I can talk to Evan about working for the veterinarian? Even if I can't heal the animals until Catherine says it's okay, I'll at least feel useful."

Scott didn't seem thrilled at her working with his brother, but he didn't object either. "I'm sure Evan could arrange something."

They fell back into silence until Hannah couldn't hold back one last question. "Scott, do you want to kiss me?"

He blinked a few times. "Why do you ask?"

"The way you've been touching me since you brought me out here. Holding my hand, massaging my face, kissing my nose." She held her breath, but Scott went completely still.

"I'm sorry," he whispered. "I should have asked first."

He sounded so contrite, but it wasn't the answer she wanted. "No, it's my fault. I asked the wrong question."

"No, you didn't. You have the right to not be touched and you shouldn't have to..."

He was all cop now, about to chastise himself for not asking for consent. Did other women have this much difficulty getting a kiss? "What I mean is," she interrupted him, "Scott Grey, will you please kiss me?"

He shut up. She waited, but he still just stared at her. Crap. He really didn't want to kiss her. "I'm sorry I asked."

"No!" He started to reach for her, but stopped. "It's not that I don't want to kiss you. I've been thinking about it since I found you in the quarry. But Hannah, have you seen your lips?"

No she hadn't. She'd avoided the mirror while getting dressed. All the pain from Miranda's damage scared her. Did she really look that bad?

"It's just," Scott continued, "My face is all busted up too. I figured if you're in as much pain as me, you wouldn't want me to kiss you."

Oh, good grief. "Scott Grey, if you can manage to not hurt either one of us too badly, I would really appreciate it if you would kiss me."

He chuckled at her formal request. "Yes, ma'am, I'll do my best."

He did. Oh, so slowly and feather light, he kissed her on the top lip, holding her close, but not so close he risked hurting her. After she nipped him, he moved lower to her bottom lip, licking her with his tongue. Oh, yeah, this is how every woman should be kissed.

"How'd I do?" he asked, when he finally pulled away.

"Heavenly," Hannah said, because it was true.

Scott's hand brushed her hair away from her face. "I've never had my kisses described as *heavenly* before."

"I can't imagine why not. Can we try for heaven again?"

He laughed. "How about I bring you below deck instead. It's been a rough couple of days and our lives aren't going to get much easier any time soon."

He was right, unfortunately.

"I've also heard my kisses are far more heavenly when experienced from the horizontal position."

"Oh, really?"

She could see what he was up to. The second he got her back into bed, she'd probably fall asleep. If she could squeeze one more heavenly kiss from him it would be worth it, though. "Very well. If you insist."

Far more gently than even his kiss, Scott carried her below deck. As he laid her down, Hannah reached up to touch his face. She didn't bloodsurf, not yet, but

335

soon. She'd heal him, and maybe together, they would heal each other.

THE END

Coming Soon

November 2015
Valley of the Blind
A Thunder City Short Story
Six months before the events in Blood Surfer

The first rule to kidnapping an alternative human is to understand their power. No, wait a sec. That's rule number two. Rule number one is: don't kidnap an Alt in the first place.

Asher Brooks tested his arms and legs, but there was no give to the plastic flexcuffs around his wrists and ankles. Whichever idiots had forgotten the rules and grabbed him had also discarded his glasses and covered his eyes with a thick blindfold. Instead of making it harder for him to see, his captors had made it easier.

January 2016
Slow Burn
A Thunder City Short Story
Three months before the events in Blood Surfer

Heat seared Spritz's lungs as she sprayed water from her hands over the fire hell-bent on scorching her and her partner. On the other side of the ferry terminal, Cobalt created fire retardant foam from the elements found in her body and shot the thick mixture along the flaming north wall.

Not today, you son-of-a-bitch. You're not killing anyone today.

A snap louder than a flashbang broke her concentration. A ceiling support beam snapped. The jagged end, still on fire, tumbled down toward her partner's head.

Acknowledgements

Contrary to popular belief, writing a novel is a group activity. Even before I put words on the page, I had the help of so many people: critique partners, beta-readers, workshop lecturers, editors, and cheerleaders. Without every single one of these people, this novel would never have happened.

I would not be the writer I am if I had not attended the Viable Paradise writers workshop (Class XVI). Many of you have read all or parts of this manuscript in one format or another. Your feedback has been invaluable. In particular I would like to thank Debra Doyle for editing this novel not once, but twice, and Jim D. MacDonald for guiding me through the squishy anatomy parts. Any mistakes made are mine.

I have also benefited from the skilled and generous knowledge of the Volusia County Romance Writers and the First Coast Romance Writers, both chapters of the Romance Writers of America. I couldn't have asked for better groups with bigger hearts than what you have given me.

Many individuals have gone above and beyond, answering my phone calls and panicked emails when the story just was not working: Jan Jackson, D.C. Black, Michele Lellouche, Holly Crawford, Gina Storm Grant, Penny Cairns, Carla Mueller, and Sean Patrick Kelley. All of these people have shared their wisdom, insight, and encouragement, and this book could not have been completed without them.

Thanks also to Cliff Weikal of Cliff's Books (Deland, Fla.) who offered to stock print copies of my novel in his book store. In a time when digital books are more popular than ever, I never thought I would see my book in print, sitting on a bookshelf. Now I have, and it has made the journey worth it.

Thank you, everyone!

COPYRIGHT

ABOUT THE AUTHOR

A Connecticut Yankee transplanted to Central Florida, Debra Jess writes science fiction, romance, urban fantasy, and superheroes. She began writing in 2006, combining her love of fairy tales and Star Wars to craft original stories of ordinary people in extraordinary adventures and fantastical creatures in out-of-this world escapades. Her manuscripts have won the Golden Pen Award (Paranormal category) and the Golden Palm award (Paranormal/Sci-Fi/Fantasy category).

Debra is a graduate of Viable Paradise and is a member of Codex. She's also a member of the Romance Writers of America and RWA's Fantasy, Futuristic, & Paranormal chapter, the First Coast Romance Writers, and she is the Vice President of the Volusia County Romance Writers. Visit her online at www.debrajess.com.

Debra Jess
Risk. Reward. Romance.